THE AUSCHWITZ DETECTIVE

AN ADAM LAPID MYSTERY

JONATHAN DUNSKY

The Auschwitz Detective

Jonathan Dunsky

ISBN: 9798684988608

Visit JonathanDunsky.com for news and information.

BOOKS BY JONATHAN DUNSKY

Adam Lapid Series

Ten Years Gone

The Dead Sister

The Auschwitz Violinist

A Debt of Death

A Deadly Act

The Auschwitz Detective

The Unlucky Woman (a short story)

Standalone Novels

The Payback Girl

For Tal, Liora, Netta, and Nitzan

1

_____

I had never seen a man cry like that.

He lay prone on his bunk, second level of three, and bawled as though he had been driven mad. As he howled his pain out, his entire body quaked in jerky spasms, like an exposed heart beating erratically. His limbs jolted and flailed about, banging hard against the rough wooden slats that bore his weight.

Each sob was so deep it must have originated in the center of the Earth. It then chewed its way upward through rock and dirt, pierced the crust of the hard Polish ground on which the camp sprawled, burrowed through the floor of our block, and wormed its way into the crying man's soul. From there it finally erupted from his mouth in a scream of such primal agony that it would have shattered our hearts at any other time, in any other place. Right then, it only hurt our ears.

The man had arrived at Auschwitz-Birkenau eleven hours ago. Soon after that, his wife and six children were led to the gas chambers and exterminated. Someone had informed him of this fact five hours ago. His denial had lasted for three. He had been crying for the past two.

Other prisoners were giving him as much space as our over-crowded block allowed. Not out of kindness, but because his wailing was so unpleasant. No one comforted him, not even me. And I sat very close to his bunk, looking at him and wishing he'd shut up already and feeling ashamed for thinking that.

Not that I could have lessened his pain. No words held such power. His wife and children were dead. You couldn't console a man in such circumstances. You had to let him cry.

He wasn't the first man to cry in our block, as Auschwitz prisoner barracks were called, nor would he be the last. I had cried my first night there myself, knowing with an uncanny certainty that my wife and two daughters were dead. But no one had cried like this man. Even those who were loud, and many were, did not scream with such abandon, nor did their muscles clench and release as though they had come into contact with a live wire. Nor did their mouth gape wide in tortured silence before a delayed shriek burst through like fire from a flamethrower.

He cried like a man possessed by demons, like a man dispos-sessed by devils. I wasn't sure about the former, but the latter was definitely true. For all had been taken from him, as it had been taken from each and every man who now had to hear him scream. And those who had taken everything from us were the closest things to the devil any of us would encounter on this side of death.

The man was in his late thirties, of average height, and had the fullness of flesh of a new prisoner. This would not last, of course. In the coming days and weeks, his muscles would dwindle, his fat would melt, his skin would shrink around his skeleton. He would look like the rest of us—gaunt and hollow-cheeked, with huge eyes and sharp bones and a sickly complexion. He would not look like a man any longer; at least not like any man he'd seen before the war, before he'd arrived here in Auschwitz.

In a way, he did not look like a man even now. Not with the endless tears leaking from his eyes. Not with the thick snot running from his nostrils. Not with the bubbles of spittle dotting his lips and the film of sweat on his forehead and shaven scalp. I wasn't sure what he looked like. I wasn't sure what I looked like. I wasn't sure what I was anymore.

Apart from a number.

The number tattooed on my left forearm in bluish ink. That number was me, and I was that number. Sometimes it felt that this was all I ever was. That everything I had once been—father, son, husband, policeman—had been expunged, erased, eradicated so thoroughly that even the memory of those things was suspect, as though my life prior to arriving in the camp had been an illusion or a fevered dream.

I knew nothing of the crying man's past. I did not know how he had made his living. I did not know his exact age. I did not know his hobbies or passions. I did not know his political or religious beliefs. I did not even know his last name. What I did know was that he was a Hungarian Jew, like myself. I knew that his first name was Gyuri. And I knew that he had married a woman, had fathered children, and, judging by the ferocity of his wailing, loved them dearly.

He and I had never exchanged a word. What I knew of him I'd learned from other prisoners—those who had greeted him upon his arrival in our block; those who had shared with him the grim new reality of his life.

And once it had sunk in, he had begun crying and hadn't stopped since.

Another howl, this one achingly high-pitched, exploded from his mouth. It echoed around the dim interior of the block, making my ears ring. A number of the other prisoners groaned. Someone swore. A few cast baleful looks at the crying man. As usual, everyone was hungry and tired. We all craved sleep. But if Gyuri kept crying like that, sleep would be impossible. Even exhausted men cannot sleep in such noise.

There was tension in the air: a sense of impending trouble, like a honed blade poised for deadly use. That was why I was sitting so close to Gyuri, in spite of my throbbing eardrums.

There was a heavy thud from my left. A man had jumped down from his bunk partway up the block and was stomping his way over, his wooden clogs tapping an angry rhythm on the packed-earth floor. He was tall and angular, with a face as hard as a brick. There was murder in his eyes. I noticed his hands were balled into fists.

I knew who he was: a gruff, truculent Dutch Jew by the name of Hendrik. He'd been in Auschwitz for over a year. That alone said he was tough. But I had also seen him use his fists on more than one occasion. Once he had fought another prisoner over a crust of bread found under the shirt of a man who had died during the night. Another time a bunkmate had snored too loudly in his ear. Hendrik had won both altercations. His first opponent emerged from their skirmish with nothing but bruises. The second had not been as fortunate. He had suffered a fractured wrist, rendering him unfit for work. Three days later, during selection at the camp hospital, an SS doctor sent him to the gas chambers.

When Hendrik reached Gyuri's bunk, he snarled in German, "Shut up already, you bastard! Stop wailing!" and he grabbed Gyuri by the armpits and yanked him off his bunk, throwing him to the floor.

Incredibly, Gyuri kept on crying, apparently oblivious to his surroundings. He lay on his back, his knees half-bent, his arms still twitching. A thin trickle of blood dripped from a cut on his temple, where his head had hit the floor.

Hendrik loomed over him, an expression of utter incredulity on his face. He couldn't fathom how Gyuri could display no reaction to his command to be quiet, let alone being hurled to the floor. Three heartbeats later, the incredulity gave way to blazing fury. The blood rose in Hendrik's face, and a feral growl rumbled deep in his throat.

"You won't shut up," he roared, "I'll make you shut up." And he drew back his right leg, intending to kick the crying man.

Jumping to my feet, I got to Hendrik as his foot was already flying toward Gyuri's unprotected head. He did not see me coming. I planted both hands on his chest and shoved. It wasn't a particularly hard push. I wasn't trying to topple him, just keep him from burying his clog in Gyuri's face. Still, with one foot in the air, Hendrik nearly lost his balance. He staggered back, his feet doing a stuttering shuffle, and he would have fallen had he not managed to brace himself on a nearby bunk.

"That's enough," I said.

Hendrik straightened and gave me a stare full of astonishment and rage. He stood with his feet wide apart and his arms slightly bent at either side of him, a stance that hinted at barely restrained violence. His fingers kept opening and closing. I was now between him and Gyuri, who was still on the floor, still weeping.

"Who the hell are you?" Hendrik said. He had a gravelly voice that added to his threatening demeanor. It didn't surprise me that he didn't know my name. There were hundreds of prisoners in our block, and, unlike Hendrik, I did not stand out among them.

"My name is Adam," I answered.

"Why did you push me?"

"To stop you from kicking this man." I pointed at Gyuri without taking my eyes off Hendrik. I might have added an apology or a mollifying explanation, but Hendrik was a thug, and neither of those things would have appeased him.

"You know him?"

I shook my head.

"Then why do you care what happens to him?"

Back in normal life, the answer would have been automatic. Now I had to think about it.

"I just don't think we should be killing each other," I said. "That would be helping the Germans."

Hendrik scoffed. "Look at him. You think he's going to make it? He won't last a week."

"That may be. But if he dies, it won't be tonight, and it won't be by your hands."

Behind me, Gyuri let out another howl of agony. Hendrik's jaw tightened.

"I don't want to kill him—just to get him to stop making that racket."

Which might have been true. But Hendrik hadn't meant to kill the man whose wrist he'd fractured, either.

"Have a heart, Hendrik. The man just lost his wife and six children."

Hendrik was unmoved. "We've all lost family. Every one of us here. We need some peace. We need our sleep. How are we going to make it through tomorrow if he keeps us up all night?"

It was a fair question, and I had no good answer. As though to bolster Hendrik's argument, Gyuri let out a couple of sharp shrieks, which then dwindled to loud, breathy, grating whimpers. Hardly the sort of sounds conducive to sleep.

Not that our block was ever quiet at night. How could it be, with hundreds of prisoners crammed together in such close quarters, sleeping on bunks that would have felt crowded with a third of their occupants? The moans of the hungry, the groans of the sick and injured, the curses of those jostled from sleep by their bunkmates, the cries of those afflicted by nightmares—these were but a few of the nasty notes comprising the symphony of misery that served as the soundtrack of our nights.

Still, Gyuri's wails had a unique, piercing quality to them. They rattled my nerves and stabbed at my eardrums as other sounds of anguish did not.

Hendrik offered me a smile that had as much warmth in it as a Hungarian winter. "Fine. I won't kick him. I'll be gentle, I promise. Now step aside."

"No," I said.

The smile disappeared. He sized me up. He was not as tall as I was, but he had more meat on him. He was also vicious, and he liked to fight.

"Step aside," he repeated, his voice pitched menacingly low. It was probably a tone that had served him well in his previous life and also here in the camp.

I shook my head.

Hendrik pursed his lips, gave a couple of contemplative nods, and cast his eyes around us. We had attracted an audience. From their bunks, or from where they were standing or sitting, dozens of our blockmates had turned their emaciated heads our way. A few had edged closer for a better view. Some gazed with grotesque curiosity; others looked on with no hint of real interest.

Fights were not rare. You packed this many men into such a cramped space in such squalid conditions and there was bound to be friction. Were it not for our overall fatigue and the need to conserve energy for the next day, we would have been at one another's throats with much greater frequency.

Hendrik was looking aside when he made his move. It was a ploy to catch me off guard, but I was ready for it. When he swung his fist at my head, I ducked it easily. I moved in under his arm and pushed him again, this time harder. He fell, sprawling on his back with a grunt.

"I'm not looking for a fight," I told him. "Just stay away from this man."

Hendrik pushed himself up. He was fuming. But there was also a wary look in his eyes. I was turning out to be a more challenging foe than he had expected.

"You've made a big mistake," Hendrik said. "A big mistake."

I didn't answer him. There was a good chance he was right. Why was I risking myself for Gyuri? I didn't know him. I didn't really care about him. I wanted him to shut up, too. But I couldn't allow Hendrik to beat him. The state he was in, Gyuri was incapable of defending himself.

Again, Hendrik looked aside, but this time there was no subterfuge. He caught the eye of two other prisoners, a pair that was chummy with him.

"Marco, Jan, come help me teach this idiot a lesson."

Marco and Jan were smaller than Hendrik, but both had mean faces. They came to stand beside Hendrik, who gave me a cruel smile. None of the spectators moved to intervene. It seemed they were smarter than I was.

"Last chance," Hendrik said. "Don't be stupid. It's three against one."

"No," I said, feeling foolish and even angry with myself. How did I get involved in this mess? Was I really going to sacrifice myself for this whimpering stranger?

"Good," Hendrik said. "I was hoping you'd say that."

Just then, right when the three of them were about to pounce, a voice called out, "Wait a minute!" and I saw Vilmos elbow his way through the crowd of onlookers. He gazed at Gyuri, then at me, and finally at Hendrik and his friends.

"Three against two," he said, and I was gratified to note that his voice barely quavered.

He was not a formidable man by any means—short, narrow-boned, with a distinct intellectual cast to his features. His voice was equally unmenacing—soft and cultured and slightly high-pitched. The sort of voice that would scare off precisely no one.

I doubted Vilmos had ever been involved in a real brawl. From what he'd told me, his life before the war had been a sheltered one. But here he was, standing at my side, risking everything. My respect for him swelled.

Hendrik and his pals hesitated. The odds were still in their favor, but less so than a minute ago. Still, they had committed themselves. They could not back down now. Not without a good reason.

Fortunately, Vilmos proceeded to provide them with one.

He stuck his hand under his striped shirt and came out holding two pieces of bread. Brandishing them, he said, "For you —if you back off and let us quiet this man down ourselves."

Hendrik, Jan, and Marco all stared at the bread. I was staring at it too. My mouth hung open, drool dripping down my chin. I wiped it off with the back of my hand, my eyes still riveted to the bread.

My stomach grumbled. The perpetual emptiness ached deep inside me. I could taste the bread, sense its rough, dry texture as my teeth gnawed it to bits. I felt a wild, primitive urge to yank the bread from Vilmos's hand, even if it meant striking him down.

But I didn't. I managed to control myself. Maybe I was a man still.

With a grin, Hendrik snatched the bread. "You got a deal," he said to Vilmos. To me he added, "You're lucky he showed up when he did. Very lucky."

Hendrik glanced from the bread to Jan and Marco. He folded

the bigger piece and shoved it in his mouth. The other piece he tore in two and handed each a share. Around the food in his mouth, he said, "Here."

Jan wolfed down his half. Marco looked about to argue with Hendrik that all three should have gotten an equal share, but in the end, he kept his mouth shut.

When they finished eating, Hendrik asked, "Got any more?"

Vilmos lifted his shirt, exposing a hairless, pasty midriff through which his ribs showed. "That was everything."

Hendrik ran his tongue over his teeth. A calculating look entered his eyes. "Where did you get the bread?"

"From a dead *muselmann*," Vilmos said. "He was still collecting his daily ration. He just wasn't eating it."

It was a plausible story. By Hendrik's nod, I could tell he believed it. Behind us, Gyuri let out a keening wail. Hendrik glanced at Gyuri and then back at us. His upper lip curled. "He's still making too much noise. Take him to the back. All the way. If I hear him, if he disturbs my sleep, the deal's off. Got it?"

Vilmos nodded. Hendrik, Jan, and Marco walked away, the Dutchman laughing and clapping his friends on the back. The crowd of spectators turned their attention away from us.

"Help me with him," Vilmos said, and together we lifted Gyuri to his feet and led him toward the rear of the block. It was like moving a mannequin. One that was sobbing.

The deeper we went, the stronger the stench became.

Our block was a converted stable, made entirely of wood. It was divided into eighteen stalls, originally designed for horses. The two in front were reserved for prisoner functionaries: our *Blockälteste*, the block senior; the three *Stubendiensts*, who were in charge of order and cleanliness in the block; and the *Blockschreiber*, the block clerk, who maintained a record of the living and the dead. The fourteen middle stalls contained our bunks. And in the rearmost two stood buckets for human waste, for at night, we were confined to our block and could not go to the latrine.

Each morning, the buckets were emptied, but a noxious cloud always clung to those two stalls and permeated the nearby bunks. During the night, as more prisoners relieved themselves, the stench of urine and feces would grow overpowering. Consequently, no one wanted to sleep near the back of the block. Those who did were either new, weak, or very near death.

This did not mean the rearmost bunks were uncrowded. With over four hundred prisoners in our block, each sliver of sleeping space was used up. Still, Vilmos and I managed to find space for ourselves and Gyuri. Many of the inhabitants of this section of our block were weak to the point of lethargy. They did not complain as we helped Gyuri climb onto a top bunk where only three other prisoners were lying. With eyes that looked massive and hopeless and oddly childlike, they gazed at us in silence as we invaded their cramped, dismal domain. Their thoughts were unreadable. Maybe they lacked the strength to think at all.

Putting my lips close to Vilmos's ear, I said, "You didn't really get the bread from a *muselmann*, did you?"

Vilmos shook his head.

"From where, then?"

He shot me a warning look and whispered, "Not now, Adam. Not here. Someone might overhear us. I'll tell you tomorrow."

Then he began to caress Gyuri's shaved head. He moved his hand gently, as though he were caressing the downy hair of an infant who had awoken from a nightmare. It was appropriate, in a way, though none of us were children. For we were in the midst of a nightmare. One from which we could not awaken.

Gyuri did not seem to notice the touch nor Vilmos's gentle voice. Vilmos lied to him, told him everything was all right now.

Gradually, Gyuri's weeping subsided and his body relaxed. No longer did his limbs jump about.

He was still in a trance, though. In a tear-choked voice, he began intoning very fast. The words were barely intelligible, flowing into each other with no separation between them. It took me a moment to realize that he was reciting a list of seven names, the names of his wife and six children, over and over again.

2

The clang of the wake-up gong ripped my sleep to shreds. Then began the morning's mad scramble. Throughout the block, hundreds of prisoners, all worn-out and hungry, struggled to cast away the last cobwebs of their miserable sleep. Another dreadful day was dawning. There was much to be done and hardly any time to do it. To dawdle could mean death.

First order of business: make sure you had all your meager possessions. That none of your fellow prisoners had stolen them during the night. The loss of a cap or your clogs was punishable by a severe beating, if not summary execution.

Then it was time to make your bed. Some bunks came equipped with paper mattresses stuffed with straw, much too flimsy to provide true comfort, while others held nothing with which to cushion the hard wooden planks. There were also blankets, thin and coarse, though not nearly as many as the number of prisoners. The lucky ones got a blanket all to themselves. The slightly less fortunate got one to share. And those whose luck had deserted them had nothing to shield them from the cold but their clothes.

The mattresses and blankets were all filthy and stinking. Many were ridden with lice, bedbugs, and fleas. Lice were the most dangerous of the three—a potential death sentence. On one of the crossbeams in our block, a simple message was painted in bold Teutonic letters: *Eine Laus dein Tod* - One Louse, Your Death.

One of the reasons the Nazis shaved off all of our body hair was to prevent the spread of lice and any diseases they might carry, typhus in particular. Another reason was to deprive us of another aspect of our humanity, just like they deprived us of our names and gave us numbers in their place.

The very idea of making up our bunks, as though they were regular beds, was meant to degrade us even further. To mock us and our deplorable living conditions. To burden us with yet another meaningless task.

The *Blockälteste*, a perpetually scowling Pole who had been in Auschwitz since 1941, marched down the center of the block, yelling for us to hurry up, kicking those he deemed to be too slow or smacking them with a stick.

"*Aufstehen!*" he shouted, German for *Get up*. "*Schnell, schnell!*" *Quickly, quickly!*

The *Blockälteste* was our master. The block was his little fiefdom in this hell on earth. He could do with us as he pleased; the Nazis had granted him this power. They enjoyed having one of us do some of their dirty work for them. It amused them.

Other blocks had good-hearted *Blockältestes* who helped their charges as much as circumstances allowed. We were not so lucky. Our *Blockälteste* was a cruel, mean-spirited brute. He relished his power over us and was quick to dispense a curse or a well-aimed blow for the slightest or even an imaginary infraction. Some nights, while we lay hungry in our bunks, mouthwatering aromas of food would waft down the block from his room, sharpening our hunger pangs, augmenting our anguish. We all knew this food was stolen from our rations or otherwise corruptly obtained. Our *Blockälteste* did not mind that we starved while he and his cronies ate more than their fill. It did not bother him one bit that every day men in our block died of malnutrition.

Rumor had it that before the war, the *Blockälteste* had been a shopkeeper. It was difficult to imagine him as anything but our harsh master, as a regular man, but perhaps it was true. His indifference to our suffering, his casual cruelty, might well have been a product of his long incarceration in the camp. Three years in Auschwitz could unravel the moral fabric of any man. I had been here for just under two months, and I could feel mine fraying as well.

"I'll do the bunk," I told Vilmos. "You take care of him."

By him, I meant Gyuri, who had spent the night mewling softly in his sleep, periodically crying out and waking those around him. Now he stood trembling, gazing about with rounded eyes and an open mouth, a look of dumb horror on his face.

His reaction was understandable. This was an alien world. None of his past experiences, not even his darkest nightmares, could have prepared him for this. Still, I found it difficult to sympathize with him. I was too tired for that. And I had my own losses to bear.

Vilmos was talking to Gyuri, explaining what was happening and what we had to do next. "Stay close to us," Vilmos said. "Move when we move. Do what we do. It will be all right." Then, as if to underscore the enormity of the lie he'd just told, he grabbed the cap Gyuri had carelessly left on the bunk and stuck it on top of Gyuri's head. "Don't lose it. If you do, there'll be hell to pay."

The *Blockälteste* had nearly made it all the way to us. Vilmos turned Gyuri around to face the bunk and whispered to him to look busy. Vilmos pretended to be straightening a blanket. Gyuri looked blankly at him. I wanted to scream at him to not just stand there, that he might get us all in trouble, just by being close to us. But of course I kept my mouth shut.

"You, you, and you," the *Blockälteste* growled, poking three unfortunate prisoners with his stick. "Empty the buckets. Spill a drop and I'll make you eat it."

I breathed a sigh of relief that none of the three of us had been chosen for this disgusting chore.

"The rest of you," the *Blockälteste* shouted as he turned and headed up the block, "better hurry up and go to the latrines. You don't want to miss breakfast, do you?"

In truth, no prompting was necessary. We all knew haste was crucial. Because of Gyuri, we were at the far end of the block from the exit, so we had to push our way through the throng of prisoners. I took the lead. Vilmos brought up the rear, prodding Gyuri ahead of him. Some of the other prisoners did not take kindly to being overtaken, so I got my share of jabs and smacks and expletives as I cut a path for us to the exit.

The *Blockälteste* and one of the *Stubendiensts* were standing just outside the block. They spurred the prisoners to greater speed, often punctuating their commands with a harsh shove. Gyuri received one, which made him stumble in his oversized clogs and fall face down in the dirt. Vilmos and I rushed to help him up, accompanied by the raspy laughter of the *Blockälteste*.

It was not yet fully light, though a gray hint of dawn was already creeping from the east. We were always roused before daybreak, as the Germans wanted our morning routine to waste as little daylight as possible. That way we could be at our work stations early, and they could extract more toil from us.

Over to the west, the chimneys of the crematoriums belched long tongues of fire and clouds of sickening black-gray smoke.

That smoke used to be people not too long ago. Men and women and children. Babies too. None were spared save those the Nazis wished to exploit as slave labor, those from whom a little extra benefit to the Third Reich could be squeezed. Those spared were given but a temporary reprieve. They were to be killed through hard labor and privation.

Additional pillars of smoke billowed into the sky from the northwest, behind the trees that bordered the camp. It was said the Nazis had ordered giant pits to be dug there, that in those pits bodies were burned. The pits were needed because the transports brought so many Jews every day that the crematoriums could not dispose of them all in a timely fashion.

A dark cloud hung low over the camp like a shroud. The smell of burning flesh was thick and inescapable. Each whiff of air was like inhaling death straight into your lungs. We were breathing our loved ones, our friends, our fellow Jews. The smoke scorched our throats, singed our nostrils, seared our souls.

With Gyuri between us, Vilmos and I rushed to the first latrine block. Inside, hundreds of prisoners were waiting their turn. The many afflicted with dysentery or diarrhea shifted from one foot to the other as they fought to control their bowels. Some, their need overwhelming their shame, retreated to a corner and defecated on the floor. The block was gloomy, and the indescribable stench was an assault not only on our senses but also on our dignity.

It was a primitive facility; a structure similar to our regular block, only instead of bunks there were three sewer ditches that ran nearly the entire length of the block. Each ditch was covered by a concrete lid into which a few dozen circular holes had been cut. On each hole a prisoner sat, his trousers drooped around his ankles, his head bowed and eyes closed, no doubt striving for a sense of privacy where none was to be had. Each time a prisoner finished with his business, his seat was immediately taken by another. You had to get done quickly or you might get shouted at or worse. Thousands of prisoners had to use this latrine, and there were about ten minutes to do so.

There were no partitions and no toilet paper. We were not accorded the basic amenities human beings were entitled to, because in the eyes of the Germans, we were subhuman.

"Let's go," I said when three adjacent vacancies emerged simultaneously. Vilmos and I raced to claim them. We pulled Gyuri along with us, but when we let go of his arms to sit down, he made no move to follow suit. His eyes were wet and dismayed, and he shook his head violently. "I can't... not like this. I..."

"It's either now or you'll have to hold it in for hours," Vilmos said, with more patience than I could have mustered. He pulled Gyuri gently toward the toilets. "Just close your eyes and do what you have to."

With his cheeks flushed from a sense of embarrassment that I had lost weeks ago, Gyuri lowered his trousers and sat down quickly, hands covering his shaved groin. He flinched when his bare thigh touched mine. I had reacted similarly the first few days at the camp. The toilet holes were so close together that one could not avoid contact with those sitting on either side of him. By every sense but taste, one could not escape the public nature of the latrine. The most private act a man does was turned into a spectacle viewed and heard and smelled by hundreds.

After we had finished, we headed over to the washroom. Washing was also done in public, at rows of spigots over low troughs with other prisoners all around. The floor was wet and muddy, the water impure and murky. A warning on the wall forbade drinking it. The water was also cold, which deterred many prisoners. It seemed pointless to try to keep clean, especially since we had no soap. Our clothes were grimy, hard with sweat and dirt and bodily discharge, so why put yourself through the agony of running cold water on your skin? As soon as you put your clothes back on, you were enveloping yourself in filth.

Still, I gritted my teeth against the water's chilly bite and rubbed at my skin as hard as I could. It was torture, but I did not relent. It was a matter not just of hygiene but also of principle. A man kept himself clean, and I desperately wanted to continue being a man, no matter how hard the Germans tried to make me into something less. But I had to admit, it was getting harder to find the will and the strength to go through this painful routine each morning. I could only imagine how terrible it would feel when summer turned into fall and then winter, and the temperatures plummeted. I tried hard not to think of winter. The way the old timers described it, hell was not a place of fire and brimstone, but Auschwitz in December.

"Hey," a voice sounded from my right. It was Hendrik. He was washing his hands, not bothering with the rest of his body. A wicked grin contorted his face. "Sleep well?"

"Perfectly," I said.

"Glad to hear it. Looking kinda skinny there. You better watch it or you'll be a *muselmann* before you know it. And then it's a one-way ticket to the gas chamber for you."

I didn't answer. Hendrik glanced at Gyuri with disdain. To me he said, "Remember what I told you. One week." Then he turned on his heel and left the block.

Shivering, I put my clothes back on my wet skin. I had no towel to dry myself. A few spigots down the line, Vilmos was doing the same. He coughed as he slipped his shirt over his depleted torso. I didn't like the sound of that cough. It rattled and had a moist edge to it. A cough in the real world was nothing to worry about, but here it could be a death knell. Vilmos was the only friend I had in this place. I feared losing him more than my own life.

Our washing done, we hurried out to get our breakfast. In front of each of several large metal containers, a crude, ever-shifting line of prisoners was forming. Each container was filled with either a coffee substitute or a weak herbal tea. One could never know which of the two beverages would be offered that day. Not that one was markedly superior to the other. Both the coffee and tea had a suspicious hue and emitted an even more suspicious odor. Their taste was equally criminal. That was the extent of breakfast in Auschwitz.

Vilmos and I, with Gyuri between us, joined one of the lines. I untied the string that tethered my metal bowl to the loopholes in my waistband. It was then that I noticed that Gyuri did not have a bowl.

"Where's your bowl?" I asked him.

He shook his head and shrugged his shoulders like a fearful, confused child. "I... I don't know. I had it with me yesterday. I must have lost it."

A flash of anger heated my face. I had risked bodily injury to protect Gyuri from Hendrik. Vilmos and I had each given up a precious piece of bread on his behalf. My stomach groaned at the thought of it. I was about to lambaste Gyuri for his carelessness, but the sight of his hapless face stayed my tongue. My anger subsided. Much to my surprise, it seemed I was still capable of feeling pity for another human being. "Don't worry about it, Gyuri," I said. "You can share mine."

The tea was bitter and lukewarm. I shut my eyes, tilted my head back, and drank the whole thing in one long swallow. I tried pouring the liquid directly into the back of my mouth, so that as little as possible touched my tongue. It was easier to get it down that way. The tea was poor in nutrients, but in Auschwitz every little bit could make the difference between living and dying. Besides, thirst was as much of a hardship as hunger, since we had no access to fresh water. The tea was hardly water's equal when it came to quenching thirst, but it was better than nothing.

When Gyuri got his portion, he gazed dubiously at the brownish brew. He lifted his eyes to Vilmos and me. "Is this all there is? There's nothing else?"

"I'm afraid not," Vilmos said. "Not until midday."

"Are they trying to starve us? To kill us off slowly?"

"Or quickly," I said. "It depends on their mood. Go ahead. Drink it. Don't think about it too much. Don't look at it either. Just gulp it down and get done with it."

Gyuri nodded and raised the bowl to his lips. His mouth twisted as the tea hit his taste buds. His eyes turned wet. "Is it always this bad?"

"Yes," I said.

Gyuri handed me the bowl. "Here. You finish it." He looked downcast and dejected.

"It's all right," Vilmos said, putting a hand on Gyuri's shoulder. "You'll get used to it."

He'll have to, I thought, or he'll be dead very soon.

3

A second gong proclaimed the end of breakfast. We hurried to the *Appellplatz*, the large square where roll calls took place, to join our work unit, known in camp parlance as a *kommando*.

In Auschwitz there were all sorts of *kommandos*, one for each of the various jobs our German masters had for us. Some *kommandos* were small, numbering a dozen men. Others employed hundreds of prisoners, though these were divided into subgroups. Not all *kommandos* were equal. Some were downright cushy compared to others. Being assigned to the right *kommando* could dramatically raise a prisoner's life expectancy. The wrong one could kill a man in days.

Our *kommando* was allotted eighty men. Among them, our *Blockschreiber* announced, was Gyuri.

"Thank God," Gyuri said, evidently relieved that he would not be separated from us.

I gave him a look. What was he talking about? What kind of God allowed a place like Auschwitz to exist on His earth?

Our *Kapo*, a grim-faced Slovakian Jew, among the first of our people to be sent here, yelled at us to get in orderly lines of ten. "Move it, you lazy bastards. Move."

A *Kapo* was like a foreman, or perhaps overseer was a better word, considering we were nothing but slaves. He was responsible for the work his *kommando* did, and he had near absolute power over us. He could shout at us, curse us, beat us, or worse—anything to get our productivity up. His position was precarious, though. If the Germans decided that he was failing in his duties, or that he was too soft, he would be stripped of his title and returned to the general population of prisoners. Such a downfall could have grave consequences. A former *Kapo* was unlikely to survive his first night back among regular prisoners. Every *Kapo* knew this, which was why many of them displayed a brutality that rivaled that of the SS guards themselves.

As with *Blockältestes*, some *Kapos* managed to keep their humanity intact. They walked a fine, dangerous line—doing whatever they could for the men working under them, all while maintaining a facade of uncompromising toughness to satisfy the Germans. Our *Kapo* was not such a man.

We formed lines as ordered. Around us, other *kommandos* did likewise. It was like watching an army gather into formation. Only we weren't soldiers. We were nothing. Just flesh and bone covered by rough, dirty uniforms comprised of a striped cap, trousers, and shirt. Most of us suffered from one ailment or another. Some of us had one foot lodged firmly in the grave. None of us had had a decent meal in weeks or months. None of us had known the joy of a good night's sleep for as long. And we were all marked for death.

We were about to head out when we heard a roaring bellow. My head spun so fast my neck ached. A shiver of fear ran up my spine. Twenty or so meters to my right was the most frightening man in our camp, almost as frightening as the Germans themselves.

It was the *Lagerälteste*, the camp senior. He was the prisoner functionary in charge of the men's camp, the most powerful prisoner among us, answerable only to the SS. The king who ruled over us with ultimate authority.

He was an ox of a man, tall and muscular, with broad shoulders and a deep chest. He did not suffer the hardships the rest of us bore. He did not know hunger. Did not know the agony of trying to sleep wedged in between other prisoners. His position afforded him every privilege but freedom. On his feet were leather boots instead of clogs. On his torso was a tailored jacket that had probably belonged to a rich Jew who had gone up the chimney. An inverted green triangle had been sewn to his jacket over his heart, indicating that he was a criminal—not a political prisoner and not a Jew.

He was German and one of several criminal prisoners the Nazis had brought here. Chosen for their criminal history and penchant for brutality, these prisoners were used by the Nazis to rule the rest of us with an iron fist. Word had it that the *Lagerälteste* was a convicted murderer, and I could well believe it. I had seen him kill for almost no reason. He seemed to have an appetite for it.

You did not want to attract the attention of the *Lagerälteste*. His mood was notoriously fickle. One could never know when he would erupt.

Right now, he was enraged. His wide, craggy face was beet red, and his fists were clenched. He stomped around like a caged animal, talking animatedly to a couple of his underlings.

"What do you think brought that about?" I asked Vilmos quietly.

"I don't know. I just hope he doesn't hurt anyone."

Three seconds later, Vilmos's hopes were dashed. The *Lagerälteste*, bouncing about like a coiled spring of raw fury, caught an unfortunate prisoner by the shirtfront, landed a hard fist in his stomach, threw him to the ground, and began to deliver a string of vicious kicks and stomps.

I wanted to stop the beating. I wanted to punch the *Lagerälteste* in the face. I wanted to handcuff him, throw him in jail, shoot him if that's what it took. But I had no gun, no handcuffs, no authority as a policeman anymore. So I did nothing. Nothing but watch and be shamefully grateful that someone else's luck had run out and not my own.

The attack went on for about a minute. At first the fallen prisoner cried out in pain. Then his voice gave out. Blood spattered through the air with each kick.

Finally, out of breath and sweating, the *Lagerälteste* stepped back from his victim. His boots and the cuffs of his trousers were red with blood. He turned away without a second glance at the beaten man and walked off. A minute later, a couple of prisoners picked up the dead man and threw him on top of the pile of bodies of those who had perished during the night.

4

_____

Accompanied by five SS guards armed with machine guns, we marched out of the men's camp to the sound of music played by the camp orchestra. The music was gratingly cheerful, probably some Nazi officer's idea of a joke, and it did nothing to raise our spirits. I did my best to ignore the merry tune. I couldn't tell you what melody the orchestra played that day, nor any other day. All I knew was that this was another insult meant to ridicule us and our torment.

Past the gate, we turned left on the road running parallel to the rail spur that had brought us to this place. We walked past the train platform where we were let out of the cattle cars in which we had journeyed from Hungary. Here we got our first sight of the camp. Here the men were separated from the women and children. Here we left all our belongings, apart from the clothes on our backs. Here was where the first selection took place, with SS doctors deciding who would live and who would die. Young children and their mothers, and those too old or feeble to work, were herded straight to the gas chambers. The rest were inducted into the camp as slave labor. My wife and daughters had been among the first group. So had my mother, probably. I wasn't sure about my sisters, though, and as we walked down the road toward the main gate of Auschwitz-Birkenau, my eyes scoured the women's camps on either side of our column.

The main women's camp was just across the train tracks to our right, and there too *kommandos* were forming. Looking at those skinny women with their shaved heads and filthy, ill-fitting uniforms was like seeing an alien species. Were these really women, or a new kind of creature, a denizen unique to the separate world that was Auschwitz? There was a morbid sameness to them, as though they had been cast from the same decrepit mold. As though all trace of their personality and uniqueness had been expunged, so that now they were no longer separate women but part of a multitude. I doubted I would recognize my sisters even if I saw them. Would they recognize me?

On our left, in the camp section directly east of our own, more women resided. This section was filled to the brim with Hungarian women, the newest and largest group of unfortunates to fall prey to the Nazis. Here many women simply squatted on the dry ground or walked around aimlessly, searching for food or any respite from their suffering. Apparently, the large influx of Jews from Hungary had created a situation in which the Auschwitz authorities did not have enough work for all the prisoners. Almost daily, trains or trucks arrived to take some of these women away— not to the gas chambers but to work camps to the west. At least, that's what the rumors said.

I did not see my sisters among these miserable women. I could only hope that they were spared the initial selection and that they too had been sent away from here. Any Nazi work camp would be terrible, but nothing could be worse than Auschwitz-Birkenau.

A little further on, we came upon a rare glimmer of light in the spiritual darkness of Auschwitz—one that drew the eyes of every prisoner in our column to the left. We were walking by the family camp of Czech Jews. Here, for some mysterious reason, the Nazis housed Jewish men and women and children together. And none of the prisoners' heads were shaved. As we marched past, I heard the singing of children from what was known as the children's block, where it was said that the Nazis had allowed a school of sorts to be established. It was the only place in Auschwitz where small Jewish children were permitted to live.

Hearing those beautiful voices raised in song, I felt my pulse quicken and a tiny spark of optimism ignite somewhere close to my heart. Here was life. Here was the possibility of a future. It made my steps lighter, my exhaustion a touch less severe. It wouldn't last—it never did—but for the moment, the world was not entirely dark.

The last camp section before the main gate was a bleaker place. It was the quarantine camp for men, where new male prisoners were housed. Here they were initiated into Auschwitz and taught its harsh rules, and here a good many of them died due to mistreatment and the shock of their new reality.

All new male prisoners were supposed to spend a few weeks in quarantine, but due to the recent explosion in the prisoner population—an increase made up almost entirely by the Jews of Hungary—the system had broken. Some prisoners were immediately shipped to one of the many smaller work camps that surrounded Auschwitz. Others, like Gyuri, were placed in the regular men's camp without going through quarantine at all. Some were not tattooed.

Prisoners did not work in *kommandos* while in quarantine, but that didn't mean they were idle. Rather, they were subjected to endless roll calls, where they were made to stand for hours, or ordered to perform grotesque calisthenics, which sapped their strength and shattered their spirit, all to the amusement of the guards. Many *kommandos* were terrible, but quarantine was worse. My two weeks there had nearly killed me.

As we walked past the quarantine camp, clumps of fresh prisoners huddled on the other side of the barbed-wire fence, looking at us. They did not make a sound. They watched us with eyes that were less than alive. The disbelief on their faces, a silent plea for help, cut me like a blade. I could not help them, could not even offer a word of encouragement. I'd be beaten if I said anything.

Our workplace was about two kilometers east of the camp. The trek there was torture. My tight clogs had chafed the skin of my feet, raising painful blisters, and each step brought a stab of pain. I'd stuffed some rags I'd found into my clogs to lessen the friction, but it was an imperfect solution. How I missed having a proper pair of shoes. I'd never thought my life might depend on having one.

Our task was to dig several trenches, for what purpose no one told us. One of the other prisoners speculated that these were anti-tank trenches, and they certainly could have been, given their planned width and depth. Vilmos saw this as a positive sign.

"The Russians can't be far off if the Germans are taking these precautions," he said. "We need only survive a short while longer."

I wasn't so sure. True, the Nazi advance in the east had faltered and was then reversed. The news we'd heard before leaving Hungary in May 1944 said the Red Army was advancing across the entire front. But no one knew where the Russians really were. I did not think they were that close. Guns are loud and artillery more so. If the Russians were truly close, we would have heard the rumble of canons. But there was no rumble.

I did not share my opinion with Vilmos. Let him believe whatever gave him strength and hope. Both were in short supply.

A truck carrying shovels and picks and buckets arrived, and

the *Kapo* ordered us to start digging. I hefted my shovel and cast a furtive glance at the five SS guards who were standing about a dozen meters from the lip of the trench. A hit on the head with a shovel could cave in a skull. There were eighty of us and five of them, six if you counted the *Kapo* among their number. If we all acted together, we might be able to overwhelm them before they finished us off with their machine guns.

But what would be the point? Even if some of us did survive the initial battle, we would still be within the administrative area of Auschwitz. For kilometers all around, there was nothing but SS patrols, watchtowers, and the German army. Even if we managed to slip past all that, where would we go? Where would we hide? We were in Poland, a foreign country. We did not know the geography. We did not speak the language and had no contacts among the local population. We did not have civilian clothes, and our shaved heads and extreme thinness would mark us as escaped prisoners. We had no food and could not count on any assistance. The Poles were not known for their love of Jews.

Escape from Auschwitz was not impossible. There had been a couple of escapes since my arrival in the camp, and I'd heard of others that took place beforehand. But it was never the result of violent rebellion, nor a mad dash toward freedom. Rather, it was the result of trickery, planned long in advance, and likely also coordination with the Polish resistance that operated in the vicinity of the camp.

In addition, there was no guarantee that if I attacked the guards, any other prisoners would join me. We had made no such plans, and every single one of us knew that such an attack was akin to suicide. If I acted, there was every chance that I would find no one at my side. Maybe Vilmos, but likely no one else.

Still, the desire to strike a blow against our oppressors was powerful. If I was destined to die in this place, at least I would take a Nazi or two with me. My palms tingled around the shaft of the shovel, and a crazy, furious voice in my head urged me, *Do it! Do it! Do it!*

Vilmos, sensing my frame of mind, touched my forearm. "Let's get to work, Adam. All right?"

I turned to look at him, my face hot, the blood humming in my ears.

"Today is not the day in which you die," Vilmos said, his voice gentle and yet authoritative. "Do you understand?"

I drew in a deep breath and let it out slowly. Then I nodded twice, a wave of defeat and self-loathing washing over me. I couldn't say whether I would have indeed gone through with my mad fantasy if Vilmos hadn't intervened. It wasn't the first time I'd had it, and I'd never had the courage, or perhaps the naked despair, to carry it out. "All right, Vilmos," I said. "Not today."

The day grew hot, and the sun beat down on us mercilessly. It didn't take long before I was itching with sweat and my throat was as dry as sandpaper. I was desperate for water, but there was none to be had.

Vilmos and I filled buckets with earth, and Gyuri carried them up the side of the trench. The buckets were heavy—they had to be full or the *Kapo* might get upset—and I could see Gyuri straining with each step. He wasn't used to such labor, and his energy was waning fast. At some point in midmorning, he stopped and set down his cargo, dropping to his hands and knees to catch his breath.

Seeing this, the *Kapo* charged over and screamed at Gyuri to get up. When Gyuri didn't, the *Kapo* hit him on the side of the head. "Get up, I tell you! Stand, you swine!"

Gyuri, his ear bleeding, struggled to his feet. He appeared to be unsteady and disoriented. I was afraid he might say something that would only invite more violence, so I ran up the side of the trench, grabbed hold of the two buckets, and said to the *Kapo*, "He's new. Only got here yesterday. Let him go to the latrine for a few minutes, will you? I'll carry these."

The *Kapo* eyed me maliciously, and I could tell he was considering hitting me as well. But then a glint of humanity entered his eyes and he said, "Fine. All right." He blinked, and the glint was extinguished, and he growled at Gyuri, "You got three minutes. Not one second more. And if you stop working again before lunch break, I'll tear up your other ear too."

Tears streamed down Gyuri's face as he hurried off toward a nearby makeshift shack that served as the latrine. He did not utter another word until lunch, but retreated into himself, stooping more and more with each bucket load he carried.

Vilmos and I continued filling buckets and handing them over to Gyuri and other prisoners to be emptied. The work was mindless and endless. It would take weeks to finish. As the minutes dragged by with agonizing slowness, I could feel the little strength I had fade away. My muscles ached all over, my head swam, and a few times I saw dark spots dancing in my vision. The thirst was killing me. Vilmos, it appeared, was faring even worse. He was taking shallow, raspy breaths, and each time he lifted a full shovel, his stick-like arms trembled and a low groan escaped his lips. A few times he coughed as he had that morning, and it sounded as though his lungs were tearing to shreds.

We kept a lookout for the *Kapo*, slowing our pace whenever his back was turned. The SS guards were no trouble. They had retreated under the shade of a few nearby trees, and they couldn't see into the trench.

At one point, Vilmos and I found ourselves relatively isolated from other prisoners, and I repeated the question I'd asked him the night before.

"Where did you get the bread, Vilmos?"

Vilmos cast a nervous look around. "Off a dead boy."

"A boy?"

"Fifteen, sixteen, maybe."

Which was a boy, I supposed, back in the ordinary world. But here, a fifteen-year-old, sixteen certainly, was a man, bearing the same hardships, subjected to the same horrors as nominal adults.

"There's something you're not telling me," I said. "Getting bread off a dead body is nothing special. Why didn't you tell me this yesterday in the block?"

Vilmos looked at me, and I saw tears in his eyes. "Because the boy was murdered. That's why."

5

"Murdered?" For a second I was confused. Weren't all the people who died in Auschwitz-Birkenau murdered? Even those who perished from disease or starvation or hard labor? "You mean he was killed by another prisoner?"

Even that wasn't unheard of. Just this morning we had witnessed the brutal murder of an anonymous prisoner by the *Lagerälteste*, who, for all his power, was a prisoner himself. And there were also killings among the regular prisoners. Violent fights over bread or contraband cigarettes or better position on the bunks. Minor things in the world from which we'd been expelled, but gigantic, all-encompassing things here.

"I think so," Vilmos said. "I didn't see it happen, but I don't think a guard killed him. A guard would have shot him."

"How was he killed?"

"Someone stabbed him." Vilmos raised a hand to his Adam's apple. "Right about here." He closed his eyes and swallowed hard. "It was terrible. His face..."

"Where was the body?" I asked.

"In the ditch behind the latrines."

I had discovered that spot a month after I'd arrived in Auschwitz.

Between the rear of the latrines and the fences ran a dry ditch with a mound of earth along its western bank. It had obviously been dug for some purpose, perhaps as a drainage or sewage ditch, but for one reason or another it had never been put to its intended use. The ditch itself, and the small piece of ground between it and the latrines, was a blind spot, where the lights from the watchtowers did not reach. This could not be used to escape the camp, but it was perfect for clandestine meetings, being out of sight of both guards and prisoners. There were several such spots in the camp. The Germans probably knew about most of them, but they cared little about what went on among the prisoners, as long as there were no escapes or revolts, or anything that interfered with the wholesale destruction of Jews or the extraction of slave labor from the prisoners.

This particular spot was not as popular as others because the stench wafting from the latrines hung over it like a pestilence.

"What were you doing there?" I asked.

Vilmos looked at his clogs. "I was meeting someone."

We were quiet for a moment as Gyuri came to collect our filled buckets and to give us two empty ones.

"Who did you meet?" I asked when Gyuri had climbed out of the trench and Vilmos and I were alone once more.

"No one. The only person I saw was the dead boy."

"All right, but who did you intend to meet?"

"It doesn't matter, Adam."

"It does if this man heard or saw anything, or perhaps did worse."

Vilmos's eyes flashed. "He's not a murderer, I can assure you that."

"Yes, but—"

"And you're not a police detective anymore, Adam. Not here."

To that I had no answer. It was the absolute truth.

Vilmos was the only person in Auschwitz who knew of my work history. I refrained from telling any other prisoner for fear word of my former occupation would reach the ears of one of the criminal prisoners. Since many of those had higher status in the camp and were likely to hold an unfavorable opinion of cops, such a revelation could prove detrimental to my continued existence.

Vilmos's gaze softened. "I'm sorry, Adam. I didn't mean for it to sound like that."

"Nothing to apologize for, Vilmos. You're absolutely right. I didn't mean to pry into your business. You don't have to share anything with me."

"Please don't be angry with me, Adam. Your friendship means a great deal to me."

"And yours to me," I said, thinking that Vilmos's friendship was by far my most prized possession.

Vilmos's smile was faint and sad. "This place, this dreadful place. It makes it so hard to remain a human being, doesn't it?"

I nodded, unsure of where I currently stood on the spectrum of human morals and values. Since my arrival at the camp, I had slipped a ways toward the corrupt end and felt myself straining to keep from slipping further. But at least I did not stab boys in the throat. Which raised a question...

"You went through the boy's clothes?" I asked.

"Just a quick search. I was stunned when I found the bread."

"Was it difficult to find?"

"Not at all. It was tucked under his waistband."

"That's strange, wouldn't you say? Why didn't the murderer take the bread himself?"

"I don't know," Vilmos said. "But you're right. It is strange."

The *Kapo* had turned around and was coming back our way, so we ceased our conversation and resumed working at a regular pace. I considered the unclaimed bread as I worked, and it felt good to have something to occupy my mind. Something not related to the family I'd lost or the incessant struggle for survival. When the *Kapo* went to inspect the work of other prisoners, I resumed my questioning.

"Was anything done to the boy?" I asked.

"Apart from the stabbing, you mean?"

"Yes. Something sexual, for instance. Were his trousers lowered?"

"No," Vilmos said. "He was fully clothed."

"Was he lying on his back or front?"

"On his back. Why?"

"Because if he had been lying on his front, I'd have asked you if you noticed any blood on the seat of his trousers. You didn't happen to turn him over, did you?"

Vilmos looked sick to his stomach. "I didn't move him. I only searched his clothes for, you know, whatever he might have had."

It was obvious Vilmos was deeply ashamed of what he'd done. He too had not slipped all the way. At least, not yet.

"What about other wounds or cuts? Did you see any?"

"I don't think so."

"Nothing on the hands or arms?"

Vilmos closed his eyes in concentration. "It was already pretty gloomy when I saw him, and there was a lot of blood. His hands were drenched all over. I don't know if it was because he tried to stanch the blood flow from the wound in his throat or because he sustained other injuries."

Which told me absolutely nothing. If the boy had no cuts on his hands and arms, it might have meant that he had been caught by surprise or killed by someone he knew. You come at someone with a knife, and he'll instinctively raise his arms to protect himself. Not that it does much good, usually. Flesh is no match for sharp metal. But it would leave clear marks—cuts and slashes on the victim's hands and arms.

"You're sure it was a stab wound?" I asked. "Not a slashing one?"

"A stab wound. I could see the hole. His throat was all bloody, of course, but I'd have noticed if he'd been slashed."

Which might or might not have been true. Some people's powers of observation deteriorate significantly at the sight of blood and death. Vilmos's recollection could be faulty. For all I knew, the boy's throat had been slashed. For all I knew, there had been defensive cuts on the boy's hands and arms, and Vilmos did not remember seeing them. I wished I could study photographs of the dead body, but of course there weren't any.

"Is this how you were as a detective?" Vilmos said. "Asking all these terrible questions?"

I clenched my jaw, dug my shovel into the crumbling earth, hoisted it up, and dumped the load into a bucket. I'd forgotten myself again. In my mind, I was already picturing myself examining the boy's body and looking for clues at the murder scene. I was being ridiculous. That life was over. "Yeah. That's what the job entails."

"It was quite impressive. I wish I'd known you then, before the war."

"I wish so too. But let's talk about other things. Like you said, I'm not a detective anymore, and this isn't my case. I doubt if it's anyone's."

"Probably not," Vilmos said.

And why should it be? What did the death of one nameless boy matter in this place where thousands, perhaps hundreds of thousands, of other boys lost their lives? The answer was that it mattered not at all.

6

At lunchtime, we formed a line again, this time to claim our soup. One's position in the line was of the utmost importance. Because the fact of the matter was that one bowl of soup was not the equal of another. It all depended on the soup's composition, the depth of the vat holding it, and the manner in which the prisoner distributing the soup ladled it out.

If the soup contained chunks of potatoes, for example, the upper half of the soup would not be as nutritious as the lower, since the potatoes would naturally sink to the bottom. So positioning yourself at the back of the line might prove more rewarding.

But if, instead, the soup was enriched by thin strips of unidentifiable meat, which happened now and then, you might find these morsels of protein bobbing on the surface. In that case, you would be wise to stand near the front of the line.

It was a complex puzzle, with many variables, as intricate as any mathematical theorem that had frustrated great minds over the centuries. And one, arguably, upon whose solution much graver matters hinged.

If we'd been given any information regarding the makeup of the soup, we might have planned our moves in advance. As it stood, we never knew what lay in store for us until the final moment. And still, some prisoners fared better than others. Partly that was due to experience: the longer your imprisonment, the better your eye for such matters. And partly it was due to nothing but dumb luck, which seemed to cling to some prisoners while turning its back on others.

The one person who did know was the prisoner who distributed the soup. Be on his good side, and he might plunge his ladle deeper to dump a hunk of turnip or potato in your bowl. Be on his bad, and he might skim the thin liquid off the top.

Regardless of what you got, it was never enough and far from satisfactory. The vegetables were often rotten, the potatoes were past their prime, the meat had a strange texture. And the overall taste was invariably foul. But if I were ever offered a greater portion, I never refused.

The line was as orderly as starving men could make it. There were shoves and the occasional punch, punctuated by curses and threats in multiple languages, and the sizzling desperation of men whose empty stomachs were driving them to the brink of madness. Everyone jostled for position, attempting to switch places as they got closer and thought they could spy what ingredients the soup held.

Our place was at the middle of the line. During the morning, one of the other prisoners had died. One minute he was hauling buckets of dirt, the next he was lying prone on the ground, unmoving. Gyuri had inherited his bowl, which he now held toward the prisoner in charge of the soup.

"Hungarian, are you?" the prisoner asked Gyuri. He had a Carpathian accent.

Gyuri nodded, and I said, "All three of us are."

The prisoner dipped his ladle low, bringing up two pieces of potato, and filled Gyuri's bowl almost to the brim. He did the same for us. His mouth stretched into a smile at once sad and kind. "I'll try to keep some for you," he said. "Check with me after everyone gets their share."

We thanked him and sat on the ground to eat. The soup was watery and had a muddy hue. The potatoes were speckled with dark spots. The smell would extinguish the appetite of anyone who wasn't starving. Trying to ignore the taste, I finished my portion quickly and licked the bowl clean. Vilmos ate more slowly. Gyuri didn't touch his food. He just stared at his bowl with a disgusted expression.

"Go ahead," Vilmos told Gyuri. "You have to eat."

Gyuri nodded shakily, tilted the bowl, and worked one of the potato pieces into his mouth. He gave it two chews, swallowed, and then his face spasmed. He gagged, retched, and the bowl slipped from his grasp, tumbling over and spilling its precious contents on the ground. I stared dumbstruck at the soup seeping into the dirt. The waste horrified me. Another surge of rage at Gyuri pulsed through me. How could he be so stupid?

The second hunk of potato lay on the ground like a diamond coughed up by the generous earth after a flood. Two other prisoners, gaunt and bony, scuttled toward it on all fours like rats. I hurled myself at the potato, clutched it in my fist, and snarled at the would-be marauders like a wild animal. My teeth were bared, the hand holding the potato pressed to my chest and the other balled into a fist so tight that my fingernails dug painfully into my palm.

The two prisoners stopped dead in their tracks. Their eyes glit-

tered with ravenous, mad hunger. Saliva coated their lips. Both
were breathing hard. Both weighed me, and each other, with their
eyes, each determining whether he could beat the other two and
whether the prize would be worth the inevitable bruises, cuts, or
worse.

For my part, I was not a man at that moment but a starving
mongrel, with a piece of raw meat under its paw it would die to
keep. Not only die, but kill as well. In that moment, I would have
gladly torn those men apart with my bare hands. I would have
ripped their throats with my teeth. I would have gouged their eyes
out with my fingernails. All to keep possession of a single hunk of
potato the size of a small lemon. It was mine. I would have given
up my last shred of humanity before I'd let them have it.

We stood like that for what seemed an eternity, but in truth
was no more than a second or two. My heart pounded in my
scrawny chest. My pulse drummed in my ears. My skin vibrated
with insane craving and burned with anger—at the two prisoners,
at the Germans who had forced us to descend to such bestiality, at
the Hungarian authorities who had expelled us with such glee, at
God who had deserted us.

"It's mine," I said at length, my voice rough and barely recog-
nizable. "Back off."

The two other prisoners eyed me for a second longer, then the
tension left their bodies, their heads slumped between their
narrow shoulders, and they turned and slunk away like dogs who
had been struck on the snout by their master. In their wake, they
left a cloud of shame as suffocating as the one that now enveloped
me. *My God, what have I become? What have I allowed the Nazis to
make of me?*

A hand touched my shoulder, and I jumped and swirled
around. It was Vilmos, his face full of compassion and understanding.

"It's all right," he said. "It's all right, Adam."

But it wasn't, and we both knew it. We knew that each time we squabbled over food like alley cats, or searched through the clothes of the dead like grave robbers, or felt a shameful relief when we survived a selection while our fellow prisoners were marked for the gas chambers, that we were shedding another layer of the men we'd once been and becoming something less than human beings—which was just what the Nazis considered us to begin with.

Gyuri had crumpled to the ground after spilling the soup. He now sat off to the side, his head buried in his hands, moaning in a low, broken voice, "Oh God, oh God, oh God," over and over again. His shoulders were quaking, though it did not sound like he was crying.

I unclenched my fist and stared at my bounty. It was a sorry treasure—mottled with age, streaked with dirt, shapeless and crumbling. But a treasure nonetheless. I looked at Vilmos and saw him licking his lips. He offered an apologetic smile and gave a tiny shrug as if to say, *What else can we do? We have to live, don't we?*

I nodded wordlessly. It was best to say as little as possible. Whatever I could say would sound like an excuse, similar to a criminal attempting to justify his crimes. With a dirty finger, I carved the hunk of potato into two pieces, as equal in size as I could make them, and offered Vilmos the bigger one. He blew on it to dislodge whatever dirt had not embedded itself into the potato and shoved it in his mouth. I did the same, and we both chewed, not looking at each other until the food had disappeared down our throats.

7

The Hungarian prisoner in charge of the soup shook his head sadly when Vilmos and I came to collect a second helping. "Nothing left, I'm afraid. The bastards did not even give me enough for everyone."

Gyuri, exhausted, had curled up on the ground and fallen asleep almost instantly. Vilmos and I sat close to him. With a short stick, Vilmos scratched a large square in the dirt between us, then divided it into an 8x8 grid of smaller squares. In some of these squares, with his forefinger, he drew letters. Each letter corresponded to a chess piece in Hungarian—K for *király*, king; V for *vezér*, queen; B for *bástya*, rook; and so on. Some of these letters were capitalized, indicating my pieces; the other letters were Vilmos's. His army was bigger and also better positioned.

This particular game had started two days ago and had been played in installments since, whenever we had the chance. Vilmos remembered the disposition of the pieces from one session to the next. The first time he'd suggested playing chess, soon after we'd arrived in Auschwitz, I scoffed at the idea, saying it would be impossible. But he had proved me wrong.

"It's not so hard," he'd told me soon after we'd started playing together. "It looks complicated, but it isn't. There are sixty-four squares on a chess board, which means all I need to remember are sixty-four positions, and at all times, at least half of those are empty. All I need to do is attribute a letter to each piece—capital letters for yours and non-capital letters for mine. And another letter to signify an empty square. It's quite simple when you look at it that way."

"I couldn't do it if my life depended on it," I said. "You have an exceptional memory."

Vilmos smiled a humble smile. "Nothing of the sort, I assure you. Especially if you compare my abilities to those of true grand-masters. Have you ever seen Salo Flohr play?"

"No."

"But you've heard of him?"

"He's a chess player from Czechoslovakia, isn't he?"

"Not just a chess player, but a true master of the art. He's also Jewish, but that's beside the point. He hasn't lived in Czecho-slovakia since the Germans took over. Last I heard, he'd fled to Sweden, and if only we were all so lucky, eh? But that has nothing to do with the story I was meaning to tell you. Which is that I saw Salo Flohr play, and it was one of the greatest moments of my life." Vilmos's eyes sparkled at the memory.

"When was this?"

"1936. In Prague. I traveled especially for the tournament. I watched Salo Flohr beat a florid Russian who scowled perpetually as he examined the state of the board, a state that deteriorated gradually and irremediably as the match progressed. Salo Flohr played with his usual quiet elegance, which was a pleasure to behold, but that's not what amazed me most."

He paused and looked at me, and I saw a tiny mischievous smile play at the corner of his mouth. He savored the role of the storyteller, and he was inviting me to draw out the story from him.

"What amazed you most?" I asked, giving him what he wanted.

"After the tournament was over," Vilmos said, "Flohr arranged a meeting with a local club of hobbyist players. They set up twenty-five tables in a semi-circle on stage at a theater hall, and on each table they placed a chess board. Flohr then proceeded to play against each of the twenty-five lucky men who'd been selected to face him, and he did so simultaneously, making a move at one table and then stepping over to the next to do the same. Of course, the state of the board was different at each table. Flohr won twenty-two of those matches, and drew the other three. Afterward, Flohr recited the sequence of moves in all those matches. Can you imagine that? Twenty-five matches!"

"It's unbelievable," I said.

Vilmos nodded, enthusiasm lending color to his face. "I saw it with my own eyes, Adam. With my own eyes. So you see, my own memory is nothing extraordinary."

Our lunch break was short, and during it we had to eat and relieve ourselves, so we had little time for chess. Consequently, we played a lightning game, without thinking, fingers moving quickly, rubbing out letters from one square and scrawling them in another as we moved our pieces across the board. "It's not the proper way to play," Vilmos said, "but nothing is proper about this place, so this will have to do. After the war, after liberation, we'll play a proper match. We'll sit in a café on the banks of the Danube and play, all right?"

"All right, Vilmos," I said, trying not to show my doubts that I would live to see liberation, if it ever came. "But not on the banks of the Danube. Not anywhere in Hungary."

"Where, then?" he said, taking a bishop with his queen, leaving my left flank horribly exposed.

"My father was a devout man. Not like a yeshiva man, but he took his religion seriously, visited the synagogue regularly, and said his prayers every day. Nothing moved him as much as saying those words at the end of the Passover Seder and the *Ne'ila* service on Yom Kippur. *L'Shana Haba'ah B'Yerushalayim.* Next year in Jerusalem."

"Your father was a Zionist?"

"Yes," I said, the old twinge of grief over his passing still sharp in my gut. I moved a rook three squares forward. "He gave money to Zionist organizations and said he would like to immigrate to the Land of Israel. My mother was dead set against the idea. She didn't want to uproot herself and her family, and he was not the sort of man who put his foot down. Maybe he would have managed to persuade her with time, but he got ill and died before he had the chance. I was heartbroken when he died, but now I think it was for the best. At least he was spared this place."

Vilmos was quiet for a moment. From the trees came the raucous laughter of the SS guards. They were stuffing their faces with thick sandwiches and swigging from canteens. Fresh water. My mouth burned with desire for it. I had been thirsty before I came to Auschwitz, of course, but it had been a different species of thirst. This one was a continuous torture. Just like the hunger.

"So that's where you'll go when you're free again?" Vilmos said. "To Jerusalem?"

"It doesn't have be Jerusalem specifically. But I'll be going to Palestine. To the Land of Israel. Which is where we should have all gone long before the war started."

"We didn't know," Vilmos said in a voice made brittle by regret. "How could we have known it would come to this?"

We couldn't, of course. Only the devil could have imagined

Auschwitz. And yet men had envisioned it, designed it, caused it to be built. So maybe we should have been able to foresee it. Maybe we should have known it was time to leave.

Again Vilmos was silent. Thought lines creased his forehead. He might have been thinking about his dead loved ones. I was thinking of mine.

"If not Jerusalem, then where?" he said eventually, in a light-hearted tone that sounded a bit forced. "A kibbutz?"

I shook my head and allowed myself a wry smile. "I don't think living in a collective fits my nature. So maybe I will go to Jerusalem. Or maybe to Tel Aviv. I've seen pictures of the beach there, and of some of the buildings. I think I might like it there." I paused, trying to conjure up those pictures, and was surprised and gratified when they appeared crystal clear in my mind. And I wondered how it was possible to feel a longing for a place where I had never been. "Yes," I said. "I think I might like it just fine."

Right then, the *Kapo* shouted that lunch break was over, and we got back to work.

8

We worked until late afternoon. By that time, I was so tired my awareness had blurred, and I barely noticed what I was doing. My movements had turned automatic. Sink the spade into the ground, raise it, dump the contents into a bucket. Then repeat. Dozens, no, hundreds of times.

When the *Kapo* finally announced that the workday was over, I could hardly climb out of the trench. My legs were wobbly, and I kept slipping down, dirtying the knees of my trousers.

Vilmos helped me over the top, though he looked as worn out as I was, if not more. We returned our shovels to the truck and formed lines again. Two prisoners did not join the ranks. They lay on the ground like discarded rag dolls. Dead.

The *Kapo* berated us for our laziness and warned us to not shirk our duty the next day. "I've gone easy on you," he shouted, "but no more, you understand? No more." He pointed at Gyuri and me and then at a pair of other prisoners. "Take the bodies and let's go. Quick march or you'll miss your dinner, not that you deserve any."

Gyuri took the feet of one of the dead men, I grabbed his arms, and we began the trek back to camp. The dead man was nothing but skin and bones, but tired as we were, he felt as heavy as a sack of bricks.

Gyuri walked with his head lowered. Something seemed to have gone out of him. He hadn't said much since lunchtime, and there was a heaviness to his step that looked like more than just tiredness.

Somewhere along the way, two other prisoners relieved us of our load, and I went over to Gyuri and laid a hand on his shoulder. "It gets a little easier," I told him. "Not better, but a little easier."

He looked at me, and for a second I thought he was going to say something, maybe call me out on my outrageous lie, but he just nodded and turned his head away.

As we neared the main gate, we heard music—the camp orchestra, playing a military march to greet us upon our return. The *Kapo* shouted at us to look sharp and quicken our stride.

"Walk straight," Vilmos told Gyuri. "Head high, eyes forward."

Gyuri looked at him questioningly, but he followed our example and did as he was told. We all fought to find the energy to straighten our stooped backs, raise our chins, and add a swing to our arms.

Because at the gate stood a gang of SS doctors. They were scrutinizing us closely. These doctors were angels of torment instead of mercy; purveyors of death instead of healing. Their job was to cull the prisoner population by identifying the sick and those too exhausted to perform slave labor for the Third Reich. They looked for signs of illness, lethargy, an extreme depletion of body mass— the latter relative, of course, because all of us had lost a great deal of weight.

And if one of them pointed at you, or inscribed your number

in his little black notebook, you were on your way to the gas chambers, and then up the chimney.

So I lengthened my stride and tried to look as healthy as possible. I kept all trace of the pain each step was causing me off my face. I tried to swell out my sunken chest, to project an air of robustness. And all the while I prayed that I would not be chosen, and felt a great shame at being so weak and helpless.

I kept my gaze straight ahead as we entered the camp. Looking into the eyes of an SS officer was a grave offense. But in the periphery of my vision I could see the faces of our tormentors. They were chatting and laughing even as they glanced at us contemptuously. They were as sure of their superiority as a cat who toys with a captured mouse.

I carved their faces into my mind, searing them into my memory with a blazing hatred. As long as I lived, I told myself, I would not forget these faces; I would not forget these men. If a miracle happened, if by some chance I survived this place, I would hunt these men down. Hunt them down and kill them.

9

Vilmos and Gyuri and I hurried to the *Appellplatz* and joined the other prisoners for *Appell*—roll call. We stood in lines of ten, utterly silent, and waited to be counted. Sunset came late in Poland in July, so there was still light, but the western sky was black. The crematoriums still devoured the victims. The chimneys continued to spew the smoke of death.

We were supposed to stand motionless, but all around I could see prisoners swaying with exhaustion or squirming with agony as their bowels spasmed with diarrhea. I was suffering from a mild case of it myself and could only hope I'd have the strength to not soil myself. We had not been allowed to go to the latrines upon our return to camp. First, the Germans had to ensure there had been no escapes.

I prayed there hadn't been, and hated myself for it. Because if the count revealed that a prisoner was missing, we would be made to stand here for hours until he was accounted for.

SS officers walked up and down the lines of prisoners, counting. We, and the other *kommandos*, had laid those who had died during the workday beside our lines, and the SS officers, sticklers for accuracy, made sure to include the dead in their count.

There were thousands of us, so this took some time. As happened more often than not, the count arrived at by one SS officer did not match that of his colleague, so they commenced counting from scratch. And all the while, as they counted, as they compared results and argued over discrepancies, we continued to stand.

Gradually, a deep ache settled in my lower back. It started out as a whimper, progressed to a cry, and eventually grew to a wailing shriek. I gritted my teeth against the pain and told myself it would soon be over, that the pain would diminish when we were allowed to move.

But it was not over soon. There was a problem with the count. Or the Germans simply wished to torture us. Some of them liked to see us suffer. Others viewed us with utter indifference. A couple of weeks earlier, I'd overheard two guards make a bet as to how many of us would collapse during roll call that evening, as though they were betting on a horse race and not the lives of human beings.

Two rows in front of me, a prisoner toppled to the ground and was still. No one tried to help him up. No one dared. We were not allowed to move. I kept my eyes on the fallen man, and under my breath muttered, "Get up, get up, get up," but he remained lying there, motionless.

Finally, roll call was over. Thousands of prisoners began moving in all directions, like an ant colony prodded with a stick. Surrounded by the noise of hundreds of conversations in a medley of languages, I rushed to the fallen man. Another prisoner had already knelt beside him and had turned him over. His open eyes left no room for doubt or hope. The man was dead. I helped place his corpse with the other dead bodies and sprinted to the latrine.

The short while between the end of roll call and night curfew was the only free time we truly had. One could barter with other prisoners, or wash up, or visit friends or relatives in other blocks—provided any of them were still alive.

But first there was dinner.

Vilmos and Gyuri and I stood in line for our evening bread. Dry, rough, moldy, and infused with sawdust, eating it was like munching on sand. The quantity of bread was as inadequate as its quality—barely enough for a grown man who had spent his day lounging at the office; gravely insufficient for one who had done hard physical labor for ten hours. In addition, each prisoner received a small pat of margarine. Other nights we got a bit of cheese or sausage or a tablespoon's worth of marmalade, but nowhere near enough to smear across the entire bread.

Decision time. Should I eat the entire bread now? Or would it be better to save a portion for breakfast tomorrow? On the one hand, my stomach was sending distress signals; it wanted the whole thing right now, tomorrow be damned. On the other, a breakfast of only coffee or tea would leave me with nothing solid to eat from now until lunchtime at the earliest. There were no good options, and the hunger was making it difficult to think.

"Is it really true?" I heard a small voice say. "Are they really all gone?"

The speaker was Gyuri. He was holding his bread in both hands, staring at the columns of smoke rising from the chimneys and fire pits. His face was a mask of agony and grief.

"I'm afraid so," Vilmos said. "I'm so sorry." He made a motion as if to lay a comforting hand on Gyuri's arm, but he stopped midway and let his hand fall back to his side. He was a good man, Vilmos, and he longed to help Gyuri in his mourning. But none of us had been prepared for this place. None of us knew the proper way to console a man whose entire family had been gassed to death, a man who in one day had lost everything and been turned into a slave. We didn't even know how to console ourselves.

Gyuri bit his lip. He took a deep breath and gave a determined nod, like a man reaching a fateful decision. Alarm bells began ringing in my head. I took a step closer as realization began to set in. Gyuri's eyes met mine. He offered me a sad smile that had the odd effect of making him look happy. He shifted his gaze from me to Vilmos. "Thank you both," he said. "Thank you for all you've done for me."

Vilmos frowned, unsure of what to make of this. I, on the other hand, understood perfectly. "Don't!" I said, taking another step toward Gyuri, my hands reaching to grab hold of his shirt. But then he surprised me by tearing his hunk of bread in two and tossing the two halves high in the air—one at me, the other at Vilmos.

Reflexively, I halted to grab hold of the bread. Gyuri had started running as soon as he'd tossed it. He ran straight toward the nearest fence. By the time I caught the bread and started giving chase, he had opened a formidable lead. I shouted for him to stop, and heard Vilmos shout as well, but Gyuri paid us no heed. He no longer lacked energy. Propelled by his grief, his pain, and his decision, he had grown wings. I did not think I could catch him, but I had to try. I had to save him. I pumped my arms and ordered my legs to move faster. I willed myself forward, finding a strength I thought was long gone. I started gaining on him. I was going to make it.

Then I nearly collided with one prisoner, and then with another, which broke my run. Gyuri experienced no such trouble. He bumped into no one, nor did any other prisoner attempt to stop him. His path appeared to have been cleared by a heavenly hand—the same hand that had once cleared a path through the

Red Sea for Moses and the People of Israel, a path toward safety and freedom. Though Gyuri's path led to neither of those things.

Again I shouted for him to stop. Again I sprinted to catch him. All to no avail. I was a good distance behind him when he crossed the dead line near the fence, the line no prisoner was allowed to cross on pain of death. The guards in the watchtowers could have shot him, but why waste bullets? They knew what Gyuri intended to do. They'd seen it before.

"Stop!" I yelled, as Gyuri hurled himself forward, leaping into the air with arms stretched wide, like a bird spreading its wings as it launches into a clear blue sky.

He hit the fence with a dull twang. Then his body tensed, his head rearing back, his mouth gaping wide in a soundless scream. He hung on the fence with his arms spread horizontally, like Jesus on the cross, attached to the wires by the electric current that ran through the fence and now him. His body jittered and twitched. His flesh started to burn. I could smell his singed skin.

He died as soon as he'd touched the fence. My brain knew that. But the rest of me didn't. I was intent on reaching him, on saving him. Logic and caution had deserted me. I was gripped by one all-consuming need—to save Gyuri. At that moment, it was not merely the most important thing in the world but the only thing in the world.

I was two strides from the dead line when someone tackled me, falling on top of me and trying to pin me down. I bucked, meaning to throw whoever it was off me and continue my senseless sprint toward Gyuri. But the man pressed me harder to the ground, his arms hugging my torso, his knees tight around my thighs.

"It's no use, Adam. It's too late," Vilmos said in my ear. His voice was strained and breathless. He was smaller and weaker than me, and he knew he couldn't hold me down for long. "He's dead, Adam. It will do no good if you kill yourself, too."

It wasn't true. It couldn't be true. I tensed my muscles, gave a great cry, and jerked upward with all my strength, hurling Vilmos off me. I rolled and pushed myself to my feet, meaning to run again toward Gyuri, but Vilmos was in my way, and he raised both hands, palms out, and shouted, "Don't, Adam. Look at him. He's dead. Gyuri's dead."

This time the words penetrated, stopping me like a slap to the face. I looked at Gyuri's lifeless form at the base of the fence, then at Vilmos sitting on the ground with tears running down his face. He had saved me. He had stopped me before I'd crossed the dead line and killed myself. But I had failed to save Gyuri.

I sank to my knees and started to cry. It made no sense, because I'd barely known Gyuri. Why was his death more meaningful than that of any of the other men I'd seen die in the camp? Why did it hurt so much?

Maybe because I'd become invested in his survival. I had saved him from Hendrik. I had shared my bowl with him. I had tried to help him make the transition to camp life. And all that effort had been for naught.

A short while later, our faces wet, Vilmos and I rose to our feet. With a final glance at Gyuri, we turned and walked toward our block. Neither of us spoke. It was a few minutes before I noticed that the bread Gyuri had tossed at me was still clasped in my hand. Camp instincts. Vilmos had tucked his half into his sleeve when he ran after me. I did the same now. I'd save it for breakfast tomorrow.

We ran into Hendrik, who grinned when he saw me. "I told you he wouldn't last. He was weak."

Red fire erupted in my head. I turned to Hendrik with violence in my heart. I wanted to rearrange his face, to replace that grin with blood and broken teeth.

"You son of a bitch," I said, marching toward him. "I'm going to—"

My voice died mid-sentence. For at that moment, in the mass of prisoners milling behind Hendrik, I saw a man that I knew. And he saw me. His appearance was different from the last time I saw him. His hair was gone, his face thinner. But I recognized him all the same. And by the widening of his eyes and the twitch of a smile on his lips, I could tell he had recognized me as well.

A bolt of fear shot from my belly button to my chest, supplanting my hatred for Hendrik. I rushed past him, ignoring his shouts, but the man had already turned and disappeared into the crowd. With mounting dread, I pushed my way after him, but he was gone. I weaved through the prisoners, searching for the man, but it was like trying to find one specific grain of sand in a beach. In their striped uniforms, with their starved physiques and shaved heads, the prisoners provided the perfect camouflage for one of their own.

Vilmos caught up with me. "What is it, Adam? What's the matter?"

"Did you see him?"

"See who?"

I was about to say Andris Farkas, the man's name, but Vilmos didn't know him. "The man who smiled at me. He was standing right there." I pointed to where Farkas had been standing when we'd locked eyes.

Vilmos shook his head. "No, I didn't. But if he was smiling at you, why do you look so distraught?"

Because Andris Farkas was trouble. Andris Farkas meant that, in all likelihood, I had no more than a day or two to live.

10

"His name is Andris Farkas," I told Vilmos after we found a relatively isolated spot, out of earshot of other prisoners.

"Okay. Who is he?"

"He's from Hungary. A Jew. And a thief. One night in '38, I caught him as he was climbing out a window of an apartment he'd broken into."

"Oh," murmured Vilmos, understanding where this was going.

"He knew my name," I said. "Knew I was Jewish. So when his attempt at bribery failed, he appealed to our common ethnicity and asked me to look the other way while he made a quick getaway."

"But you didn't?"

"No. We'd been looking for him for months. He'd committed a string of robberies, which was bad enough, but in one of them, he'd beaten an old woman who lived in the house he broke into. She had to be hospitalized. So I arrested him. He got eighteen years."

Vilmos let out a low whistle. "A harsh sentence, isn't it?"

"Yes. The prosecutor in the trial used Farkas's Jewishness against him, portrayed him as a slimy rat who robbed good Hungarian folk even though he had plenty of money. It wasn't true; Farkas had grown up poor, and his robberies never netted him much. But the prosecutor didn't let that get in the way of a good story. It was right before the government started enacting anti-Jewish laws, and the atmosphere was darkening by the day. So Farkas got eighteen years. I remember sitting in the courtroom, hearing the sentence and feeling sick to my stomach and thinking that maybe I shouldn't have arrested Farkas after all. Maybe I should have let him go with a warning and a little roughing up to make him reconsider his life of crime."

"You couldn't have known he'd get that kind of sentence."

"Maybe not. Don't get me wrong, Vilmos. Farkas certainly deserved jail time. He was a professional criminal. Arresting him was my job. I was protecting the public." I sighed. "And soon after that, I was thrown off the police force for being Jewish."

Vilmos was silent for a moment, perhaps reliving a similar indignity he'd suffered at the time. "And he's here? You're sure?"

"One hundred percent. The Germans must have cleared Hungarian prisons of Jews. They're certainly thorough, aren't they? And I'll tell you something else: Farkas recognized me. I'm sure of it."

"It doesn't mean he'll tell anyone about you."

"Maybe not. But the bastard smiled at me, Vilmos. And then he fled so I wouldn't find him."

Vilmos gave it some thought. "Maybe he won't know where to find you. He knows your name, but he doesn't know which block you sleep in."

I pointed at the number stitched to my uniform, the same number that was tattooed to my forearm. "He saw this. I could tell by how his eyes shifted down and then back up to my face."

Vilmos understood the implications. My number could be used to locate me. Not by Farkas himself, perhaps, but some of the criminal prisoners, those who held functions in the camp—*Block-ältestes*, for example—could use their contacts to find me.

"You don't know that he'll tell anyone," Vilmos said after a minute, probably because he could think of nothing else to say.

I didn't reply.

"And even if he does," Vilmos continued, "maybe nothing will come of it. All the criminal prisoners are German and Austrian. You didn't arrest any of them. Maybe they'll leave you alone."

Again I said nothing. Vilmos did not understand how prisons worked, not fully, even though he was now living in one.

The worst thing to be in a prison is a former cop. Criminals detest policemen. They view them as the cause of their misfortune. So when a cop falls from grace and is incarcerated, he becomes a target, the outlet through which all the hatred criminals have for the police is vented. It doesn't matter who the cop is, or whether he personally arrested any specific prisoner. The hatred is universal.

An imprisoned cop is very much like a *Kapo* or other prisoner-functionary who loses his position and returns to live among the regular prisoners. You wouldn't want to bet money on his longevity.

A cold, heavy fear settled in my bones. It weighed me down, like I was walking with ankle chains.

"We can go block by block and look for him," Vilmos said, sounding utterly unconvinced of the efficacy of his suggestion.

"Just like he would have trouble finding me without my number, I would have trouble finding him," I said. "Besides, what would I do if I found him? Talk to him? Appeal to his conscience? I'm not sure he has much of one. And even if by some miracle I persuaded him to keep his mouth shut, what's to stop him from changing his mind tomorrow? There's only one certain way to stop him from talking."

Vilmos raised a questioning eyebrow, but then he understood, and his eyes dilated.

"Exactly," I said. "So I either kill him or live in fear. And I don't see myself killing a man to prevent him from maybe doing something in the future, even a thief like Farkas. Because there's a chance—a slim one, but a chance nonetheless—that he'll say nothing. If I kill him now, I'll have to live with the possibility that I've committed murder, and I can't see myself doing that."

Which meant that if I indeed died over the next couple of days, I would do so more as the man I'd been before I got to Auschwitz than I thought I was now. It didn't make me feel a whole lot better about my future prospects, but I thought my father would have been proud of me, and that made the notion of dying a little more bearable.

11

Vilmos told me he was going to pay a quick visit to the latrine before bedtime. I went to our block to see if I could reclaim our former bunk, the one we had given up the previous night due to Gyuri. I was ready to fight for our place if need be.

Hendrik was sitting on the stone heating duct that ran down the center of the block. The stoves did not work in summer, and I'd been told they provided inadequate heating during the winter. Prisoners used the heating duct as a bench, since the bunks were too low for men to sit in.

Upon seeing me, Hendrik jumped to his feet and blocked my way. "Hey, you miserable coward. You have a filthy mouth, you—"

A blood-red mist shrouded my vision. I moved in close, clamped one hand around Hendrik's throat, and drove him back until he smacked hard into a bunk. Bringing my face close to his, my nose filled with the stink of his breath and acrid sweat. He saw something in my eyes that made his gape with dread. Maybe it was death that he saw. Maybe that was why he appeared to be paralyzed and made no attempt to break loose.

For a moment I said nothing, just slowly tightened my grip on his throat. My fingers dug into his flesh, compressing the tendons and airway beneath. He whimpered in pain, opened his mouth to say something, but changed his mind when I shook my head.

"Not another word, Hendrik," I said, my voice low and rippling with grief and rage. It was a warning I wasn't sure I wanted him to heed. On the one hand, I had already decided that I did not wish to end my life a murderer. On the other, I knew that if Hendrik said the wrong thing now, there was a good chance I would tear his throat open with my fingers. The latter option had an undeniable appeal.

"You listen to me now," I said, increasing the pressure further. "I just watched a man I cared for die. A man you ridiculed. A man you were about to hurt last night when he was at his most vulnerable. His death means nothing to you, and that's fine. None of us can care for every person that dies here, or we won't be able to function. But you took pleasure in his death, and I don't appreciate that. It makes me believe that I would take pleasure in your death, and trust me, you don't want that. So if you say another word, you do so at your peril. And if you want to fight, I'll fight you. But fair warning: I'll likely kill you. Your decision."

With that, I let go, removing my hand from his throat and stepping back. Suddenly free, Hendrik stumbled forward a little before whirling around and grabbing hold of a bunk. Bending over, he coughed several times, sucking in raspy gulps of air.

I gave him a minute, then said, "Well? What's your decision? Are you going to give me any trouble?"

Hendrik straightened and looked at me. His face was a mask of fury, but I noticed he kept his back pressed to the bunk behind him, as far from me as he could get. Lowering his eyes, he gave a quick shake of his head.

"I want to hear you say it," I said. "Are you going to give me any trouble from now on?"

Hendrik raised his eyes and glanced around him. We had attracted a crowd. I did not see any smiles, but I could sense the delight some of the other prisoners were deriving from Hendrik's humiliation. Right then, I knew I had made a mistake. I had taken it too far; had caused Hendrik too much shame. He would want to get even. But maybe it didn't matter. If my fears regarding Andris Farkas proved accurate, I would soon be dead anyway.

Seeing Hendrik's eyes pause on a certain point, I allowed my gaze to drift a little sideways. There was Marco, one of Hendrik's pals. He and Hendrik had locked eyes, and I could sense the invitation—no, the command—by Hendrik for Marco to come fight alongside him. But Marco lowered his eyes, pretending not to comprehend. Perhaps he was still bitter about Hendrik taking a bigger share of the bread Vilmos had given them the previous night. Or maybe he was scared to fight me.

"No," Hendrik said after realizing he would get no help from Marco. His voice was hoarse. I must have damaged his vocal cords. "No," he said again, but his eyes belied his words. For in them I saw naked, unalloyed hatred. Yes, he would want revenge. Probably not tonight, but soon.

With a quick final glance at our audience, Hendrik pushed himself off the bunk and sauntered out of the block, trying to inject a bit of swagger in his step even in defeat. I watched him until he went outside, then continued toward my former bunk. All desire for conflict had drained out of me. I did not wish to hurt any other prisoner tonight.

As it turned out, I did not need to fight for our place. One of our bunkmates had died during the day and another had gone to the hospital, so there was space for Vilmos and me.

My dreams were wretched that night. Again and again, I

chased Gyuri as he sprinted toward the fence, toward his death. Each time, I was closer than I had been in real life—a mere step behind, within arm's reach, my fingers even brushed the back of his shirt once—but I never managed to catch him. I always ended up short and watched as he leaped on the fence.

But unlike in real life, he didn't strike the fence with the front of his body. Instead, he did a weird turn in midair so that he was facing me as he hit the fence with his back. And each time he did so, his face was different. Once it was my wife's face. Then it was the face of my elder daughter, and after that the face of my younger. All dead because I had failed to save them.

I watched their faces contort in agony as the electricity burned their bodies. Their hair caught fire. Their clothes blazed. Their mouths stretched wide, wider than was possible anywhere but in dreams, and flames shot out of them, like they sometimes did out of the crematorium chimneys. Their cries were uniformly shrill, daggers of sound stabbing at my core. I fell to my knees, covering my ears, but their cries pierced through, unimpeded. There was no escape from my guilt, no clemency for my failure to save my loved ones. Not even wakefulness could rescue me. I did not emerge from sleep until morning wake-up.

The next day began much as the previous one. I awoke into a haze of exhaustion, shook it off as best I could, arranged my bunk, rushed to the latrine, cleaned myself, and drank my morning tea. Vilmos and I still had the bread Gyuri had bequeathed us before he'd killed himself, and that made our breakfast a little richer. I said a silent thank you to Gyuri as I chewed on my inheritance, and made an equally silent apology that I had failed to save him.

My anxiety mounted throughout breakfast and reached a summit as we gathered on the *Appellplatz* to form our *kommandos*. I fully expected my number to be called out, to be summoned to one of the prisoner functionaries who'd learned of my existence from Andris Farkas.

But this did not happen. Rather, we marched off to work in the usual fashion. As we passed by the Czech family camp, we heard no children singing. Instead, I saw a sight that made my heart sink. In the open ground between the blocks, a few tables had been set up. Behind these tables SS doctors were lounging in their crisp uniforms and polished boots, while standing around them were about two dozen guards, all heavily armed.

Female prisoners, fully naked, were made to jump up and down before the SS doctors who examined their stamina with a clinical eye. The guards, however, did not cloak themselves in an air of studious examination. Many were grinning or laughing outright. Some jeered. Many of the women were weeping and trembling—from shame or fear or both—and did their best to shield their nakedness. But they weren't allowed to. The SS doctors wanted to see everything. Whether the women had sores on their bodies. How much fat remained on their buttocks and breasts. If they had suffered an injury that would render them incapable of hard labor.

Each man in our *kommando* knew what this was. A selection. A process by which the SS would winnow the sick and worn-out prisoners from the general population of the family camp. Those selected were deemed useless to the Third Reich and therefore condemned to death.

And the children? What about the children?

They were probably cowering in their block, covering their ears so they wouldn't hear their mothers and sisters and aunts crying. In all likelihood, this would prove just as futile as my covering my ears in my dreams. I couldn't help but think that since a selection was taking place among the grown women, another would likely follow among the children.

The thought made me want to weep, just like these women. But I held the tears back by sheer force of will. I did not want my vision to blur. I wanted to clearly see the faces of all the SS doctors and guards performing this selection, and I added them to the growing list in my head. A list of those I had already judged and sentenced to death—if I survived this place.

I toiled in the trenches under the blazing sun, Vilmos by my side. It was hotter than yesterday, and sweat poured down my back and stung my eyes. That morning during washing, I had discovered a rash along my left side and lower back. I needed an ointment, but of course there was none to be had. The inflamed skin itched and prickled maddeningly. I scratched at it through my clothes, unable to stop, suspecting as I did so that I was only aggravating my condition. My left foot was an even bigger problem. The blister around the knuckle of my big toe had burst, and judging by the swollen red skin around it, infection had set in. I had cleaned the area as best I could that morning, but every step in my heavy, tight clogs was like rubbing salt into the wound. It was not the only sore on my feet, just the worst one. Each morning, when those who had died in the night were heaped outside the blocks, I scoured their feet for larger clogs. But so far, I had come up empty.

Lunchtime soup was distributed by the same kindhearted prisoner as yesterday. He smiled at Vilmos and me, but then his smile faltered.

"What happened to your friend?" he asked. In the ordinary world, the question would have been different. *Where's your friend?* perhaps, or *Is he on holiday?* But in Auschwitz people did not have other places to be. They were expected to follow a routine. If they didn't, one tended to assume the worst.

"He died yesterday," Vilmos said.

"Already? But he was new, wasn't he? Way he looked, I would have thought he'd been here just a few days."

"He threw himself at the fence," I said.

The soup distributor grimaced. "Poor fellow." Then a sort of dreamy look entered his eyes, and I knew he was thinking that maybe Gyuri was the smart one among us. At least his suffering was over.

He blinked back to the moment when I asked about the soup. "Rather poor today. Just turnips and parsnips, and not much of either. But I'll do my best for you."

He did precisely that, and Vilmos and I sat with our bowls and proceeded to empty them. As usual, we ate to blunt our hunger, not for enjoyment.

As I ate, I gazed at the spot where Gyuri had spilled his soup, where I'd nearly come to blows over an overripe piece of potato encrusted with dirt, and I could scarcely believe that what I was experiencing was reality and not some ultra-vivid nightmare.

This place, this hellish place—it shouldn't exist. It couldn't. The mind rebelled against it. It was an insane delusion brought to life, a psychopathic hallucination made real. And it infected every single person it pummeled and trampled, breaking not just their body and spirit but their mind. Detachment and insanity each offered its siren song—a means of escape from some of the hardships Auschwitz imposed upon us. And, of course, there was the ultimate escape, the one Gyuri had chosen; perhaps the most seductive of them all. I struggled against all three and was never sure how far I was from succumbing.

Following my gaze and sensing my thoughts, Vilmos said, "We did everything we could for Gyuri, Adam. It wasn't our fault."

I nodded but said nothing. Vilmos drew a chess board on the ground and filled it with the remaining pieces from yesterday's game. It didn't take him long to defeat me. He was the far better player even in regular circumstances, but on that day I was incapable of focusing on the game.

"Another one?" he asked.

"No," I said. "Let's start a new game tomorrow, okay?"

Vilmos nodded and busied himself with wiping out the board. Neither of us voiced what I feared—that I would not be there tomorrow.

Vilmos's shirt had torn at the collar. I had a needle and some thread, acquired in exchange for a third of my bread ration on the camp's black market. I sewed the collar back together, then threaded the needle into a seam in my trousers.

"Where did you learn to sew like that?" Vilmos asked me.

"My mother taught me. She said a man should not expect a woman to mend his clothes. That women might have more interesting activities with which to fill their time." Sadness squeezed my heart. "She was a special woman, my mother."

Unlike yesterday, all the prisoners survived the day. We trudged back wreathed in our exhaustion and various aches and pains. No SS doctors inspected us at the gate, yet our *Kapo* still yelled at us to hasten our step, straighten our backs, and walk in tight formation.

A train made up of twenty or so cattle cars squatted by the platform like some mythological monster slumbering while it digested its latest prey. The cars were open, and swarms of flies buzzed in and out of them. Hills upon hills of luggage and other belongings lined the platform: suitcases of all sizes and styles, bundles of blankets and bedclothes, sacks and satchels, various loose garments, boxes tethered with string, all lay jumbled about together. The final belongings of a plundered people, the dregs that remained after several rounds of confiscation in their country of origin. I saw a couple of empty baby strollers, a girl's doll with one arm missing, and a single wheelchair lying on its side. Its occupant had either perished during the horrific journey to Auschwitz, or had been yanked out of the wheelchair and thrown onto a truck that had taken them and other invalids to the gas chambers.

How many people had been brought here on this train? Judging by the amount of luggage, it had to be over two thousand.

A few dozen prisoners moved among the loot, sorting the various belongings or loading them onto trucks or large carts. Several SS guards stood watch over them. All this was Reich property now. To the murderer the spoils.

And what of the people who had packed these suitcases? Those who had worn the clothes within them? Most were already dead. Some were now being incinerated in the crematoriums and fire pits. The rest, those who might be considered lucky, were living through the worst day any human being could ever experience: the first day in Auschwitz. A day in which they lost their loved ones. A day in which they were stripped of their name and identity. A day in which they became slaves.

One of the prisoners working among the luggage turned and stared at our passing column. Tears glittered in his eyes. But they didn't spill, perhaps signifying that his sadness was a constant and unchanging emotion, one from which there was no release or respite. His work was physically easier than ours, but it brought him closer to the wholesale murder of our innocent brothers and sisters. A soul might shatter under such proximity.

Roll call was relatively short yet still an ordeal. A few times, my legs wobbled under me and I was sure I was about to keel over. I had to bite the inside of my cheek to keep from passing out. As the count was held, a high-ranking SS officer harangued us about our supposed laziness and low productivity. He reminded us that we were not on vacation but were expected to work hard for our German masters. He called us pigs and filthy Jews and various other names. He also warned us that anyone trying to escape would be caught and dealt with harshly, and that those who stayed behind would be punished as well.

After roll call, we got our bread rations, and Vilmos and I joined a few other prisoners to eat our dinner. As was often the case, the conversation revolved around the various rumors swirling about the camp.

"The Allies have landed in France," one of the prisoners said. "They have over ten thousand tanks."

"The British have crossed the Rhine and are rolling toward Berlin," another claimed.

"The Russians have liberated Warsaw."

"Over one hundred thousand Nazi soldiers have died in the past week."

"Tito's partisans have expelled the Germans from Yugoslavia."

"Hitler has been wounded in an air raid. He might even be dead by now."

As usual, the rumors were highly positive and as equally suspect. If all the calamities purported to have fallen upon Germany were true, why was the war still raging?

It was easy to see why these rumors abounded. They were a manufactured hope for miserable people who had none. We were almost completely cut off from the outside world. Some information did manage to trickle in, but as it spread, it became almost impossible to tell the truth from the lies.

But maybe it didn't matter. Maybe these rumors served a purpose regardless of their veracity. They made us think that if we held on for just a little longer, we might actually survive this place. Without such a belief, more people would be throwing themselves at the fences.

After visiting the latrine, Vilmos and I headed back to our block. Our *Blockälteste* was standing near the entrance. Beside him were two other prisoners, both functionaries, judging by their armbands. One had gray eyes and a single conjoined eyebrow. The other had a long nose and a square jaw. Both were well-fed and had an air of brutality.

The *Blockälteste* gave me a vicious smile. "There you are. We've been waiting for you."

12

The two men ordered me to come with them. They did not give me a minute to say goodbye to Vilmos. I scolded myself for not giving him my needle and thread, and also for eating my bread ration. Now both would be lost.

I thought of Gyuri. Maybe this was the right time to emulate him. If I were going to die, better to do so by electrocution than at the hands of some demented criminal. But it appeared my escorts had been given firm instructions to prevent such an escape. They flanked me, and each grabbed one of my elbows. Both had tight grips.

"Where are we going?" I asked them.

"You'll see," the square-jawed man said. It was the only answer I got.

They led me to another block. Just outside, stood another prisoner functionary, this one fair-haired and long-faced, with a nasty pink scar that curved down one cheek to the corner of his mouth. The scar looked to be about fifteen years old. The age of the man who carried it was about twice as much. On his jacket was an inverted green triangle—another criminal prisoner.

"Is this him?" he asked in German.

Square-jaw confirmed that I was.

"Show me your arm," the fair-haired man told me.

I pulled up my left sleeve and angled my forearm so he would have a clear view of my number. He studied it without expression, nodded once, and told me to step inside the block.

"Go on," Square-jaw said unnecessarily. The other escort gave me an equally pointless hard shove, and I stumbled toward the open door. The fair-haired man followed me. The two escorts didn't.

"Wait here," the fair-haired man told me once we were inside the block, standing near the rooms in which the functionaries lived. He knocked on a closed door, and a gruff baritone voice called out from within. The fair-haired man opened the door a bit and poked his head in. My heart was hammering so loudly that I could not make out the ensuing exchange of words. The fair-haired man retracted his head from the opening and told me to go in. He closed the door behind me.

I stood just inside the door and gawked about me with an open mouth. The room was another world, a separate planet from the rest of the camp. There was a real single bed with clean sheets, a folded blanket, and a fluffy pillow. There was a night table, topped by a Hanukkah menorah with all nine candles blazing, doubtless the property of a murdered Jewish family. There was an oval rug on which stood a table covered by a fine linen cloth, and on that were a bottle of wine and a long-stemmed glass. There was an armoire, its doors hanging open, revealing hanging shirts and jackets and trousers. There was a framed painting; not a very good one, but still a shocking display of culture in a place devoid of any. There were three pairs of shoes and boots in a corner, and all had been polished to a high gloss.

And lastly, there were shelves bearing rows of canned food. Olives, fruit, various vegetables, sardines... even meat. For a moment, I couldn't breathe at the sight of these riches. My stomach let out a grumble like a starving tiger at the sight of easy prey.

"What do you think, Jew? Nice, isn't it?"

The voice was the same gruff baritone I had heard a minute ago. The man it belonged to was lounging in a chair on the opposite side of the table. Seeing what he wore around his neck was so astounding that for a moment my fear evaporated. It was a cravat. Black dots on a field of navy blue and made of silk. The kind one might expect to find encircling the neck of an affluent merchant or a university professor sitting in a well-appointed living room, perusing that day's newspaper or a book of verse.

But the moment passed and the fear flooded back in, nearly liquefying my knees. I had to angle my foot to increase pressure on my wound. The pain helped steady me. Andris Farkas could have turned me in to any of several criminal prisoner functionaries. But he had chosen the worst one by far.

The *Lagerälteste* beamed at me. He had read my fear and was basking in it. He reached forward, grabbed the bottle, and poured himself a hefty dose of red wine. Picking up the glass, he took a large slurp that would have fit better the consumption of beer or ale and let out a loud, satisfied "Aaah," all the while not taking his eyes off me.

The bottle, I noticed, had an ornate label with old-fashioned French script. The sort of wine one kept in a cool cellar. The sort of wine to be drunk by a refined man in a refined setting. Not by a deranged thug in the middle of hell.

The *Lagerälteste* drained the rest of his glass, then wiped his mouth with the back of his hand. He had big hands, their backs and fingers covered by a thick growth of hair. I had seen him use those hands to kill five prisoners since my arrival in Auschwitz, and rumor had it that he'd killed many more beforehand. I knew what he was: a born killer. A man who found pleasure in inflicting pain, in snuffing out life, in instilling dread. The Nazis had chosen him precisely for those traits.

"You look hungry, Jew," the *Lagerälteste* said. "Are you hungry?"

For a few seconds I said nothing, unsure of how I should respond. I was confused by my presence here. This room was immaculate. The floor swept, the shelves dusted, the bed made. Everything looked as clean as the interior of a block could be. So why was I here? Obviously, the *Lagerälteste* liked his room to be spotless. Yet he had summoned me here in order to kill me, probably in a brutal fashion, and such a killing would be messy. There would be a lot of blood. So why hadn't he told his goons to take me someplace else? He didn't need to hide his crimes. He could kill me in public. No one would lift a finger to stop him.

"Well?" he said, his voice deepening. "I asked you a question."

I licked my lips, which had gone bone dry. "Of course I'm hungry."

He smiled again, nodding. His face was a gruesome mix of the Neanderthal and the Aryan. His brow ridge protruded, shadowing a pair of startlingly clear blue eyes. His complexion was fair, but his cheeks were pitted with acne scars and webbed with broken capillaries. The bridge of his large nose had been flattened in numerous past fights. More broken capillaries surged across it. His chin was flat and bulky. Beneath it was a short, thick neck that suggested great physical strength.

"A new experience, I bet," he said. "I've never known a Jew who did not have a full belly. When I was little, after the Great War, when much of Germany was starving, I remember the Jews were always plump. Well, you're not plump anymore, are you?"

"I'm not from Germany," I said.

"As if that makes a difference. You Jews are the same all over. Money grubbing, controlling, looking down your big noses at the rest of us. Always in your fancy clothes and expensive shoes." He regarded my uniform with a sneer. "And look at you now."

I didn't need to look. My uniform and clogs were so uncomfortable and humiliating, I was always aware of their presence. "I can assure you that I've never worn anything as fine as what you have on."

He was wearing a navy double-breasted jacket with six shining buttons. His trousers were black and stainless. A white handkerchief protruded sloppily from his breast pocket.

Each article of clothing was exquisite, but something about their combination and the way they sat on the *Lagerälteste* made him look ridiculous, as though he were a failed actor, trying without success to slip into his role. He had obviously never worn such clothes before Auschwitz. He did not know how to hold his body to carry them well.

He smiled at me with genuine pleasure, which meant he had not read my thoughts. His smile revealed large, stained teeth.

"Do you know what I did before the war?" he asked.

"You were a criminal," I said.

"Yes. So imagine my surprise when I learned that there was a genuine policeman living here, right under my nose."

I said nothing. My intestines had twisted themselves into a tight knot.

"I've never known a Jewish policeman. You people like to be lawyers, accountants, landlords, that sort of thing. Easy work with lots of money. You leave the hard, dirty jobs to Christians. At first I didn't believe it, but the prisoner who brought me the information swore on it. He said you were a detective. Is that true?"

It occurred to me then, a little too late, that I might have tried to lie myself out of this predicament. I could have claimed another occupation. And if confronted with Andris Farkas, I could have said that he was lying, trying to settle a grudge from our previous lives in Hungary.

But looking at the *Lagerälteste*, I realized that this would have been futile. He might have failed to see the cop in me when I was just another face in a sea of prisoners, but now that my secret had been revealed and he was looking at me in isolation, he would not have been fooled.

I nodded slowly, wondering if this revelation would mean a more agonizing death than the one I would have suffered had I been a mere patrolman. "I was a detective on the police force in Hungary."

He pursed his lips while weighing me with his hard eyes, as though contemplating whether to punch me or kick me to death.

After a while, he said, "Do you know what I went to prison for?"

I shook my head.

"Why don't you make a guess?"

I wondered what sort of answer he was after, and whether giving him the right one would make an iota of difference to my fate. Death can come in many forms, and it is best to arrange for yourself the one which is the least excruciating.

On the one hand, he might be flattered if I said that he'd been some sort of kingpin, the head of a criminal organization, much like he was now. On the other, it was clearly not the case, and he might see through my pathetic attempt to win favor. I opted for what I thought was the truth.

"You were imprisoned for an act of violence," I said. "Likely several of them. You did not use a gun, I think. Nor did you run anyone over with a car. Those would have been too remote. You did it up close, with your hands or maybe with a knife or a hammer or another such implement. And you either hurt someone badly or killed them. I would say the latter."

"You're right about that," he said, grinning.

"This wasn't the first time you had hurt someone, and not the second, either. Maybe the police couldn't pin all those cases on you, but you had a reputation."

"Indeed I had. What else can you say about the criminal I was?"

Again, I considered whether to speak honestly or not. The crazy glint in his eyes convinced me to stick to the truth.

"You became a criminal as a means to make money. And you hurt people while committing other crimes—robbery, extortion, that sort of thing. But you didn't beat or kill just when you had to —to get rid of witnesses or prevent bodily harm to yourself. You enjoy hurting others. A few times, you took it too far. You killed some people when a simple beating would have sufficed.

"As a criminal, you always hovered near the bottom rung of the underworld. You never ran a sophisticated operation. You never masterminded a clever heist. You did not own an illegal gambling joint or run a brothel—though you might have been a pimp at one time, but never of high-class prostitutes."

I paused, my breath catching in my throat, because he had lowered his chin and set his jaw, and his eyes were smoldering. His hands were on the table and curled into fists. He had enjoyed my depiction of him as a murderer, but he did not like how I'd correctly pegged him as a low-level criminal. He gave the impression of a volcano about to erupt. And I knew that once he did, he would not stop until I was a bloody, pulpy mass at his feet. I had to mollify him quickly, or I might not get the chance.

"But in prison," I said, my voice cracking on the first words, "things changed. You discovered that your particular set of talents was well-suited for prison life. Your strength, your penchant for violence, your ability to dominate other prisoners physically—all these qualities helped you thrive behind bars. For the first time, you became a leader, with other prisoners doing your bidding, much as you had done the bidding of others on the outside."

I held my breath and waited a beat. Some of the tension left his face and his fingers loosened a little, though his hands were still fisted.

"You did it the only way you knew how—by instilling fear among the prisoner population and meting out severe punishment for any infraction. You also took care to eliminate any competition that might have threatened your new exalted position. If I had to guess, you killed quite a few men during your imprisonment."

"Quite a few," he said, with a smile of reminiscence. His fists unclenched all the way, and his posture returned to what it had been when I'd entered the room. I let out a low exhalation, feeling a sense of relief so acute that my hands trembled. I grew aware of how weary I was, how hard it was to remain standing here before this ruthless maniac. Again I wondered why he was asking me all these questions. Why this lengthy prelude to what had to follow—my violent death?

"In prison," I said, fearful that I would anger him again but figuring I should keep talking for as long as he let me, "you made a second discovery; one that you did not anticipate, perhaps. You realized that the authorities cared much less about what happened to prisoners than they did about the citizens on the outside. If two prisoners got into a fight and one stabbed the other, there would be an investigation, but not a comprehensive one. As long as there were no revolts or widespread disobedience or escapes, the authorities largely turned a blind eye to the internal dealings among prisoners. Which meant that there was room for certain understandings between the authorities and any prisoner who could maintain order and discipline in the general population. This was a golden opportunity for you. And it further cemented your position."

"I was like a king," he said, but his expression was incongruous with his statement. Which led me to think that he had failed to hold onto his royal position for long. I scrambled for the reason, sensing it was important I discovered it. Gazing about the room, with its ostentatious display of relative luxury, a possibility came to me, and before I had the chance to examine it properly, I gave voice to it.

"You went too far," I said. My tone was tentative, because I was uncertain of my guess. "You hurt too many prisoners. Or you killed someone in a manner that could not be swept under the rug. Or maybe one of your victims, despite being imprisoned, had some connection to people in high places. You crossed the line, perhaps without knowing it was there, and the authorities reacted."

He stayed silent, neither confirming nor denying my guess. But the way his eyebrows knitted suggested I had hit the nail on its head.

"You lost the position you'd worked so hard to attain, along with its attendant privileges. That must have been difficult. Your life might even have been at risk. But then the Nazis came, and your fortunes turned."

"Mine and yours as well," he said, again showing me his teeth.

I nodded to mask the flare of anger I felt at his wanton cruelty. Then experienced a spark of surprise that I could feel anything but dread in the presence of this man. For a second I allowed myself the exquisite pleasure of imagining the two of us in the ordinary world before everything had gone crazy—he the criminal and I the policeman. How I would have loved to slip the cuffs around his wrists.

"The Nazis needed men like you for their concentration camps," I said, returning to reality. "To save manpower, they came up with a system in which prisoner functionaries ran the daily operation of the camps—ensuring a high level of productivity, maintaining order and discipline, and keeping everyone afraid at all times. Which camp did they put you in?"

"Dachau. The first camp the Nazis built. Right after Hitler came to power."

"It was a perfect fit. A win-win situation. You had all the qualities the Nazis were looking for in a prisoner functionary, and the camps were just the sort of prison where you could employ your natural abilities with little fear that you would once again overstep the mark. The Nazis have a very dim view of their prisoners. Dimmer than the previous German government had of theirs. In Dachau, prisoners must have had very few rights."

"Nearly none," he said.

"You excelled at your new job. And why wouldn't you? It was the perfect outlet for your proclivities. You could be cruel. You could hurt people with near impunity. You could watch them tremble just by walking by or glancing in their direction."

Again I stopped, shocked by my frankness. What was I doing? Was I angling for a harsher death than necessary?

But the *Lagerälteste* did not appear to be offended or annoyed. In fact, his clear blue eyes were thoughtful and assessing. "Go on. Finish the story."

"Dachau was a good place for you. You must have been concerned when you were informed that you would be moved to a new camp, and in Poland, of all places."

"Auschwitz is not in Poland," the *Lagerälteste* said with a bite to his tone. "Not anymore. It was annexed to Germany in 1939."

How odd it was that despite his status as a prisoner, he was staunchly patriotic.

"When were you moved here?" I asked.

"Right in the beginning, in 1940. There were thirty of us."

"So you were sent to the main camp, not here to Birkenau."

"Birkenau didn't exist back then. Only the main camp, what the SS boys in administration now call Auschwitz-I. The prisoners there were mostly Polish; still are. It was before they started bringing in all you stinking Jews from everywhere. Birkenau, or Auschwitz-II, was built by Russian prisoners of war, at least in the beginning. You should have seen them. There was nothing here. They had to build the blocks by themselves. They lived like animals, out in the open, exposed to the rain and snow. Some dug holes in the ground in which to take shelter. They died like flies."

He said all this without a hint of sympathy; with a gleeful twinkle in his eyes, even. Those Russians were as inconsequential to him as cockroaches one crushes underfoot. For a couple of seconds, I could not move a muscle, not even to breathe. I was plunged into total immobility by the thought of those poor Russian soldiers who were treated so cruelly, instead of being accorded the proper treatment owed to prisoners of war.

"Don't stop now," the *Lagerälteste* said. "We're near the end."

I swallowed hard and tried to work some saliva into my mouth. I said, "In Auschwitz you came into your element. The life of a prisoner had very little value in Dachau, but it was still worth something, so there were limitations to what you could do. In Auschwitz, the value of such a life is zero, especially if the prisoner happens to be Jewish. Because the goal of this camp is to destroy Jews, to kill them in whatever way suits Germany. This means that for the first time, you're free to indulge fully in your violent cravings. You can do anything you want. Because Jews have no rights, no powerful friends. They are to be disposed of."

"That's right. You Jews are worth nothing. Absolutely nothing. You're the scum of the earth." He said this with utter conviction, as much of a zealot as the SS officers who ruled the camp in which he too was a prisoner.

For a few seconds, there was silence. I kept expecting him to say something, but he seemed to be deep in thought, his gaze fixed on me. There was hatred laced with insanity in his eyes, but also that assessing look I had noticed before.

I was afraid to speak, because I knew that the end he had referred to, the one to which we had arrived, was not merely that of the story, but of my life as well. I had no idea why he'd had me talk at such length about his life, but we had come to the present day. And try as I might, I could think of nothing more to say. Nothing that would further postpone the inevitable.

Finally, I mumbled, "That's it. That's the sort of criminal you are." Then I waited, resigned to my fate, knowing for the first time what standing under the hangman's noose truly felt like for an innocent man. A blend of bleak despair, deep remorse over much that I'd done or hadn't done in my life, and a sizzling current of anger at my fate, strangely coupled with an almost tranquil acceptance of it.

He kept on looking at me for a long moment, his mouth set in a hard line, and I kept expecting the trapdoor to open under my feet. Then would come the drop and the pull of the rope. If you were lucky, your neck would snap in an instant, and you would feel nothing. If you weren't, you'd dangle at the end of that rope for minutes while the noose squeezed the life right out of you, turning your face purple, pulling your tongue right out of your mouth. Whatever death he had in store for me, it would be as long and painful as that of the unlucky hanged man. And much more bloody.

With each passing second, my innards turned increasingly to mush. My bowels contracted. A fresh surge of panic hit me. If I peed or worse on his clean floor, my death would be even more painful.

In my mind flashed the faces of my loved ones. All the family who had come with me to Auschwitz and was no more. *I'm so sorry*, I told them, *I'm so sorry I didn't save you.*

I did not find any comfort in the thought that I would soon be reunited in death with my wife and daughters. I wasn't sure I believed that would happen. I didn't know what I believed in anymore.

The *Lagerälteste* drew a loud whiffing breath through his nose. "You know how much I hate cops?" he asked in a low growl. "Even more than I hate all you filthy, good-for-nothing Jews."

Then he showed me his clenched teeth, his hands bunching once more into fists. There was a feral look about him. A wild animal about to pounce for the kill.

13

But the *Lagerälteste* didn't pounce. Nor did he rise from his chair. His face continued to hold that bloodthirsty stare that stabbed a spear of ice into my gut. His fists tightened even further. His eyes narrowed to slits. He wanted to kill me, but something was holding him back.

Finally, after what seemed as long as roll call, his teeth unclenched and his thick tongue emerged to slither wetly over his lips. He relaxed his hands and offered me a morbid smile.

"Normally, I would find great pleasure in killing you. But this is your lucky day, Jew. I need you."

It took me a moment to register what he was saying. Then a breath I didn't know I'd been holding leaked from my lungs, leaving a dull ache in my chest. I felt like I was about to fall down, as though something I'd been leaning on had been pulled away. He wasn't going to kill me. I was going to live. The urge to laugh came over me, but I tamped it down. I was not out of danger yet.

"Maybe you're wondering why I let you ramble on about my history," he said. "It was a test. I wanted to see how good of a detective you are. If you'd failed the test, I would have killed you. But you were right on the money. How did you figure all that out?"

I weighed my words, fearful of squandering the stay of execution I'd been granted. "I took what I knew about you and made an initial deduction. Once you confirmed it, I made a second deduction, and so on."

He wagged a finger at me, chuckling. "You Jews are clever as hell, that's for sure. Too clever for your own good, usually, but just what I need today." The levity vanished from his face, replaced by an angry scowl. But I realized that I was not the cause, nor the target, of his ire.

I waited. There was no need to ask what he wanted from me. He was going to tell me.

"Someone in this camp did a bad thing. A very bad thing. I want you to find out who it was."

"What sort of bad thing?" I asked.

"A murder. Someone committed a murder."

I looked at him, unsure if I'd heard him correctly. He'd said it as though a murder in Auschwitz were something shocking and unusual. Hell, the entire camp was dedicated to murder. He himself had done his fair share of it.

"You're going to have to be more specific," I said. "People are murdered here every day."

He waved a hand. "I'm not talking about that. What goes on in the gas chambers is none of my business. But what happens inside the men's camp is." He jabbed a forefinger on the tabletop. "This is my domain. I am king here. If I want something, I take it. If I want someone dead, I kill him. And if I want someone protected, no one is allowed to lay a finger on him."

"And someone did?"

He nodded, his face darkening. "Two days ago, someone murdered a boy of mine."

A boy of his? He couldn't mean his son, could he?

"A boy?" I asked.

"A servant boy of mine. Fifteen years old."

It hit me then. The dead boy Vilmos had stumbled upon. The boy who had been stabbed in the throat. I tried to keep the realization off my face, but the *Lagerälteste* caught it.

"What is it? What are you thinking?"

"I was just wondering how and where he was killed," I said.

His answer confirmed that the servant boy and the dead boy Vilmos had told me about were one and the same.

"I don't suppose the body's still around."

"Of course not. He went to the crematorium like any other body. Is that gonna be a problem?"

"I don't think so," I said, knowing full well that it might be, but thinking it did not serve my interest to make him suspect I might fail in my mission. "Who was this boy?"

"His name was Franz. A Dutch boy."

"Jewish?"

"Yes."

"What happened to his family?"

Again he waved a hand. "Gassed to death. He was the only one left. I took him under my wing."

"When was this?"

"Three weeks ago."

"That's when he came to the camp?"

"No. That's when I saw him for the first time. He arrived here eight months ago."

"What did he do for you?"

"Various chores. Cleaned this room, shined my shoes, that sort of thing."

"You didn't have someone to do all that already?"

"Another boy. But he died."

I was about to ask how, but something in the *Lagerälteste's* expression made me hold my tongue.

"Do you know why Franz had gone to the place where he was killed?"

"No."

"It's one of those places prisoners use for clandestine meetings," I said. "Any idea who he might have been meeting there?"

"If I knew that, I wouldn't need you, would I? I would just kill the bastard."

"The person Franz met and the killer might be two different people."

The *Lagerälteste* shrugged in response, which I took to mean the prospect of killing a host of innocent men did not bother him in the least, as long as he also got the guilty one.

"Can you think of anyone who might have wished to harm Franz?"

He shook his head.

"Was he in possession of any items that might have tempted someone to attack him?"

"No. And nothing was taken."

"You saw the body?"

"Yes," he said, his face tightening.

"Do you remember whether there were any other wounds on it? Especially on the hands and arms?"

He pushed out his lips, then shook his head. "I didn't stay there long. I saw he was dead and left. I didn't want to look at him anymore. What difference does it make?"

A great deal, perhaps, but I didn't tell him that. As with there being no body to examine, I wasn't about to make him think I'd have trouble solving this crime.

"When was the last time you saw Franz?"

"Early afternoon, two days ago."

"And when did you discover he was dead?"

"Yesterday morning."

That explained why he had exploded that morning, beating an unfortunate prisoner to death. It didn't occur to him that what he'd done to that prisoner was every bit as bad as what had been done to Franz.

"How did you find him?"

"He wasn't here in the morning," he said. "So I sent men out to search for him. One of them found him."

"I'll need to talk to him. See if he remembers anything about the scene."

"That's no problem. It's Mathias. The guy who brought you in." He gestured with his chin toward the door at my back, indicating, I thought, the fair-haired man with the scar on his cheek. "He'll tell you everything he knows."

"I'll also need to be able to talk to whoever worked with the boy. Which *kommando* did Franz work in before you took him in?"

"Kanada," he said. "He worked in Kanada."

Kanada was the name given by prisoners to the group of warehouses where the belongings of the murdered Jews of Auschwitz were sorted and stored before being shipped to Germany. It was Polish for Canada, a country of legendary wealth and abundance, which was the association conjured up by the massive amount of property plundered from the victims.

"Can you arrange for me to be stationed there?"

He raised a thick eyebrow, and the corner of his mouth tilted upward. "You would like that, wouldn't you? Better than what you do now, I suppose?"

Kanada was considered among the best postings a prisoner could get. The prisoners of the Kanada Kommando worked in the warehouses or on the train platform. The work was less strenuous than in other *kommandos*, and one might find food and various other treasures among the belongings of the dead.

"Much better," I said. "But the reason I need to be there is to be able to talk to prisoners who knew Franz. He worked there until recently. Someone there might have held a grudge against him or know of someone who did."

The *Lagerälteste* nodded. "That makes sense. But if you're thinking of stretching this out so you can take it easy in Kanada, you'd be making a big mistake. I want results, and I want them fast. Four days from now is Sunday, when for some stupid reason you lazy Jews get a day off work. Well, if you fail to catch this killer, you don't deserve any rest. So you have until Saturday night to solve this case, or I'll return to my original plan for you. Is that clear?"

I nodded, trying to hide my fear. I didn't bother telling him what Sundays were really like for us—that we had to stand in endless roll calls, often punctuated by stretches of degrading physical exercise, and witness brutal punishments administered to our fellow prisoners or be subjected to them ourselves. That we had to clean our block, have our body hair shaved, and take a communal shower under blasting jets of freezing water, without soap or anything to dry ourselves with.

"I understand," I said, trying to come to grips with the fact that I had three days to solve a murder or die.

"And just so each of us knows where we stand," he went on, "you will get nothing for this job. No food, no clothes, no cigarettes. Absolutely nothing. Your only compensation is your miserable life. Not that it changes the overall equation, because here in Auschwitz, your life *is* worth nothing." He grinned, pleased with himself.

"All right. But I do have one request," I said.

His self-satisfaction gave way to angry astonishment. "Don't push me, Jew."

"It's not a material request. I think you'll find it to your liking." I told him what I wanted, and he broke out laughing.

"You are a wily son of a bitch, aren't you?" he said. "Very well, I'll allow it. Anything else?"

"Just one more question. Where did Franz sleep?"

Again he gestured with his chin. "The other room. With Mathias and the *Stubendiensts*. You can talk to them too, if you like, but it will have to be tomorrow. They're busy with the prisoners now. And it's time you left as well. You need to get back to your block. I'll see you out."

With that he rose from his chair and rounded the table, approaching me. For a heartbeat I thought he was actually going to offer me his hand. Instead, faster than I could blink, he drew back his right fist and drove it forward like a piston, right into my solar plexus. I was not prepared for the blow, and it folded me in half. An eruption of pain and nausea engulfed me. I crashed to the floor and lay there with my knees drawn to my chest. I gasped for air, bile clawing at my throat, tears pumping out of my eyes.

A shadow fell over me. Through the blur of tears, I could see the *Lagerälteste's* boots, shiny and black, very near my face. This had all been a game, a cruel, depraved game, meant to give me false hope. He was going to kick me now. Kick me right in the face. He was going to split my lips, bust my teeth, crush my nose. He wasn't going to stop until I was dead.

But he didn't kick me. Instead, he crouched next to me, bringing his head so close to mine that I could smell the wine on his breath. He said, "Just so you know what will happen to you if you fail."

Then he rose to his full height, opened the door, and bade Mathias inside. "Help him up and see him to his block. Make sure he's posted to Kanada until further notice. Oh, and one more thing." He told Mathias of my request. "Let him do what he wants. He certainly has cause."

The tears had dwindled, so I could make out Mathias's face. He took in my request impassively. Maybe he was good at hiding his thoughts, or maybe he didn't find it strange. He nodded understanding, bent down, grabbed me under the armpits, and hauled me out.

The *Lagerälteste* shut the door to his room. Through it, I could hear his gruff laughter.

14

Outside the block, Mathias gave me time to recover. The pain in my torso was so sharp, I could not stand straight and instead was on hands and knees on the dirt. I'd received my share of blows over the years, but I had never been punched as hard as this.

"It'll pass in a minute or two," Mathias said, his voice flat. "At least the worst of it."

He was right, though I could not swear on how long it took. Severe pain makes it difficult to estimate time. But after a while, the pain subsided sufficiently for me to push myself onto my feet, wincing as I did.

Mathias gave me the tiniest smile. "He certainly packs a punch, doesn't he?"

I grimaced. "And he knows where to place it."

"At least he didn't hit you in the face. You'd be missing teeth if he did."

We started walking. I ran my tongue over my teeth. They were grimy and gritty, having not been brushed since my arrival at the camp, but at least I still had all of them. Many prisoners lost some of their teeth, due to fights or their inability to care for them. Every morning, I checked my teeth to see if any felt loose. I had no idea what I'd do when one of them actually did.

"I'll make sure to count my blessings," I said.

"You should," Mathias said. "If he didn't need you, you'd be dead right now. Or on the way to being dead."

"You know of my history?"

"Yes. The prisoner who ratted you out came to me first."

"And you took him to the *Lagerälteste*?"

"Yes."

"I suppose you hate cops as much as he does?"

"Not really."

"No? I thought all criminals hated cops."

"Don't get me wrong—I don't like cops very much, but most of them just do their job, what they have to. Like we all do here."

I studied him as we walked. Like the *Lagerälteste*, he was not wearing a striped uniform and clogs. Instead, he had on black leather shoes, black trousers, and a fine jacket with a wide collar. Unlike the *Lagerälteste*, Mathias carried his classy outfit well. He looked like a man on his way to a social outing rather than a prisoner in Auschwitz.

His gait matched his manner of speech—easy and even. He had a long, straight nose, symmetrical features, and a light complexion with smooth skin, apart from the scar. Slightly above average height and well above average weight—average for Auschwitz, that is. In the ordinary world, he would have been considered trim.

He was a handsome man, despite the scar. I wondered how he'd gotten it, but I didn't ask.

Instead, I said, "Do you also know of my mission?"

He nodded. "I'm to be your contact. If you learn anything, or need anything, you come to me."

"You're not a suspect?"

Mathias looked at me. In the dim light of dusk, his eyes were black and inscrutable. "The *Lagerälteste* trusts me."

"I would have thought a man like that would trust no one."

"He does me."

"Why is that?"

"We've known each other for a long time. Been through some tough things together."

"Does this mean you don't have an alibi for when Franz died?"

"I do, actually. I was inspecting a part of the camp with another functionary during that afternoon. And later, I was with the *Lagerälteste* in his room throughout that evening. I didn't leave the block until the next morning."

"Not even to get your evening meal?"

He allowed himself a small closed-mouth smile. "I get my food another way."

Of course he did. He wouldn't stand in line like an ordinary prisoner. Nor would he subsist on the same miserable diet.

"When did you last see Franz?"

"Sometime during the afternoon."

"Late afternoon or early?"

"Early, I think."

This meant that the time of death was between early afternoon and when Vilmos discovered the body, which was shortly before curfew. It also meant that the killer could have belonged to one of the *kommandos* that operated outside the camp and returned before the evening meal. So basically, any prisoner in our camp could have committed this murder.

"You share a room with Franz?"

He nodded.

"Didn't it strike you as odd that he wasn't there when you turned in for the night?"

"I went to sleep early that day. I was drunk, you see."

Which wasn't uncommon among prisoner functionaries, nor among the SS guards. It seemed that drunkenness made it easier to do evil unto your fellow man.

"Was that usual, you going to sleep when Franz was still out?"

"It happened."

"What about during that night? Did you see him?"

"I slept the whole night through."

It said a lot about my circumstances that this answer nearly caused me to trip over my own feet. "You did not wake once?"

"No. I usually don't."

I was speechless for a moment. I had not had a full night's sleep since I'd arrived in Auschwitz. The noises other prisoners made in their sleep, every tiny motion of my bunkmates, not to mention the need to urinate several times during the night—the result of our mostly liquid diet—jolted me awake repeatedly. Not that I should have been surprised. Prisoner functionaries slept in separate rooms, much less crowded rooms, and they ate better. Why shouldn't they sleep full nights?

"Who else sleeps in the room you shared with Franz?"

"Two *Stubendiensts*. The two men who escorted you to our block."

"I suppose you asked them the same questions I asked you?"

"Just about. They said that Franz wasn't there when they went to bed."

"Did they also go to sleep early?"

"I don't know," Mathias said. "I was already asleep."

"Do they also have alibis?"

"No. I'm the only one."

"I take it both of them have committed murder before."

"I don't know of any reason either of them would kill Franz, if that's what you're getting at."

"Would it take a reason? Maybe one of them did it for fun."

The corner of his mouth twitched in subtle amusement. "Look around you. There's no shortage of men to kill here if that's what gives you pleasure."

Like all truths in Auschwitz, this one was blunt, harsh, and unimpeachable. Mathias was right—if one of the *Lagerälteste's* assistants had murdered Franz, he must have had a damn good reason.

"Did both of them sleep the whole night through as well?" I asked.

"One of them didn't. He said he got up in the middle of the night to piss. He sleeps on the opposite side of the room from Franz's bunk, so he says he didn't notice if Franz was there. As it so happens, he did see me, because my bunk is below his." He paused for a moment. "So I guess I have an even stronger alibi than I thought."

It seemed he was right. But I would have to hear it from the witness myself.

"I understand you were the one who found the body."

"Yes."

"Did you see any other wounds apart from the one in his throat?"

Mathias thought about it and shook his head. "I don't remember seeing any, but I wasn't looking for them either."

"Was there a lot of blood?"

"Yes."

"At some distance from the body?"

He glanced at me. "Some of it. Why?"

"Because when you sever an artery, blood spurts, often to a surprising distance. Some would have almost certainly hit the killer."

"I see."

"It would be a good idea to conduct a search for a bloodied shirt. And if you happen to find the murder weapon, that would be great too."

"All right. I'll see that it's done."

We walked a few more paces before I asked my next question.

"Can you think of anyone who would have wanted to hurt Franz?"

"No."

"Someone he had a fight or an argument with, maybe?"

"The boy was well liked."

"What sort of boy was he?"

Mathias considered this. "Quiet. Smart. Adaptable."

"Adaptable? What does that mean?"

"He knew how to survive in this place," Mathias said, stopping outside a block not that far from my own. "This is it. You wait here. I'll go get him."

It took less than a minute before Mathias emerged from the block in the company of a second prisoner, this one not a functionary.

"What goes on?" the prisoner asked in broken German. "Where you taking me?"

Mathias stopped a few meters from the block and pointed to where I was standing. "To him," he said, and took a step back.

Andris Farkas turned his face in my direction and squinted. His eyes widened as I stepped out of the shadows. He took a frightened step backward, bumping into Mathias who had unobtrusively moved to block Farkas's retreat. Farkas turned his head to see who was behind him, then shifted back to me. He managed to say, "No. Wait, I—" before I hit him. I punched him right where the *Lagerälteste* had punched me. And into that punch went all the fear I'd felt since Farkas had made me out the previous day and all my anger at him for informing on me, knowing he was sentencing me to an agonizing death.

The punch knocked the air out of him. He folded into me, and I pushed him away and onto the ground. He lay there much as I'd lain on the floor of the *Lagerälteste's* room. The main difference was that I did kick him. I kicked him several times, each kick venting a portion of my rage—both at him and at the world at large. I kicked him in the crotch. I kicked him in the stomach. I kicked him in the face. That last kick broke something, and blood spurted onto my clog. Farkas lay whimpering on the ground, his body squeezed into a small knot, one hand held to his bloodied face, the other raised in a pathetic attempt to ward off the next kick.

But there was no next kick. Seeing Farkas there on the ground, hurt and bleeding, made me pause and step back before I gave in to the desire to do more damage. Bent over with my hands on my knees and panting for breath, I felt like screaming at the sky, at God, at everything and everybody. I felt like crying for the man I used to be and the one that I'd become.

When I had my breath back, I said to Mathias, "Can you get him into the hospital tonight?"

Mathias gave me a look. He had not twitched a muscle when I was kicking Farkas, nor did his expression shift. But now he was frowning. "Why? I thought you wanted—"

"I know what I wanted," I said, cutting him off. "I've changed my mind. Can you get him into the hospital or not?"

The prisoner hospital was said to be a place of horrors, overflowing with the wretchedly sick and weak, almost entirely devoid of medicine and medical equipment. It was also where frequent selections took place, the Nazis not wishing to waste food on those who would not be able to return to work in the very near future.

Yet it was also a place in which the prisoners performed no

labor, where a man with a minor injury might rest for a few days and regain his strength. Farkas's injury would be considered minor. A few missing teeth and a broken nose do not prevent a man from digging trenches or laying bricks, not if he's allowed a short respite from work. The hospital would offer Farkas such a respite. And given that he was not emaciated, compared to the other patients, he would likely survive any selection that might take place there. It was the best place for him.

Mathias studied my face. What his thoughts were I couldn't say. Maybe he thought I was weak, that I lacked the stomach to go through with what I'd asked the *Lagerälteste*. Which was to kill Andris Farkas.

He certainly deserved it. When he'd gone to the *Lagerälteste* and told him I was a former cop, he had sentenced me to death. I was within my rights to do the same to him. And when I followed Mathias to Farkas's block, when I was waiting for him to come out, when I punched him and kicked him, I had every intention of ending his life. But that moment, that sickening moment when I heard the crunch of something break in his face, had switched off that desire like a light bulb. I did not pity him. Nor did I regret injuring him. But I no longer wished to kill him.

"Well?" I said.

Mathias nodded. "Yes, I can do that. You're going to your block?"

"Why? Do you need help carrying him?"

"I'll manage. If your *Blockälteste* gives you any trouble—"

"I'll tell him that by order of the *Lagerälteste,* I've been posted to Kanada. That would make him think."

Again, Mathias smiled his tiny smile. "I'm sure it would." He looked around. We were alone in the empty stretch of ground between the blocks. Already, the lamps atop the fences had been switched on, and the watchtower searchlights were scratching their insidious yellow claws across the camp. All the prisoners had gone into their blocks for the night. Very soon, night curfew would go into effect, and any prisoner roaming outside would be liable to get shot. "Just so you know, Adam, nobody but the *Lagerälteste* and me know about your history. Nobody else but this lowlife right here." He gestured at the groaning Farkas. "If other prisoners learn that you used to be a cop, they might target you. So let me ask you this: Are you absolutely sure you want to keep this man alive?"

"Yeah, I'm sure," I said, noticing that this was the first time Mathias had used my name, while the *Lagerälteste* hadn't done so once. I wished I could have more time with Mathias, because I had a slew of questions I had yet to ask him. About Franz. And about the *Lagerälteste*.

"Very well," Mathias said. "I'll warn him to keep his mouth shut. That if he tells anyone else about you, he'll pay even more dearly than he did tonight. But he might still talk, you understand?"

"I understand."

"All right. You better go now."

I did, glancing behind me once to see Mathias pull Andris Farkas to his feet and drape one of his arms around his shoulders. There was something oddly gentle about the way Mathias was supporting Farkas, or maybe it was a trick of the dwindling light. I turned my head forward and could see them no more.

The *Blockälteste* was standing outside the block like a high-wayman ready to extract a toll from every passing traveler. He frowned when he saw me. I was supposed to be dead, and here I was without a mark on me. I told him of my new posting, getting a cheap but delicious spark of pleasure at watching his jaw drop.

Inside the block, I encountered another man who was surprised to see me. It was Vilmos. He was sitting hunched over on the heating duct right next to our bunk. When I called out his name, he turned a tear-streaked face toward me, his eyes growing big.

"Adam?" he muttered. "Adam, I can't believe it."

"I can hardly believe it either," I said.

"How? What happened?"

"I explained that I was in the middle of a chess game, and that I might actually win this time."

"Come on. Be serious. Tell me."

I motioned with my eyes to indicate the hundreds of men surrounding us. "We'll talk about it tomorrow morning, Vilmos, all right?"

Vilmos nodded, wiping his eyes, which had overflowed yet again, this time with tears of joy. I was moved by his reaction. It was nice to have at least one person who would mourn me if I died and rejoice if I lived.

Vilmos climbed to our bunk, and I went to the back of the block to piss. On the way back to our bunk, I caught sight of Hendrik lying in his. He gave me a baleful look but said nothing. I didn't say anything either.

As I lay squeezed in, Vilmos on my one side, a short Norwegian Jew who stank with sweat on the other, I thought about the incredible events of that day. And also about how I was no longer merely a number.

I was a detective once again.

15

In the morning, after a trip to the latrine and collecting our breakfast, Vilmos and I found a secluded spot, and I told him I would not be joining him in our regular *kommando*. "I've been assigned to Kanada."

"Kanada? How did that come about?"

I told him about the *Lagerälteste* and the mission he'd given me. "It's the dead boy you saw, Vilmos. His name was Franz. He was from Holland. Fifteen years old."

Vilmos took a moment to absorb this. "All right. But why Kanada?"

"Before Franz became the *Lagerälteste's* servant, he was stationed in Kanada. He worked there until three weeks ago. Perhaps I can find the reason for his murder there."

"Even if you don't, I'm glad you'll be working there. It's much better than digging trenches, that's for sure."

I looked at him. If he harbored any envy toward me, he didn't show it. "Don't be too happy on my account. The *Lagerälteste* gave me until Saturday night to find this murderer. Which is less than three days from now. If I fail, he'll kill me."

Vilmos took that in with a stricken expression. "That's a very short time, isn't it?"

I shrugged, though my stomach felt heavy with dread. "Most murders get solved within a couple of days of being committed. Of course, that's in the ordinary world, with laws and police. Here..." I cast a look around at the multitude of prisoners, each hunched over their meager breakfast, all around us the stench of dead bodies burning. I did not complete the sentence. I had no idea how to conduct a murder investigation in this place.

But there was one person who might be able to help me.

I turned my eyes back on Vilmos and fixed him with my gaze. "Who were you meeting the night you found the body, Vilmos?"

"I told you, Adam. He had nothing to do with it. He's not a murderer."

"I believe you. But he might have seen something. Or someone. I need to talk to him. Who is he? Where can I find him?"

Vilmos bit his lower lip, and his eyes did a wild dance. He looked like a cornered animal. "I can't tell you. I'm sorry, but I just can't. I don't believe he saw anything. He would have told me."

"So that's where you went last night, when you told me you were going to the latrine? You went to meet this man?"

My tone had changed, and it took me a second to recognize into what. It was the tone I'd used to interrogate suspects or uncooperative witnesses when I'd been a policeman. A twinge of shame pricked at my heart for using it on Vilmos.

I took a breath and placed a hand on Vilmos's shoulder. I brought my face a little closer to his, our eyes locking. In a soft voice, I said, "I know, Vilmos. You don't need to hide things from me."

"Know what?"

"That you should have a pink triangle stitched to your uniform."

In Auschwitz, prisoners were classified and marked according to a number of categories. Criminal prisoners with an inverted green triangle; political prisoners with an inverted red one. Jehovah's witnesses with an inverted purple triangle; gypsies with an inverted brown or black one, the latter also used to mark what the Nazis referred to as asocial prisoners. Jews were marked with two triangles, an inverted red one over a regular yellow one, the two triangles forming a Star of David. And homosexuals were marked with an inverted pink triangle.

Vilmos blanched. "How..." he began, but his voice faltered.

"I suspected it very shortly after we met," I said, regretting using the word 'suspected' the instant it left my lips. "And I don't care one bit."

"You don't?"

I shook my head emphatically. "Not one bit, Vilmos."

Vilmos searched my face, disbelief in his eyes. He had obviously spent a lifetime hiding this secret. He had clearly suffered negative consequences whenever it was revealed. And now he discovered that the man with whom he spent the majority of his time here in Auschwitz had known it all along and did not judge him for it. His lack of belief was understandable.

"Most cops do care," Vilmos said, still scrutinizing my face.

"I did too, before I got here. Now I think I'd rather judge a man by who he is than by what he is. Do you understand?"

Vilmos nodded, his breath quickening with emotion. "You're a good friend, Adam."

"And you're the best friend a man could have," I said. "The best one I've had in my life."

We looked at each other without speaking a word or moving a muscle. Yet a lot was said silently in that moment. Words that men don't usually say to one another. Or maybe men like Vilmos do, but only to each other.

It didn't last long. Time was a luxury we did not have. Vilmos broke the silence. "I need to talk to him first, before you do. I'll do it tonight, after dinner. You can meet us where I found the dead boy. All right?"

I nodded. "Thank you, Vilmos."

"Thank you, Adam," he said. "For more than you can imagine."

Then he started coughing, his thin body quaking. His cough had worsened. It sounded as though he were tearing up on the inside. He spat a glob of phlegm onto the ground. I did not like its color one bit. I did not like Vilmos's color either. It was sickly, despite the tan.

"Are you going to be all right?" I said.

He wiped his mouth. "I'll be fine, don't you worry."

But I did worry. What I'd said was true: Vilmos was the best friend I'd ever had. The only friend I had in Auschwitz-Birkenau.

"Is there anything else you remember about the murder scene? Something other than what you've already told me?"

Vilmos looked away. "Not about the murder scene. But about the boy, yes."

"What about him?"

Vilmos's eyes drifted back to mine. "He was beautiful. Even in death, with his eyes open and vacant. His face was delicate and smooth and... just beautiful. That's the only thing I remember that I did not tell you."

I nodded, knowing full well why he'd kept it to himself until that moment.

We made our way to the *Appellplatz*, and there said goodbye for the day.

"I'll try to get something for you from Kanada," I said before we parted. "Food, or something we can exchange for it."

"Don't be a fool, Adam. It's your first day. Get the lay of the land first."

My *Blockschreiber* spotted me and indicated where I should stand. I joined the group of men who'd been assigned to Kanada. Some of them were as thin as the rest of us, but many were fuller. All of them looked dejected and tired. Some of the men nodded a greeting at me; others gave me suspicious looks. No one smiled. The *Kapo* shouted "*Antreten!*", the command to form lines. "We've got a busy day today," he bellowed almost cheerfully. "A train is coming. Maybe more than one."

He spotted me and marched over. "You're new, aren't you?"

"Yes," I said.

"Well, let me tell you something. I'll tolerate no trouble from you, are we clear? You disobey one order, you cause any disruption, and you'll be joining the rest of them in the gas chambers. You got that?"

"Yes."

"Good." He pointed to the man standing to my right. "You. You're responsible for this man. He makes any trouble, you'll pay for it too. So you tell him what to do and what not to. And he'd better behave, or it's your head." With that he walked back to his position in front of our formation and shouted at us to maintain order.

"What's your name?" my appointed guardian asked me. He was in his forties, short, with a bulbous nose and a hangdog face. His eyes were a wet nutmeg, and one of his front teeth was chipped.

I told him my name was Adam and he said his was Jakob. He was a Pole, and he'd been in Auschwitz since early 1943. His German was impeccable.

"The *Kapo* is a real bastard," he said, "and he meant every word. You're not thinking of doing anything stupid, are you?"

"Stupid?"

"You know what I mean. You can't save them, so don't even try. All you'll do is make the Germans kill them all, including those who would have been selected to go into the camp, and us as well. So just do what you're told. You've got no choice."

The *Kapo* yelled an order, and we marched the short distance from the men's camp to the train platform. There, we were ordered to stand and wait. SS officers and guards swarmed the platform, some with dogs. They chatted among themselves, sharing jokes by the looks of it. Just another day of exterminating Jews. Nothing to dampen the mood.

The guards were armed with machine guns or rifles. The officers each had a pistol. The dogs looked ferocious, their tongues hanging out between their teeth in the building heat of morning. The Germans were ready in case anyone tried to disrupt the orderly process of death. On occasion, the Nazis would have a prisoners' orchestra play cheerful music to lull the new arrivals into complacency. But that day there was no music. There was just the routine sounds of camp life, and why shouldn't there be? This was the regular order of business here. What the camp was for. What was about to happen was nothing special.

We stood motionless for a long time on the platform, the sun baking our faces. I was terribly thirsty, and sweat was making the rash on my side itch like crazy. The wound on my foot was sending dull waves of pain up my leg. Suddenly, off in the distance, a sharp whistle sounded. Then the clack-clack of train wheels. I glanced to my left. A plume of smoke rose into the sky, a harbinger of worse things to come.

The train materialized like a living nightmare. A black snake carrying a cargo of the soon-to-be dead in its belly. It entered the camp like the needle of a syringe full of poison, rolling on the rail spur between the women's and men's camps, and screeched to a halt in front of us. The engineer leaned halfway out of the locomotive. "They're all ready for you," he hollered to a group of SS guards, his mouth gaped in a psychotic grin. The guards laughed. A few of the dogs barked, straining at their leashes. The SS doctors, a separate group among the officers, continued their conversation, but now they were looking not at each other but at the train, as though they were guests at a dinner party, their eyes on the covered main course just before the lid is removed.

Stenciled on the cattle cars in large letters were the words *Deutsche Reichsbahn*, German Reich Railway. From inside the cars came the sounds of frantic banging and pleading. The cargo was desperate to get out.

"Remember," Jakob whispered to me. "You can't save them. So don't be stupid. Just follow me and do as I say."

But I was barely listening. My eyes were roving about, counting the number of guards and officers, noting their positions and weapons. The train was long, with many cars. Two thousand people at least. Maybe more than three. And four dozen or so men in our *kommando* to lead them in revolt. Enough to overwhelm the German soldiers, to tear them apart and take their weapons. This was our chance. To kill them. To stop them killing us. To avenge the victims. Gyuri's family. Vilmos's family. My family. And all the other families the Nazis had wiped out.

An SS officer barked a command. The guards hustled, some moving to take up controlling positions on the platform, others going to the train cars. The *Kapo* shouted at us to do our duty and obey orders.

My heart was pounding a manic rhythm. I thought nothing of the boy Franz. Of my mission. All I could think of was that this was the moment in which I would strike back at the oppressors. The moment in which Jews would rise up to show the Germans that we could fight and we could kill. It would be glorious. Some of us would die; maybe many of us. That was unavoidable. But it was worth it.

"Don't warn them," Jakob whispered. The panicked urgency in his voice made me turn to look at him. He knew what I was thinking. "It wouldn't do any good. They're already dead."

He was lying. I was sure of it. Surer than I'd ever been of anything. He was a miserable coward, nothing else. He wanted to live, and he didn't care that so many others would die.

"You think you're the first one?" He grabbed the sleeve of my shirt. "You think I haven't thought of it a hundred times? It won't work. You'll only get everyone killed."

I pulled my arm free, not bothering to answer him. My face was hot, and not because of the sun. I was burning up on the inside with rage and, yes, with blood lust as well. My nerves vibrated with anticipation. My fingers tingled. I was aching to spill German blood. I looked at the train, where my army of Jews awaited. An army that would crush these German soldiers to dust.

Another command sounded. The guards unbolted the train cars, pulling the doors open. They shouted and motioned for those inside to come out. And from the black holes of the cattle cars, the vanguard of my Jewish army emerged.

They jumped down onto the platform, blinking around in disorientation, their eyes blinded by the glare of sunlight after days of near total darkness in the cars. They shrank under the shouts of the SS guards and the frenzied barking of the dogs, then turned to help their fellow passengers out. Those they helped were women and children, some infants, and also the middle-aged and the elderly. Some were so exhausted, they could hardly stand straight. A few leaned on canes or crutches. Some simply sprawled on the ground, utterly spent. Many had a dazed look on their faces. This was no army, I realized with a slap of grief and resignation. These were terrified, bewildered, exhausted citizens.

Unarmed and disorganized. Many of them were too old or too young to be soldiers. And as for the women, many of them were holding children.

They had not had a proper meal in days. Nor sufficient water. Nor a breath of fresh air. If they'd slept at all, they'd done so fitfully. They had traveled in cattle cars so crammed with people that sitting or lying down was possible only for a fraction of them at a time. They'd had to relieve themselves in a bucket, in the company of strangers. They'd had to fight each other for every sliver of space. They were in no shape to fight the Germans.

And I had been a fool to believe otherwise for even a second.

For hadn't I been in their shoes not too long ago? Didn't I remember with frightful clarity how exhausted I'd been coming out of the train? How confused? How my mind had struggled to make sense of all I was seeing and hearing and smelling: the fences, the blocks, the stench of death, the SS officers, the strange men in striped uniforms and clogs. Didn't I remember that all I'd wanted was to make sure my family was safe? That even if someone had tried to tell me that soon all of my family would be dead, I would not have believed him? For who could believe a place like Auschwitz existed?

Seeing how these poor Jews held onto their luggage, the tiny bit of former property they'd been allowed to bring with them, I knew they would not believe me either. I knew that Jakob was right. I could not save these people. They were beyond my help. They were already dead.

All the other prisoners in the *kommando* knew this already, like Jakob did. They would not join me in an uprising. They knew how pointless it was, and they wanted to live. To my infinite shame, I had to admit I wanted to live, too.

Someone was tugging on my sleeve. I turned and saw it was Jakob. His face was tight with anxiety, but at the sight of my welling eyes, his expression softened. He knew I understood. He knew I would not cause trouble. He gave me a nod, telling me without words that he understood my pain, and that he shared it.

The wailing of infants, the shouting of family members desperate not to lose each other in the teeming mass of humanity now crowding the platform, the howling pleas for water that went unanswered, the barking of dogs, and the yelling of SS guards—all combined into a palpable cloud of painful cacophony. It was pandemonium, with people still coming out of the cattle cars, while others jumped back in to bring out more of their luggage. They did not know their luggage was of no further use to them.

Our *Kapo* ordered us forward. Jakob brought his mouth close to my ear. "Don't warn them. Just tell them to leave the luggage on the platform, and help us bring the rest of it out."

On the platform, the SS guards were trying to instill order, yelling at everyone to be quiet, to put their luggage aside and start forming lines. Following Jakob among the new arrivals, I was bombarded by their fear. Some of them looked at me in horror or disgust, and why shouldn't they? I was incredibly thin, dressed in filthy striped clothes—what sort of creature could I be? Was this what lay in store for them?

Words in Hungarian swirled all around me. Mothers promising their children that everything would soon be all right; people telling each other to watch it when they stepped on or jostled one another; someone beseeching God for mercy or salvation. I wanted to shut my eyes and plug my ears, to see and hear nothing. But these people deserved better. If I could not help them, I could at least bear witness. So I ran my eyes around, trying to imprint my mind with as many faces as I could.

An old bearded man with a black yarmulke asked Jakob in German where we were, and Jakob answered that we were in

Auschwitz, in Poland, and that the old man should leave his suitcase where he stood. Then he simply carried on walking.

Cutting through the crowd in Jakob's wake, I spotted two redheaded teenage boys, clearly brothers and both white with fright, and an ember of defiance glowed hot in my belly. I paused and asked them how old they were. Fourteen and thirteen, the older one said.

"Tell them you're seventeen and sixteen. You understand? Seventeen and sixteen."

They gulped and nodded. I turned away without another word and hurried after Jakob. I could not save all these Jews, but maybe I had just saved these two boys. And maybe one day, I'd be able to convince myself that I had done enough.

A German voice blared over a loudspeaker, ordering the people to divide into two groups: men on one side, women and small children on the other. "You'll be reunited soon," the voice promised. "Leave your luggage on the platform. You'll get it back later. There's coffee and water and food waiting for you."

The people looked at each other. They did not know what to think. They could sense the wrongness of this place. But the voice had promised food. Had offered hope. And most chose to cling to it.

Still, there were some who resisted parting with their loved ones. The guards acted swiftly and without mercy. Kicks, punches, and shoves were their method of persuasion. A few prisoners of the Kanada Kommando helped in the process, though they used nothing but words. Then came the voice over the loudspeaker again. "Please follow orders. You'll be with your family again soon. After a brief medical examination, you'll be able to eat and rest."

Slowly, the Jews on the platform formed two columns. Men shouted exhortations to their wives to take care of themselves and their children, words of love, and promises that soon they'll be together again. I followed Jakob into one of the cattle cars.

The car stank of feces and urine, and something else too. Death. Two bodies were stacked against one wall. A third lay near the center of the car. Old people—two men and one woman. They had died of suffocation, or maybe heart attack or stroke, caused by the severe conditions on their journey from Hungary. Judging by the smell, at least one of them had been dead for more than a day. The woman was the one who lay in the center of the car. She had likely died without any of the other passengers noticing until they'd arrived here. Otherwise, she would have been placed aside with the other two corpses. Her eyes were open, staring up at the ceiling. One of her arms was stretched out horizontally, and I noticed that her fingers were crooked and broken. They had probably been stepped on when the people scrambled to get out of the stifling car. A large purse was hooked over her arm. Jakob pulled it off her and tossed it out of the open door. Then he went deeper into the car, where three suitcases and a few bundles of linen lay. "Come," he simply said, and I did, but not before I knelt down and closed the dead woman's eyes.

We removed the remaining luggage. Then it was time for the bodies. We carried the woman to the lip of the car, and Jakob made to throw her out. "Don't," I said, and set down her feet, which I'd been holding, jumped down, and began to drag her out. Jakob gave me an inscrutable look, but he did not laugh or complain. Wordlessly, he followed me down and together we took the woman out of the car and laid her on the platform.

When we climbed back into the car, I turned and stared at the two columns of Jews. Those at the front were at this moment being examined by SS doctors who would determine their fate. Some Jews were sent to the left, others to the right. One side signified death, the other a miserable life in the camp. At the tip of the men's column, I spotted two fiery-red spots. The two boys. I watched with bated breath as they stepped forward together to talk to the SS doctor. *Remember*, I pleaded with them in my mind, *you're seventeen and sixteen. Seventeen and sixteen.*

The SS doctor was talking to them, then listening. Naturally, I could not hear what they were saying. It seemed that the SS doctor was peering at the two boys, and I imagined that he was suspicious of their purported ages. Time stood still as I waited for his verdict. Then, with a snap of the wrist, he motioned them to go left, toward life. I exhaled, then grinned, for a second forgetting about all those other poor people, most of whom would die today.

But the two boys would live, at least for now, and that was wonderful.

"What did you say to them?" a voice asked from behind.

It was Jakob. He was staring intently at me with his watery eyes.

"Who?" I asked, acting dumb.

"You know who. Those two boys."

With a tilt of my chin, I answered, "To tell the Germans they were seventeen and sixteen years old."

For a moment, Jakob just looked at me, his morose expression unchanging. Then he gave me a nod. "You did good. Now let's get back to work."

16

We cleared cattle cars until noon, heaping up luggage and bodies on the platform, emptying buckets of excrement. Gradually, the columns of arriving Jews dwindled to nothing as they went through selection. The majority were sentenced to immediate death. I watched them—men, women, and children—shamble toward the gas chambers.

Invalids and those too weak or old to walk were loaded onto trucks that took them to their death. Other trucks waited for the plunder.

It lay scattered all over the platform. Mounds of property. Linen and clothes, suitcases and kitchenware. Here a metal pot. There a briefcase with tarnished clasps. Here a pair of spectacles, their lenses broken. There a discarded coat with a yellow star stitched over the breast pocket. An incredible quantity and variety of small items caught in this final sieve of thievery.

Other prisoners were loading the plunder onto trucks. Little sorting was done. The goal was to clear the platform as quickly as possible. All the property. And all the bodies, too.

There were a few dozen of them, those who had perished en route to Auschwitz. Most of them elderly or middle-aged, but among the dead was also a single baby boy, his hair as fine as a feather. He could not have been more than three months old. The adult bodies were thrown like luggage into a waiting truck, but the baby boy received a different treatment. A prisoner carried him reverentially to the body truck, weeping with each step, and laid him down as gently as though the baby were still breathing.

We were all used to death. We'd seen too many dead bodies to give each new one the respect it deserved. But a baby was special. The death of a baby cut deep.

We had lunch on the platform, where there was still some loot to clear. Jakob and I sat in the slim shade cast by the empty train. From under his shirt he produced a lump of bread, likely soaked with his sweat. He cast me a glance, obviously considering whether to share the bread with me. I decided to make it easy for him.

"It's all right, Jakob. We barely know each other."

"That's right," he said. "We don't." But he tore off a small piece of the bread and handed it to me nonetheless. He dunked the tip of what remained in his soup and chewed on it. My piece was too small for that, so I simply tossed it into my mouth.

"Thank you," I said, though, of course, that tiny morsel did little to dispel my hunger.

He didn't answer for a moment, just sipped his soup and ate his bread. You could tell a lot about a man by the way he ate. Jakob did so slowly and methodically, like he was completing a task. "You had me worried there in the morning. Real worried. I'm glad you changed your mind."

"I'm not sure I am."

"I know what you mean."

"Do you?"

He gave me a stern look. "Yes, I do. You think I haven't imagined what it would be like to rise up against them? But like I said, it would do no good. You know that now too."

I looked away from him, a little ashamed. Because he was right. I did know. Which was why I hadn't acted. I was like him now. Like all the men in the Kanada Kommando. I had taken part. I was a small cog in the machinery of murder and plunder, and nothing I did would ever change that.

"It's a lousy feeling," Jakob said, finishing his soup and setting his bowl aside. "The worst feeling. But if you want to stop it by dying, go jump on a fence. Don't take the rest of us with you."

The image of Gyuri in the instant of death flashed before my eyes. I tightened my lips and said nothing. Jakob was right. I drank the rest of my soup and forced my mind away from Gyuri and the events of that morning. I had a case to solve.

"You've been in this *kommando* for long?" I asked.

"Five months."

"Ever met a Dutch boy named Franz?"

"Franz? You know Franz?"

"So you have met him."

"Sure. Up until two months ago, I knew almost every man who worked in Kanada. It was a smaller *kommando* back then. These days, it's much bigger, because so many Hungarian Jews are being brought here. You're Hungarian, aren't you?"

"Yes."

"So you're new in the camp."

"Almost two months. I was on one of the first transports from Hungary."

"I was probably here on this platform when you arrived. But I don't remember you. I don't remember any of the people who pass through here."

I wondered why that was. Was his memory shaky by nature, or

was it a way in which his mind shielded itself from the horror it witnessed?

"Did Franz work here with you?" I asked.

"Sometimes. Mostly, he worked in the Kanada warehouses. Then one day I heard he'd been assigned someplace else. Haven't seen him since. How's he doing?"

"He's dead."

"Dead?" Jakob shook his head. "Goddamn the Germans."

I studied him. His expression was as lugubrious as always, but he did not appear to be mournful. Then again, apart from when I'd scared him that morning, his emotions never rose above a low guttering flame.

"He wasn't killed by the Germans," I said. "Someone stabbed him to death."

"Another prisoner?"

"That's what it looked like."

Jakob was thoughtful as he took that in. Then he shook his head again. "It's a damn shame. He was just a boy."

"Was there anyone who might have wished him harm?"

He narrowed his eyes at me. "Why are you asking all these questions? What was Franz to you?"

"I never met him."

"Then why the questions?"

I had prepared for this, had contrived a reason for my interest in Franz.

"A fellow prisoner, a friend of Franz's family who heard I was being assigned to Kanada, asked me to look into the matter." I had deliberately not said that this prisoner was a cousin or an uncle of Franz, fearing that the boy might have talked about his family. For all I knew, there had been no uncles or cousins. I had also decided not to say I was working for the *Lagerälteste* unless there was a good reason to do so.

"The matter?" Jakob asked.

"Franz's murder."

"What do you mean, look into it? It sounds like you're conducting an investigation."

"I suppose I am."

"What makes you qualified to do that?"

"I used to be a criminal defense lawyer back in Hungary," I said. "I picked up a few things on how to conduct an investigation." The lawyer idea had come to me during the night, mostly as a way to explain to the prisoner functionaries who had shared a room with Franz why the *Lagerälteste* had chosen me to investigate this case. I was relieved when Jakob seemed to readily accept this falsehood.

"And you actually plan on doing this?"

"Yes, I am."

"Why? It's a damn shame that Franz is dead, but people die here every day."

It was a good question, and I needed a different answer than *Because if I don't, the Lagerälteste will beat me to death.*

"Because I don't like murderers," I said.

Jakob blinked, caught off guard, perhaps, by the blunt simplicity of my reply. He pursed his lips, then said, "I guess that's a good enough reason. But what's the point? Suppose you find out who killed Franz, what then? You're going to put him on trial?"

I didn't tell him there would be no trial. Just a summary execution, and a brutal one at that. Instead, I said, "I don't know. I'll cross that bridge when I get to it. First, I need to know who he is."

Jakob stuck a hand under his cap and scratched his head. "A murder investigation in this place. I don't know... it seems bizarre, ridiculous even."

"Maybe it shouldn't. At least not among ourselves."

He contemplated this and shrugged. "I still don't see the point of it. But if you got some questions, I'll answer them as best I can."

"I appreciate it. Do you happen to know if anyone had anything against Franz?"

"Not that I know. Mind you, I don't think I ever talked about him with anyone. Nor did I know him too well. He started out working on the platform like we did today, but a few months back he was moved almost exclusively to the warehouses. Lucky him."

"Why do you say that?"

"Because it's easier to get things in the warehouses. Food, and stuff you can trade for it. They open the luggage there and sort it for shipment to Germany. Here we mostly just haul it to the trucks. Also, in the warehouses, you don't work among the soon-to-be-dead, just with their stuff. And you don't carry bodies. It's not as physically demanding as what we do here on the platform. That's why most of the work in the warehouses is done by women prisoners."

"Did Franz have a relationship with any of these women?"

"You mean a romantic relationship?"

"Yes."

"No idea. Like I told you, I didn't know him all that well. Barely saw him for more than a couple of minutes at a time since he began working at the warehouses."

I looked at him, suddenly suspicious. Why was he stressing the shallowness of his acquaintance with Franz? To throw me off? So I would not consider him a suspect?

"I can't imagine anyone having a romantic relationship in this place," Jakob said, gazing around us at the blocks and fences and watchtowers. "How would you court a girl? Bring her a piece of potato instead of flowers?"

It would be far more useful than flowers ever were, and

suggest an immeasurably deeper emotional bond. A man willing to go hungry for a woman was a man head over heels in love.

Jakob might not have believed romance could bloom in Auschwitz, but I knew otherwise. Vilmos was proof of that.

"What did Franz look like?" I asked.

"He was a good-looking boy. Sort of gentle, boyish features. Blue eyes, blond hair, though that was shaved of course. Not tall, but that might have changed with time. He still had a few years to grow. He must have been getting his hands on proper food because he looked healthy. First time I saw him, I was surprised to learn he'd been in the camp for months. He looked like he'd just gotten off the train."

I remembered Mathias telling me that Franz was adaptable and knew how to survive in the camp. Apparently, this had been true even before he became the *Lagerälteste's* servant.

"Did he ever tell you anything about his past, his family?"

"Just that he was from Holland, and that he was alone here. I didn't ask too many questions. I hardly ever do. If people I work with die, I'd rather know as little about them as possible."

Which might have explained why he hadn't asked anything about my history, or my family, or even what my last name was. Then again, I hadn't asked him any of these questions, either.

"Did Franz have any friends?" I asked.

"One that I know of. A youngster named Ludwig. He also works in the warehouses."

"As young as Franz?"

"No. Nineteen or twenty, I think. They seemed pretty chummy."

"Anything else you can tell me about Franz?"

He began shaking his head, but then he paused and examined his calloused hands.

"What is it, Jakob?"

He didn't answer right away. He obviously wasn't sure he should say whatever was on his mind. I decided not to push him. It was better if he chose to tell me on his own.

"It was shortly after I began working on the platform," he said. "A train arrived. Not as big as this one; maybe seven hundred people or so. I think they were French, but maybe I'm not remembering right. What I do remember is that about half of them were affluent. You could tell by their clothes and luggage. Apparently, the Germans over there in France didn't fleece the Jews as much as they did here in Poland and elsewhere. Not until they got to Auschwitz."

He fell silent, his jaw moving, as he relived that day in his mind.

"And Franz?"

Jakob rubbed his cheek with his thumb. "Franz acted a bit strange when we moved the luggage onto the trucks. He grabbed just the nice luggage and took it all to a single truck, even when there was a closer one he could have used. When I asked him about it, he said it would make it easier to sort the stuff in the warehouses. Then he winked at me, which I thought was inappropriate, given that the owners of that luggage were at that moment being gassed."

"Why do you think he did that?"

"I don't know." Then he sighed and ran a tired hand over his face. "I don't know why I'm telling you this. The boy's dead. I shouldn't be saying anything that might paint him in a bad light. Don't ask me any more questions, all right? The boy's dead, and nothing's going to change that. And your whole investigation or whatever you may call it is stupid and worthless. There is no justice here, Adam, can't you see that? No justice whatsoever."

17

I had hoped that after lunch I'd be sent with the trucks to the Kanada warehouses, but the *Kapo* informed us that another train was coming. The hungry monster of Auschwitz had not had its fill for that day.

We hurriedly cleared the platform of every trace of property. The new victims needed to have no clue of what lay in store for them. The Germans wanted them to suspect nothing. It would keep them hopeful. And obedient. Which would make the process of killing them tidier and smoother and more efficient. Like a conveyor belt in a factory. Only this factory produced nothing but death and ashes and tears.

Jakob worked in ponderous silence, his mouth set in a downward arc of grim isolation. He hardly looked at me. My questions had upset him deeply. I gave him what little peace I could bestow and did not speak to him anymore.

The heat of the day had turned oppressive. The sun beat down like a jackboot stomping on my head. I could see my fellow prisoners were all suffering from the heat and thirst. But there was no shade, no water, no break. Once the platform was clear, we were ordered to stand in formation and wait for the new train.

It was similar to the first one—a black beast with a cargo of victims—more than two thousand desperate, hungry, disoriented people, liberated from the nightmare of the cattle cars only to be plunged into a worse one. Mothers clutched frightened children to their bosoms; men stooped, made smaller by the crippling certainty that they were now powerless to protect their families; old people hovered near unconsciousness or death, with some having crossed the boundary during the trip. And we, the prisoners who met them, knowing what awaited these poor brothers and sisters of ours, and also knowing we could do nothing to save them.

As before, I walked among them, memorizing faces, my shoulders bent with the guilt of my silence. But as I did so, I could also feel a distance building between me and these people. A detachment. They were already dead, and I was still alive. If I got too close, I would go insane.

The loot was even bigger on this transport than the one that preceded it. We worked continuously until evening, by which time every muscle in my body felt like weak rubber. The wound in my foot screamed with each step. It was getting worse. By the end of the day, I had developed a limp, and I feared that soon I would not be able to walk at all.

We left the platform as we'd found it that morning, empty and lifeless. The train departed, vacant, but not for long. The trucks took the plunder to the Kanada warehouses.

I needed to be in those warehouses tomorrow. I needed to see where Franz had worked before he'd become the *Lagerälteste's* servant. Mathias had posted me to the wrong section of the Kanada Kommando, and now a precious day had passed with not a whole lot to show for it—just the name of another prisoner who was said to be Franz's friend, and a description of Franz carrying a specific sort of luggage to a single truck.

Whatever this information proved to be worth, I had paid a painful premium for it. I had no doubt that for as long as my heart beat and my lungs drew breath, what I'd seen and heard that day would haunt me. That and the guilt I would forever carry.

I staggered back to camp and found Vilmos. He took one look at me and said, "What happened?"

I told him a little, sparing him the worst of it. "When people say Kanada is a good posting, they must mean the warehouses. Because I'd rather dig trenches than work on the platform."

He did not look all that well either. His cheeks held an ominous pinkish flush, and his breathing was scratchy. But he swore he was feeling fine. Obviously a lie for my benefit.

Together we stood at roll call. As we were counted, I kept glancing sideways at the smoke rising from the crematoriums and fire pits. The corpses burning there were of the people I had seen on the platform. Those whose faces would forever be imprinted on my mind.

After roll call was finally completed and we had gotten our bread rations, Vilmos said he was going to meet his lover. "We'll meet in twenty minutes or so?" he said.

Neither of us had watches, so the best we could do was estimate the time. "Twenty minutes," I said.

After Vilmos had gone, I started heading for the latrine, but then I saw Mathias. He was leaning against the front of a block, given ample space by the other prisoners on account of his functionary armband. He beckoned me over.

"You're limping," he said in that even tone of his. His expression did not shift. It was a statement of fact, nothing more.

"A bit," I said. As big an understatement as I had ever made.

"What's wrong with your foot?"

"Do you want me to show you? It's not pretty."

"I'm sure I've seen worse," he said.

I pulled off my clog and showed him my wound. It was red and oozing. "The clogs are too small."

"Or your feet are too big." He displayed no reaction to the ugly sight of my injury. Then again, he had not been lying when he said he'd seen worse. We both had.

"Or that," I said. I gingerly slipped my foot back into my clog, unable to restrain a hiss of pain. "It's a strange thing about starving: Your feet don't shrink nearly as much as the rest of you."

"Did you learn anything today?" he asked.

"Not much. I was at the wrong place." I explained to him that I would need to be in the Kanada warehouses tomorrow.

"I'll see to it. I've come to take you to meet the *Stubendiensts* who shared a room with me and Franz. You said you needed to talk to them."

"I do, but I can't come right now. I'm following another lead."

"Oh? And what lead is that?"

I didn't answer for a few seconds, just looked at him, wondering what his story was. What crime had led to his arrest and eventual placement here in Auschwitz? It must have been serious. He had to be a dangerous man. I needed to keep that in mind.

"If something comes of it," I said, "you'll be the first to know."

He cocked his head. "Are you keeping secrets, Adam?"

"Hardly that. It's just that I wouldn't want anyone but the guilty party to get hurt," I said, hoping I was not stepping over the line.

Mathias gave me a look, then nodded understanding. He knew what the *Lagerälteste* was capable of.

"Tomorrow, then?"

"Yes. Tomorrow." Then I told him about pretending to have been a defense lawyer.

"That's good," Mathias said with another of his tiny smiles. "I'll let the *Lagerälteste* know."

He turned to leave but stopped when I asked him, "What did you do time for? The first time, I mean?"

"Why do you ask?"

"Just curious."

He thought it over before answering. "I killed my stepfather. He deserved it, if that makes a difference. Was a real bastard."

"What did he do? Beat your mother?"

"Among other things. He gave me this." He touched his scar.

"That doesn't seem enough to send you here," I said.

"He was just the first. In prison, I killed a few more. They deserved it too."

"Is that where you met the *Lagerälteste*? In prison?"

"Yeah. That's where we met. Any other questions?"

I said there weren't, and Mathias walked off, whistling softly. I proceeded to the latrine, and after relieving myself, I circled the building. There was that patch of desolate ground, between the latrine and the unused ditch, where secret meetings could be held. Where the body of a fifteen-year-old boy named Franz had been found. The smell was ghastly. It did not merely hang in the air but also wafted up from the very earth on which I stood. The result, no doubt, of inadequate disposal of human waste.

As I waited, I thought of Vilmos and his lover.

How was it possible to have a tryst in this place, in this stench? How could one touch the filthy, wasted body of a fellow prisoner without recoiling in horror or revulsion? Were love and passion really as powerful as that?

An image of my wife flickered in my mind, and I knew the answer was yes. Because if she were here now, even if she were emaciated and hairless, even if she were dirty and diseased, I would hold her tight and press my lips to hers.

My eyes were moist as I heard footfalls behind me. I wiped them dry and turned. It was Vilmos and another man. His lover.

He was a little man with a narrow beak of a nose and hooded light-brown eyes. Otherwise, he looked just like the rest of us. His hands were clasped before him, and his head was bent forward. He kept raising his eyes and then quickly lowering them, stealing nervous glances at me and then at Vilmos. There was a mousy quality about him. A cornered fearfulness. I wondered what Vilmos had told him about me. His nervousness might have been the result of guilt, or a deep-seated affliction. Some prisoners got that way. You live in constant fear for long enough and it will seep into your bones and ooze out of your pores.

"It's all right, Zoltan," Vilmos told him in Hungarian. "Adam can be trusted. Just tell him what you saw."

Zoltan kneaded his hands, his movements twitchy. He clearly did not wish to speak about this, which raised my antennae. Notwithstanding Vilmos's assertion that Zoltan was incapable of murder, I was keeping an open mind.

"You're in no danger," I told him. "But I need you to tell me everything you saw. It's important."

Still he hesitated, but an encouraging nod from Vilmos swayed him into speech.

"I came here to meet Vilmos," Zoltan said. "I saw the boy. He was dead. It was terrible."

"I'm sure it was. Where exactly was the body?"

With mincing steps he led me toward the ditch and pointed down. "Right here."

There was no trace of the crime perpetrated here. The earth had lapped up the blood. The body was gone. All that remained was the dry lifeless dirt of the camp. I crouched down for a closer look. Here and there were scuff marks of shoes or clogs, but none that were clear. This crime scene was as dead as the boy who had lain here with a hole in his throat.

"Was there anything near the body?" I asked.

"Nothing but blood. A whole lot of blood."

I asked him about defensive wounds and got the same inconclusive answer that I'd received from Vilmos, Mathias, and the *Lagerälteste*. I cursed inwardly. This was no way to conduct a murder investigation. Normally, either I saw the body with my own eyes or I had pictures of the victim. And if no pictures existed, I had a police report to consult, written by someone trained at solving crimes.

Who was I kidding? I was no detective. I was merely a slave trying to stay alive. This was absurd. Pointless and hopeless. And yet... what else was there to do? I wanted to live, and I wanted to feel like I was something more than just a prisoner. And investigating this crime, believing I had the power to solve it, gave me that feeling. I realized I needed that, almost as much as I needed food and sleep and something to relieve the sharp pain in my foot. So I pushed away my belittling doubts and tried to focus on the task at hand.

"Did you touch the body?" I asked.

Zoltan shook his head. "I didn't go near him. I saw him and ran away. I didn't want to be around him for one second longer."

"You didn't check to see if he was carrying anything useful?"

"No."

"Why not?"

"I was scared."

"Of what? There was no one around, was there? The killer had gone. And it's not a crime to kill a prisoner in this place, especially a Jewish one."

"I didn't want to be seen near him."

I frowned at him, and then it hit me. "You knew who he was. You knew he was the *Lagerälteste's* servant."

"Yes."

"How? Do you live in that block?"

"No. He told me."

"Who? The boy?"

"Yes. His name was Franz, you know."

"I do know," I said, feeling a prickle of excitement. "When did you speak to him?"

"Four days ago, I think? Maybe five. It's difficult to keep track of the passing days in this place."

"Where did you talk?"

"Not far from the kitchen. I saw him walk by and approached him."

"Why? What for?"

"I was hoping he might sell me some medicine."

"Why would he have any?" Medicine was one of the hardest commodities to get in the camp, scarcer and far more valuable than even food.

"Because he knew how to organize all sorts of things. About a month ago, I bought soap from him. French, with a scent of lilacs." Zoltan permitted himself a fragile smile; talking had alleviated his anxiety. "A terrible deal on my part—bread for a tiny bar of soap—but I had an overwhelming need to be clean. He said if I ever needed anything else, I should come see him."

To *organize* in camp parlance meant to acquire and sometimes trade illicit or hard-to-obtain goods on the camp's black market. And there was no better place to come into possession of such goods than in the Kanada warehouses.

"It was odd," Zoltan said thoughtfully.

"What was?" I asked.

"Him. The boy. Because he didn't seem like a boy at all. He

looked like one, but he had the air of a man of accomplishment, brimming with masculine confidence. At least he did when I bought the soap from him."

"But not when you approached him for the medicine?"

"No. His outward appearance was unchanged. He was healthy and well-fed, but at the same time he looked... dimmed, for lack of a better word. And his eyes, they were haunted and troubled and dull, like tarnished silver. He told me he didn't have any medicine to sell, and that I shouldn't bother trying to buy anything else from him. Then he said he had to hurry, that he was going to his master, the *Lagerälteste*."

I took a moment to think of what Zoltan had told me. It was obvious why Franz could not obtain any more illicit goods: He was no longer working in the Kanada warehouses. He had been cut off from his supply. But couldn't he still get certain things just by being in the *Lagerälteste's* orbit? I would have said the answer was yes, but it seemed I was wrong.

"Did he say anything else?" I asked.

"Nothing. It was the last time I saw him. Until I found the body."

"At which point you immediately left the scene?"

"Yes," Zoltan said. "I was worried that if someone saw me with him, they would think I'd done it."

I cast a quick glance at Vilmos to see if he understood the implications of what Zoltan had just said, but he had his eyes firmly on his lover.

"I take it no one saw you," I said.

"Thankfully no."

"How about you? Did you see anyone? Perhaps when you were coming this way? Someone who was going in the opposite direction?"

Zoltan started shaking his head, but then he stopped and his lips parted a little. "There was someone. Funny, but I forgot about him entirely until now. Seeing the dead boy and knowing who he was must have pushed that memory away. But I don't think the man I saw killed anyone."

"Let me be the judge of that," I said, hardly daring to hope. Was I on the verge of a breakthrough? "Who was it?"

"Other prisoners call him the Mumbler. Do you know who I'm talking about?"

"Yes," I said, my spirit sagging.

"I nearly bumped into him as he rounded the corner of the latrine," Zoltan said. "It startled me quite a bit because I didn't expect anyone to be here."

"How did he look? Did he have any blood on his clothes?"

"If he did, I didn't notice. But I admit, I didn't look at him for more than a fraction of a second. He makes me uneasy."

The same was true for me and all the other prisoners. For in the Mumbler, each and every one of us saw the future, and it was not a vision anyone wished to contemplate.

"Did he say anything?" I asked.

"He always does, doesn't he?" Zoltan said. "Nothing that made any sense to me. Not that I was paying any attention. I just stepped past him and hurried on. He didn't follow me, just kept going to God knows where."

"Do you think he saw the body?"

Zoltan shrugged his narrow shoulders. "Who knows what he sees? It's impossible to say how aware he is of what's going on around him. I'm surprised he's still alive."

It was a mystery to me as well. On more than one level.

"Anything else you saw?" I asked. "Anything at all, no matter how minor."

Zoltan shook his head with finality. "And what I did see," he said, "I wish I hadn't."

18

"I know what you're thinking," Vilmos said after Zoltan had departed. It was difficult to read Vilmos's expression, but if there was any anger there, I didn't see it. Which only served to increase my anger in turn, and also prodded me to not mince words.

"He's a coward," I said.

"Yes, I suppose he is."

"And a selfish one at that."

"Cowardice is generally selfish, Adam. We see proof of this every day around here."

"He didn't even stick around to warn you about the dead boy." I was starting to get angry with Vilmos and not just Zoltan. How could he be so casual about this? "He just scampered off to save his own hide. Do you know what would have happened to you if one of the goons working for the *Lagerälteste* had seen you near the body? Not to mention going through the boy's clothes?"

"I'd have been killed."

"That's right. And not gently either. The *Lagerälteste* would have beaten you to a pulp. And don't think Zoltan didn't know it.

He knew exactly, which was why he ran off like a frightened rabbit."

Vilmos was quiet. He just stared in the general direction in which Zoltan had gone. If my words had had any effect on him, he wasn't showing it.

The silence stretched for an uncomfortable minute. I was about to speak when Vilmos beat me to it.

"He wrote the most beautiful poetry, you know."

"Who?" I asked, thrown for a second by the abrupt change in topic. "Zoltan?"

"We met at university. Two Jewish boys hoping to expand our minds and make something of ourselves. Being who we are, what we are, we were drawn to each other. Being with him made my university days the happiest in my life. Zoltan was wonderful, and he wrote the most wonderful poetry. Love poems of such delicate and profound emotion that one could cry when reading them. Some were even published. Everyone thought they were written for a woman, of course, but they were written for me." Vilmos turned to face me, his eyes glistening with the memory of a happier lost time. "For me, Adam."

Before I could think, before I could stop myself and rise above my petty need to be right, I said, "But he ended your relationship, didn't he? Then what did he do? Get married?"

Vilmos drew a sharp breath, and I knew I had hurt him, and I cursed myself for it. Yet he didn't seem upset. He just pushed his lower lip out and gave me the saddest smile I'd seen him give.

"You don't know what it's like, Adam, living your life while needing to hide your true self. If you're not married by a certain age, people start to wonder and whisper. In certain circles, not being married, not having a family, can mean a very low ceiling on your career prospects, if not the outright end of them. So, yes, Zoltan got married. Plenty of men like us do. I came close to it myself, and I would have gone through with it if the girl in question hadn't gotten suspicious. So I don't blame Zoltan one bit for breaking things off with me, nor for getting married. It's what one has to do in order to live a secure and accomplished life in a society that frowns upon men like us, if it doesn't actively persecute them. That's not cowardice. It's self-preservation."

This time the silence was due to my not knowing what to say. "I'm sorry, Vilmos," was what I finally came up with. Far from eloquent, but genuine and heartfelt nonetheless.

Vilmos smiled that sad smile again. "Apology accepted, Adam. And you're right. Zoltan did a cowardly, selfish thing. An immoral, unconscionable thing. He is not the man I knew in university. But I don't meet with him because of who he is. I meet with him because of who he was. Because when I'm with him, I become, for a short magical while, the young student I was when I knew him. I'm transported beyond these fences, outside of this wretched camp, and back to a time when there was proper food, and proper clothes, and proper shoes, and proper hopes and dreams. Do you understand, Adam?"

"Yes," I said, shame making my voice small.

Vilmos nodded. Then his face broke into a wide grin. "Besides, Zoltan has his moments. Why do you think he bought that soap? For whom do you think he wished to be clean? A man gives up his bread to be just a little less dirty for you—it says something about how he sees and values you, doesn't it?"

"It most certainly does," I said.

"That's part of his charm. He's a romantic. That's one thing this place hasn't squashed out of him."

I nodded, and then a thought struck me.

"Is Zoltan sick?" I asked.

Vilmos coughed. The sound like unoiled cogs grinding. "We're all sick, aren't we?"

"I mean more than the usual."

"No, I don't think so. Why do you ask?"

"I was just wondering what he needed medicine for," I said, though seeing Vilmos's flushed cheeks and clammy forehead, and hearing his raspy breath and rattling cough, I knew. Zoltan had been trying to get medicine for Vilmos. He might have been a coward, but he wasn't all bad.

"I don't know," Vilmos said, though he clearly did.

"Are you all right, Vilmos?" I said, though I could tell that he wasn't, that he had gotten worse over the past few days.

"Yes," he said, trying and failing to bite back another cough. "I'm fine. Don't you worry about me. Now, shall we go and find the Mumbler?"

19

It didn't take us long to find him. He was walking by the northern fence through which one could stare across a service road into what prisoners called Mexico—a new, partially built extension of the camp, which was now home to thousands of Hungarian Jewish women.

The men's camp was horrendous enough, but Mexico was even worse. Here there were no washrooms and no latrines. Here the blocks were incomplete. It was said that some of them lacked bunks and that the women had to sleep on the hard floor.

The women themselves looked especially miserable. Many were not given prisoner uniforms. The lucky ones wore torn, bedraggled dresses—the refuse of looted clothes which the Nazis hadn't wanted for themselves—while others had to make do with rags or dirty blankets which they caped around themselves to hide their nakedness. They wandered about the desolate wasteland that was Mexico like starved sleepwalkers.

Why this section of the camp got the name Mexico was unclear. Perhaps because, unlike Canada, Mexico had the image of a poor, undeveloped country, where basic facilities were scarce. I could only hope none of my sisters had been put into Mexico. I doubted anyone could survive for long there.

The Mumbler was all alone, as usual. A *muselmann* was a solitary creature by nature. Other prisoners avoided them as much as possible, and they themselves grew more and more detached from their environment, until finally they made the ultimate departure and died, usually not long after becoming a *muselmann*.

But the Mumbler was special. Because by some mysterious manner, he had managed to live for longer than his condition should allow. Not only had he staved off death by starvation, he had also survived a camp-wide selection, the latter despite him clearly being unfit for work and on the brink of death, which would normally have earned him a trip to the gas chambers.

When Vilmos and I found him, he was plodding along at a tottering shuffle, his feet barely clearing the ground. Each step was so laborious it seemed certain to be his last, but then came another, as sluggish and onerous as its predecessor.

As we got closer to him, my ears began to pick up the steady, relentless burr of his mumbling, for which he had earned his nickname. His language was German, but his accent was nonexistent, as his flat, meandering speech was smoothed of all inflection.

"Cream tart, grilled sausage, potato pancake, sauerkraut, roast beef stew, egg noodles, pretzel, gingerbread cookies, coffee with sugar, apple strudel, black forest cake..." was just part of the caravan of foods the Mumbler was reciting.

This was a common symptom of being a *muselmann*. While ordinary prisoners generally avoided talking about the delicious foods they had known as free men, as this would only augment the pain of their absence, a *muselmann* seemed able to speak of little else. Yet another reason why prisoners steered clear of them.

"Hey," I said, but the Mumbler did not appear to have heard

me. He kept up his litany of delicacies, drool snaking from his lips, his eyes gigantic and bulging in his skeletal head.

Up close, the stench he exuded overwhelmed that of our own. As part of his descent into a *muselmann*, he had abandoned any pretense at cleanliness. Not only that, but his condition affected his bowel movements, which had become runny and continuous, and he was either unable to hold them in or he had ceased to try. He stank like an outhouse in heat. Bile rose, acidic and biting, to the base of my throat. Beside me, Vilmos raised a hand to cover his nose. The Mumbler was not offended by this show of disgust. He might not have noticed it at all.

"Butter pastries, blintzes, rugelach, crispy schnitzel with mashed potatoes, boiled asparagus with sauce..."

I stepped in front of him, blocking his path. He stopped, and also fell silent. His eyes swam over my face. They held a look of profound wonderment, as though I were an unfamiliar creature who had suddenly dropped from the sky. This was ironic because the Mumbler himself was such a creature, a nightmarish apparition of horror and deprivation.

He was a man stripped of flesh. All that remained was skin and bones, like an exhibit in a nature museum of some extinct humanoid. His cheekbones stood out like twin shovel blades under paper-thin skin stretched so tightly it looked ready to split. His cheeks were sunken, as though he were ceaselessly sucking them in. His lips were two colorless pencil lines bordering a jutting mouth missing all four front teeth. Through the gap, the tip of his tongue peeked like a bird sticking its head between the bars of its cage. His hands could have belonged to a centenarian, with elongated fingers and the bones and tendons showing starkly on the back of his hands. The stubble on his jaw was uneven, broken by patches of bald, flaky skin.

He had been partially claimed by death already. Yet some

piece of him stubbornly clung to the world of the living—enough to keep his heart beating and his lungs drawing air, though gradually shedding more and more of what made him a man.

Now he was staring at me with his huge innocent dark eyes. "Mother will be down soon," he said pleasantly. "Dinner is almost ready. Just a few minutes." He blinked, and his gaze began to roam again. "Chicken broth, potatoes with rosemary, freshly baked bread, dumplings, champagne, chocolate cake for dessert." He licked his lips, and his eyes regained their focus. "So glad you could come."

"We're not here for dinner," I said.

He paid me no mind. "I need to go upstairs." He ran a hand down the sleeve of his striped shirt, which hung on his body as baggily as on a rack. "I must change before dinner. There's not much time."

The Mumbler's uniform was an amalgam of stains and filth. The front of his shirt was crusted with a brownish stain that might have been spilled soup or morning tea, but could also have been blood. Franz's blood?

The rest of his clothes weren't much better. The seat of his trousers was dark and wet with his shit. One trouser leg was torn, revealing an ankle as thin as a stick and dotted with blue and black spots.

"Don't worry about it," I said. "You look fine."

The Mumbler's eyes bulged further. He looked horrified. "Mother would insist. Especially now that we have guests." He made a sweeping gesture with his hand, encompassing Vilmos and myself. Then his lips stretched into what might have once been the practiced smile of a young host, but which now looked like the deranged grin of a mental patient. "Toast with butter, baked apples, cool lemonade..."

"We're not here for dinner," I said again, a bit forcefully. "We're here to talk to you."

He looked delighted. "How wonderful! But let's talk after we eat. I'm famished. And mother has worked so hard to prepare everything." He sniffed and sighed in contentment, his nose tickled by delicious aromas that existed solely in his head. "Vegetable soup, cutlets of veal, peas, vanilla ice cream..."

It was no use. He was in his own world, running on his own track. He was a useless witness.

I looked at Vilmos, hoping he'd have some idea on how to breach the Mumbler's fantasy and access whatever true memories he might possess.

Vilmos shrugged, then leaned over and whispered to me, "Perhaps we should play along with his delusion. Be the guests he clearly wants us to be."

It seemed preposterous and futile, but I was desperate. If the Mumbler had seen something, I needed to know what it was. We didn't have much time. The sky was rapidly darkening, and soon it would be time to go to our block for the night.

I plastered a wide smile on my face, took the Mumbler by the elbow, and pulled him down with me to sit on the ground. Then I pretended to unfurl a napkin and spread it across my lap. "Let's eat," I said with a smile.

For a few long minutes, the three of us talked of nothing but the imaginary food on the Mumbler's make-believe table. It was a meal like none the world had ever seen. Two dozen main courses, twice as many appetizers, and more types of dessert than I knew existed.

It was also torture. Simply hearing of all those scrumptious dishes made my stomach cramp and a hungry voice wail in my head. Vilmos looked just as anguished, but he kept up the show, remarking favorably on each course, complimenting the choice of wine, and generally buttering the Mumbler up.

The Mumbler looked as happy as a man could be. And why wouldn't he? In his mind, he was sitting on a plush chair, not the barren ground of Auschwitz. In his nose were the aromas of his favorite foods, not the reek of burning flesh and his own stink. Around him were the familiar and comforting walls of his old dining room, not barbed wire and watchtowers and blocks unfit for human habitation. And in his belly there was ample food and drink, not the howling emptiness that shrieked like a banshee.

But more than anything else, the Mumbler appeared to enjoy our company. Perhaps he had been aware on some level of his solitude, and here he was socializing again, playing host. People were actually listening to him. He basked in our presence, relishing our compliments. He smiled constantly, the dark space where his teeth had once been a symbol of his perforated cognitive state.

Like his mood, his speech improved as well. A bit of modulation entered his voice, and with it a hint of a crisp German accent. The words no longer tumbled from his mouth in a rambling stream. Now they were clearly delineated, which made him sound half-reasonable.

We had finally reached the final dessert—cheesecake with fresh strawberries—when Vilmos patted his stomach and proclaimed how delightful the meal had been. I chimed in as well, saying I was stuffed. The Mumbler beamed, his smile that of a skull covered by a thin sheet.

Vilmos gave me a quick nod, then leaned a bit toward the Mumbler and said, "We were wondering about a friend of ours you might have met."

"A friend?" the Mumbler said. "What friend?"

"He was a guest at the dinner party you threw three nights ago. Do you remember it?"

The Mumbler nodded. "Of course. What a splendid night it was. Full of laughter and food. But there were so many people—

friends of friends, you know." He let out a self-conscious chuckle. "I don't actually know everyone who attended."

"Our friend is a youngster," I said. "A teenager really. He's..." I stumbled for a description, having never seen Franz, then remembered what Vilmos and Jakob said of him. "Very handsome. Fair hair, clear skin, delicate features."

The Mumbler took this all in with the utmost seriousness. "I'm not sure I know who he is. What about him?"

Vilmos and I exchanged a look, unsure of how to proceed. Then an idea came to me. During our fake dinner, the Mumbler had mentioned a large back garden in his lost home. I decided to make use of it. "After dinner, our friend stepped out into your back garden." I waited, hoping I was not shattering the Mumbler's illusion, but he seemed to be listening to me intently. "Something happened to him. He got hurt pretty badly. Bled a lot."

The Mumbler blinked a few times very rapidly, and his smile disappeared. A glimmer of dread showed in his eyes, then a haze descended over them, and he began to mumble again, "Scones smeared with marmalade, cold beer, smoked Frankfurters, cookies filled with red currant jam, pickled herring..."

I was losing him, but now I was sure he had seen something. I grabbed his forearm, wincing as my fingers closed upon what felt like nothing but bones under his sleeve. "Stop it now! You know who we're talking about. What did you see?"

The Mumbler shook his head violently. "Meatloaf in a bun, roasted goose with thyme, gingerbread with almonds..."

I was so frustrated I was ready to shake him, but Vilmos put a hand on my arm. "That's not the way, Adam."

He was right. The Mumbler was beyond such persuasion. I needed to find another way. I thought for a moment, and then it came to me.

"Shall we ask Mother?" I said. "Maybe she knows."

The Mumbler fell silent abruptly. He was utterly still. All except for his lips, which were quivering. "Mother?"

"Yes. Maybe she would know what happened to your guest."

"No, no, no. Mother saw nothing. Nothing. Nothing."

"But you did," I said. "And you need to tell us what."

"I don't want to," the Mumbler said. "I don't want to talk about it."

"It's not pleasant, we know. Not the proper way a dinner party should end. But he was your guest. You have a duty to safeguard his well-being. He got hurt, and we're here to help put things right. You need to tell us what you saw. Or shall we go ask Mother what she thinks?"

The Mumbler gave me a pleading look. "No. Oh no. Don't do that. It would only make her unhappy."

Shame washed over me. Here was another sin I was committing in this camp. I had found this man's vulnerability and I was exploiting it. He was beyond most of the suffering that had brought him to his sorry state, but he was still terrified of upsetting his mother and of her being upset with him. All this despite the near certainty that she was dead.

"We won't," Vilmos said. "You have our word. Just tell us what happened to our friend."

The Mumbler's tongue darted out of his mouth, quick as a lizard, wet his lips, and curled back into his open mouth.

I still had hold of his forearm, and now I moved my grip to his hand. It was clammy and cold like a dead fish; I had to force myself to keep my hand on his and give him an encouraging squeeze.

"It's all right," I said. "We won't judge you. We know what a terrific host you are."

The Mumbler looked at me and smiled. "We did have a wonderful meal together, didn't we? Mother was thrilled."

"Yes. Yes, she was. She's very proud of you. You're a terrific son. Now tell us what you saw."

The Mumbler gulped. An expression of such profound sadness settled over his shrunken features that my heart threatened to break. Beside me, I heard Vilmos sniffle.

"He was lying at the rear of the garden," the Mumbler said, "on the soft earth past the edge of the lawn, near a long row of flowers that Mother had planted herself. Such beautiful flowers."

A better place to die, I thought, than an empty ditch in Auschwitz.

"His eyes were open," the Mumbler said, gazing at some vacant spot over my shoulder, at the picture he had painted over his memory, a picture only he could see. "They were blue. And around him the earth was red."

"Did you and he have a fight that night?" I asked. I did not think the Mumbler had the strength to kill anyone, but I still needed to rule him out. "Did he say or do something that upset you?"

The Mumbler frowned, his forehead wrinkling like crumpled paper. "I never fight with my guests. That would be inhospitable."

"Did you see anyone else fight with our friend?"

"No. We've never had fights at any of our dinner parties. Everyone has such a wonderful time. That was the first time anyone ever got hurt." He screwed his eyes shut and then opened them. They were wet and fearful. "It was as if the world had gone mad, that such a thing could happen."

For a second or two, I couldn't speak, silenced by this poor man who had lost his connection to reality. A man who had ceased to be aware of the tragedy in which he lived and would soon die. A man who had escaped into the comfort and safety of his imagination, and whose little peace I had disturbed with my questions.

But I had no choice. If I wanted to live, I needed to find this killer.

"Did you see anyone else in the garden?" I asked, knowing that if he hadn't, this had all been a waste of time.

"Just the knight," he said after a moment, his voice barely audible and once more devoid of accent. His shoulders were hunched, arms squeezed tight to his chest. He looked small, like he was trying to fold into himself.

"What was that?" Vilmos asked, craning forward.

"The knight in shining armor I saw coming out of the rear of the garden."

Vilmos and I exchanged a look. Was this a true memory distorted by the Mumbler's delusion or a complete fantasy born in his failing mind?

"What knight?" I asked.

"He had a sword in his hand. It glinted in the moonlight before he sheathed it."

"You mean a knife? Was it a knife he was holding?"

"He had been to war before. Now he was our guest. I didn't know him, but everyone there was our guest."

"What did he look like?"

"He was resplendent in his armor, outshining all the other guests. Mother would have been impressed."

I strove to keep my frustration out of my voice. "Come now, this is a dinner party we're talking about. There was no knight there."

"He didn't see me. Just quickly walked away on the other side of the house. Then I saw the boy near the flowers." The Mumbler blinked a few times, tears dribbling down his cheeks with each blink, and when he stopped his eyes were dim and vacant. He started to rise from the ground. "Potato salad, triple-cream cheese, meat patties, onion pie, star cookies..."

I jumped to my feet and put a hand out to stop him. "No. Don't! Come back! I need to know what you saw."

But the Mumbler didn't hear me. He brushed off my arm and began trudging forward. "Noodles with melted cheese, sheet cake with a chocolate topping, veal sausage..."

I matched the Mumbler step for step, begging him to describe the man he saw, at one point grabbing his arm so hard it was a wonder his bones didn't crack.

But the Mumbler was oblivious. He continued shifting his feet, walking in place when my grip prevented his progress. My hold on his arm did not register, nor did my raised voice and anxious tone. The Mumbler had fled to a happier place, and this time he was determined to stay there. Neither my pleas nor my attempts to once more paint myself as his guest could coax him back out.

I glanced at Vilmos, who shrugged with a look of hopelessness on his face. "He's gone, Adam. You can't reach him anymore."

"I have to know what he saw," I said, my voice vibrating with desperation. "That man might have been the killer."

"Yes, but look at him. Going back to that night has taken too much of him."

"But what the hell does it mean?"

"I don't know. Maybe nothing. It could all be the fruit of his delusion."

I looked at the Mumbler. He was still treading in place, his gaze leveled at nothing, the river of words spilling from his lips sounding like a swarm of hovering bees. There was no intelligence in his eyes. He could have been a crude prototype of a machine that had malfunctioned. I let go of his arm, and he made his way forward, step by agonizing step. Vilmos and I watched in silence as he continued onward along the fence until his mumbling ceased reaching our ears.

20

I let out a long exhalation. "That's it. I'm a dead man."

"Don't say that," Vilmos said forcefully. "It's not true."

I didn't answer. I was tired and filled with a sense of doom. I had talked to two men who had seen the dead boy shortly after he was killed, and neither of them could provide me with any useful information—not even the man who might have seen the murderer leave the scene of the crime.

Vilmos said, "You'll find the solution, Adam."

I turned on him in anger, my frustration spilling over. "Really? What makes you so sure, huh? There's no physical evidence, no police report, no clues, and the only witness is a blathering moron who can't tell fiction from reality. It's hopeless, don't you see that?"

"There's always hope, Adam."

"Oh, come on. Look around you, Vilmos. Do you see any hope around here?"

Vilmos did not shift his gaze. "I don't need to look around to see it, Adam. I need only look at you."

"What are you—"

"And you need only look at me to see it, too. What else do you think keeps us alive in this place? God knows it's not the food, or the conditions, or the generosity of the Germans. So why aren't we dead? Why do we keep struggling? Why don't we follow Gyuri's example and jump at the fence?" He did not wait for me to reply, but pushed on. "It's hope, Adam. Don't you see that? We still hope, despite everything; hope that there's a future outside these fences; hope that one day we'll be out of here, that we'll be free again and could live a life worth living."

He looked so earnest, so imploring. He so wanted me to believe in this fantasy. In this lie. He didn't understand me at all.

I said, "Do you know why I want to survive this place, Vilmos? The real reason? It's not to live a life worth living, as you put it. Because my life ended there." I pointed at the smoke rising from the crematoriums. "It's over and done with. It can't be rebuilt. The reason I want to survive is not to live, but to kill. Kill as many of these Nazi bastards as I can. Not just the guards and the SS doctors, but everyone who had a hand in building this place, in sending our people here to be murdered. That's what I want. The only thing."

"No, it's not," Vilmos said. "You told me so yourself."

"What are you talking about?"

"You said that after you got out of here, you'd go to Tel Aviv, that you thought you'd like it there. Well, guess what, Adam? There are no Nazis in Tel Aviv. No one for you to take revenge on. So what are you going to do there if not live your life?"

I had no answer. But I also had no hope. It was just a dream, all of it. Exacting vengeance on those who killed my family, and later starting life afresh in Tel Aviv. As delusional as the Mumbler's imaginary feast. It had always been that and nothing more. Because I was going to die here. My body would be stuffed into a crematorium oven and there would be nothing left of me but ashes and dust.

Before I got this case, I'd thought I would die of starvation, or maybe I'd be marked for death in a selection, or an SS guard would shoot me for fun. And for some inexplicable reason, not knowing precisely how and when I would die had made it easier to cope. But now I knew the date and means of my demise: I would be beaten to death in two days, once I had failed the Lagerälteste's mission. The hopeless mission. And that inescapable certainty, that pre-determined fate, was crushing my spirit.

"I can't do it, Vilmos," I said, my voice cracking. "I'm not a detective anymore."

"Yes, you are."

"I'm not. You said so yourself, remember?"

"I was speaking in anger," he said. "And I was wrong."

"Oh yeah? What made you change your mind?"

"Seeing you in action—how you talked to Zoltan and the Mumbler. You asked all the right questions, got more out of them than I ever could."

"But nothing useful."

"It looks that way now, but if you keep asking the right questions, the way you know how, that's bound to change. Maybe the new things you'll learn will shed new light on what now seems useless, and everything will suddenly make sense."

I scoffed, kicking at a loose clod of earth. "I know you mean well, Vilmos. But I know how I feel. It's hopeless."

Vilmos looked about to say something more, but then closed his mouth with a snap of finality, as though he were throwing spadefuls of dirt into a loved one's grave. Seeing his expression plummet into dejection made me wish I had lied and feigned a hope I no longer felt. Now it was too late. Too late for everything.

"Let's go," I said. "Curfew's not that far off."

We walked to the block in heavy silence. Around us, the crackle of camp life seemed darker and more ominous than usual. Vilmos had his head down, deep in his own thoughts. I thought of the family I'd lost, all the many regrets that now weighed on my soul.

Then my mind turned to the case, to the question that had begun niggling at me. Why had the killer taken the murder weapon with him? It was a big risk. If he had been seen with it, or if it had later been found on his person, he would have been as good as dead.

Just outside our block, we saw the *Blockälteste* lurking about. He spotted me and said, "You there. Come here."

Without saying a word, Vilmos broke away from me, looped around the *Blockälteste,* and entered the block. There was no anger on my part. This was not a desertion, just common sense. He could not help me, so why put himself in jeopardy?

The *Blockälteste* looked me up and down with distaste. "What did you do, bend down with your trousers by your ankles? How old are you, anyway?"

I looked at him with bewilderment. What did he mean?

He sneered at me. "You wait here."

He was gone for less than a minute. Upon returning, he threw something hard at my chest. Two things, actually. I only managed to block one with my hand. The second robbed me of breath when it bounced against my ribcage.

"Here you go," he said, then swung around and went inside the block.

On the ground before me lay two clogs. Big ones. It took me a second before I realized who had left them with the *Blockälteste*.

I wasted no time removing my tight clogs and slipping on the new ones. I sighed, wiggling my toes while bowing my head and closing my eyes. The new clogs were too big and not comfortable by any means, but sheer heaven compared to my old ones. These would not rub the skin off my feet. Now my wound would have a chance to heal.

Why had Mathias left these for me? Why would he care? Perhaps this unexpected kindness was similar to that shown a condemned man shortly before his ascent to the gallows. The condemned man received a last meal, but here this was not possible. Perhaps this was my last meal, the chance to take my steps over my final days with reduced agony.

Or maybe this was as emotionless as oiling a machine so it would function properly. I was no longer a human being, after all, but a tool designed to perform a task for Mathias's master. If I limped, if I were in pain, I might do a suboptimal job.

Either way, gratitude suffused me as I entered the block, gratitude and something so unexpected I had to pause for a moment to examine it until I was sure I had identified it correctly.

Hope.

It was hope. Just a tiny bit of it. A filament of flame, flickering and faint, giving hardly any heat. But it was there. Unmistakable. And it did not strike me as unfamiliar. Rather, it had been hiding somewhere deep inside me, pushing me onward day by day without my knowing it.

Maybe Vilmos was right. Maybe I could solve this case after all.

I became aware of the muscles in my cheeks straining, and it took me a second to realize I was smiling. My steps lighter than they had been in many days, I hurried to our bunk to tell Vilmos of the hope I now felt.

21

That night, Vilmos took a turn for the worse. He shivered the whole night through, and he was boiling hot. It had been building up for over a week: the cough, the flush on his cheeks, his ragged breathing. Something bad had settled in his lungs, and now his body was trying to burn it out.

As the light of early dawn began to filter through the narrow high windows of our block, I could see his suffering etched on his face. His eyes were knotted shut, his forehead was creased and sheened with sweat, his mouth was pressed tight. At a rare moment of quiet in the block, I heard his teeth chattering.

I looked at him with dread and a crippling sense of impotence. I didn't know how I could help him. There was barely any medicine in Auschwitz; not for the prisoners, that is. Not even in the hospital.

The wake-up gong jolted me out of the bunk. I helped Vilmos down and, looping his arm across my shoulders, walked with him to the latrines.

"It's all right," he rasped. "I can walk."

I didn't answer; just carried him along. The heat radiating off him was intense. He needed medical attention, but the only place there were doctors was in the camp hospital, and what could they do without equipment, with hardly any medicine?

We were slow getting to the latrine and had to wait a long while. My bowels ached. Vilmos leaned against a wall, his head drooping. He looked like he would fall without the support.

But when we found two vacant holes, he managed to lower his trousers by himself and later pull them up again.

"I'm fine," he said, then went into a fierce coughing fit that bent him over at the waist.

"Yeah," I said when the fit ended, again draping his arm across my shoulders. "You're as good as new."

In the washroom, I cupped cold water in my palms and poured it over his head. He winced, swearing at me. It was so unexpected, and he'd chosen such a juicy curse word, that I broke out laughing, and was gratified when he joined me.

"I wouldn't have guessed you were capable of such profanity," I said.

"My vocabulary is quite extensive. Do that again and you'll find out exactly how much."

I poured more water on his scalp.

"Stop it!" he said. "It's freezing."

"You have a fever. I'm trying to bring it down." Again I doused his head. This time he took his treatment in silence. He looked quite miserable, dripping and shivering like a wet dog, and all trace of amusement drained out of me. Vilmos was sick, and there was nothing I could do for him.

Then I thought of Mathias and felt a sprinkling of hope. Maybe he could do something. But would he be willing?

We made our way slowly to the breakfast lines. Vilmos drank

his coffee gingerly, each swallow painful. He protested when I offered him my bowl.

"Take it," I said. "You need it more than I do."

"I'm fine, I told you."

"Take it, goddammit, or I'll dump it all on the ground."

He saw I was serious. "At least take a few sips," he said.

I did. Then, as he drank, I scoured the milling crowd around me. Where was Mathias?

Vilmos handed me my bowl back. "Thank you, Adam."

"Maybe you should go to the hospital," I said.

He shook his head firmly.

"You're sick. You need to rest."

"I'm not going to that place."

"You could die, Vilmos."

"I could die in the hospital, too. I'd rather take my chances digging trenches."

I didn't argue with him, because he might have been right. In his condition, the hospital was a gamble.

"I'll try to get you into an easier *kommando*," I said, again searching for Mathias in the sea of prisoners around us, "so you won't have to work so hard."

I was about to tell Vilmos that I was going to look for Mathias when we were summoned to the *Appellplatz*. I swore under my breath. Where was he?

We gathered with the other prisoners, and then came a loud bark of a command: "*Achtung!*"

We jumped to attention, as still as pillars. Looking around me, my heart plummeted. For there, at the edge of the *Appellplatz* were four SS doctors in their pressed uniforms and starched collars. With them were a few dozen guards.

We weren't about to form our *kommandos*. At least not yet. First, there was going to be a selection.

Only then did I see Mathias, standing to one side with his arms folded across his chest. He had nothing to worry about. He was not a candidate for death. Beside him stood the *Lagerälteste*, a vicious grin on his face.

"Form rows!" an SS guard ordered. And once we did: "Do not move! Silence!"

The four SS doctors began to amble along the rows of prisoners, as casual as though they were on an afternoon stroll. Here and there, one of them would point at a prisoner, and this unfortunate soul would be pushed at gunpoint by an SS guard off to the side.

Some accepted their fate with quiet dignity. Others broke into sobs and had to be dragged away. And yet others begged and pleaded, claiming a vigor they no longer possessed. Their pleas were ignored. Their death had already been ordained.

My mouth turned as dry as dirt as one of the doctors approached. I chanced a glance at Vilmos. His cheeks were aflame, his forehead was damp, and his breath hissed through his mouth. He stood stooped like an old man.

"Stand straight, Vilmos," I whispered. "Don't give up."

Vilmos didn't reply, nor did he straighten his posture. The doctor was now just ten prisoners away. In one hand he held a pair of gloves, which he was lightly tapping into his other palm. Five prisoners away. Four, three, two, one...

The doctor gazed at me closely. I stared ahead, careful not to look him in the eye. My stomach was flipping itself over. My heart was bouncing around my chest. My knees were quaking. Could he see that? Could he sense that somehow?

He had a pinched mouth and cold, reptilian eyes. A round, shaven face from which wafted the fresh scent of cologne. His nostrils flared as though he savored my stench. I was gripped by the irrational thought that he was feeding on my fear.

In my head I pleaded with a God I was no longer sure I

believed in to spare me, to spare Vilmos, to let us live. I offered no promises in exchange. No oaths of future worship or adherence to religious laws. Just a simple, desperate supplication to postpone our deaths.

The doctor moved on. I had not been selected. But no relief came. There was still Vilmos, and he was sick. If he was sent to the gas chambers, I did not know what I'd do.

The doctor had barely paused before me, but he stopped before Vilmos. Out of the corner of my eye I could see him tilting his head a bit as he examined Vilmos's face.

"Have you got a fever?" the doctor asked. His tone was mild and pleasant. A good doctor's voice. Calming, reassuring, inviting confidence. Camouflaging his true, evil nature. This was how the devil sounded as he tricked you out of your soul.

"No, Herr Doctor," Vilmos replied, and I was astounded at the resonance and clarity of his voice. No hint of a rasp. "I'm just hot. I ran when I heard the gong."

"Where are you from?"

"Hungary, Herr Doctor."

"So you're new here."

"Yes, Herr Doctor."

"And how do you like living here so far?"

"It's a new experience, Herr Doctor."

The doctor's sneer bloomed into a smile. He had thin, haughty lips, as pink as a girl's.

"Which *kommando* do you belong to?" and when Vilmos replied, he said, "Hard work, eh?"

"Yes, Herr Doctor."

"Are you sure you're up to it?"

"Yes, Herr Doctor."

"What was your profession before the war?"

"I was a history professor, Herr Doctor."

"Ah, an educated man. Wouldn't you rather be assigned an office job? Something less taxing, more restful?"

His amiable tone plunged a dagger of fear into my stomach. This was a trap or part of some demented game. For this was a man incapable of true kindness, at least to us. If Vilmos answered in the affirmative, the doctor would view it as an admission of physical weakness.

"I like working with my hands, Herr Doctor," said Vilmos. "And the sun does me good."

"Or maybe you'd rather go to the hospital? You look tired, perhaps even sick."

"I feel quite well, Herr Doctor."

Abruptly, the doctor's voice shed itself of all pretense of concern. Now only icy imperiousness remained. "Lift up your shirt. Higher!"

I barely restrained from wincing. For I knew what the doctor would see: Vilmos's gaunt, pasty torso, the skin so thin the blood vessels showed blue and stringy underneath. You did not need to be a doctor to see that Vilmos was sick and weak, on the brink of collapse. Any second now, the doctor would point a crooked forefinger at Vilmos, and he would be taken away.

For a few agonizing moments, the doctor neither spoke nor moved his predatory eyes from Vilmos. I heard the rhythmic tapping of his leather gloves as they slapped against his palm, like a small, wicked heart beating in anticipation of sin. So unlike my own heart, which was stuttering in my chest.

I imagined each tap of the gloves signifying the turning of a flipped coin as it somersaulted through the air. Heads, you live; tails, you die.

Then it stopped, so abruptly that I almost gasped. Next came the doctor's voice, arrogant and slick. "All right. I wish you a pleasant day of digging. Just be sure to not change your mind and try gaining admittance to the hospital. I'll be watching for you there." Then he moved on down the line, his gloves once more tapping.

I turned my head a fraction so I could better see Vilmos. I watched as his shoulders sagged like a puppet no longer held by its strings. He closed his eyes and let out an almost inaudible exhalation. His hands trembled at his sides.

It was a display of extraordinary determination. Proof of the incredible power of the will to live. A warm wave of emotion and, yes, love engulfed me as I looked at Vilmos, seeing how much of his little strength it had taken to fool this doctor of death. How I wished I could put my arms around Vilmos and lend him some of my energy. But we were not allowed to move from our spots. At that moment, I was willing to postpone my investigation, to give up this day, just to be by Vilmos's side. For I feared that the only way he would be returning to camp this evening would be on the shoulders of other prisoners. Dead.

This was not possible, of course. One could not simply pick a *kommando* to join. And if I dared to ask, the *Lagerälteste* might decide to kill both Vilmos and myself for my insolence.

When the selection was finally over and we could move and talk, Vilmos said, "Thank you, Adam."

"For what?"

"For carrying me around, and for splashing water over me. It helped. I'm sorry I cursed at you."

I laughed. "I'll accept your apology tonight at roll call, you understand? We'll meet right here, okay? Right at this spot."

Vilmos nodded. "I'll be here, don't you worry. You just focus on solving this murder."

But I did worry. Because I knew how sick Vilmos was. I'd seen healthier men drop dead during a day of hard labor.

I grabbed Vilmos by the shoulders and pulled him into a tight embrace. "You be smart today, okay? Save your energy as much as you can."

"I will. I promise. I'll see you this evening."

He gave my shoulders a squeeze and let go. Then he walked away to join his *kommando*. I looked to where Mathias had been standing earlier, but he had gone. Then I turned and gazed at the knot of forlorn men who had been selected to die, trying to remember as many of their faces as I could. My eyes paused on one of them.

The Mumbler.

He hadn't slipped the net this time. From a distance, it didn't seem that he was aware of his impending demise. He was staring off into space, at what I couldn't imagine, and his lips were moving incessantly. A last meal before death.

Why hadn't I asked him his name yesterday? Now it would be lost forever. Another stone added itself to the mountain of guilt in my belly.

I turned away from the Mumbler. He was already dead. But Vilmos was still alive. Maybe in Kanada, I would find the medicine he needed.

And maybe I would learn something that would lead me to Franz's murderer. I hoped so because now I had just two days to catch this killer. Two days before the *Lageralteste* killed me.

22

Before we set out from the men's camp, the *Kapo*, a squat German Jew with a hard-bitten face, had a few words to share with me. "You're new, so you better listen. This *kommando* is one of the best. You're lucky to be part of it. But there are a couple of rules. Follow them and you'll do fine. Don't and you'll pay for it dearly. Understand?"

"Yes," I said.

"Good. First thing, work hard and do as you're told. Second thing, don't steal anything. You get caught stealing and you're out like that"—he snapped his fingers—"no exceptions. Understand?"

"Yes."

"And you'll likely find yourself in the *strafkompagnie*, hauling rocks back and forth from sunrise till sunset. You won't last two weeks. That is, if they don't shoot you on the spot. Understand?"

"Yes." The *strafkompagnie*, the penal work unit, was the hardest and most feared *kommando* in Auschwitz. The prisoners there worked longer hours, got less food, and had shorter breaks than any other *kommando*. It was an instrument of punishment, terror, and murder rather than a real work unit.

The *Kapo* said, "You speak German, which is good. It'll make things easier for you. You wait here a minute." His eyes searched the rest of the men, and he beckoned one of them over. "This man is new. You show him the ropes, all right?"

The man nodded, and after the *Kapo* had moved out of earshot, he gave me his name. "I'm Stefan."

"Adam."

"Don't worry about the *Kapo*. He's not that bad. He just puts on a hard face for newcomers. Mind you, that doesn't mean you can do whatever you want, but he doesn't beat us for no reason and hardly ever shouts as well. No more than he has to in order to look tough for the Germans. How long have you been here?"

"Almost two months."

"I've been here eight. Where've you been working till now?"

"Digging trenches to the east of the camp."

He grimaced. "Hard work, eh?"

"Very."

"Well, working in Kanada is better. And worse."

"Why worse?"

A cloud passed over his face. "You'll see soon enough."

The Kanada section sprawled inside a fenced enclosure west of the men's camp, past the gypsy camp and the hospital. Two of the gas chambers and crematoriums stood a little to its south, two more right by its northern edge.

The closer we got, the thicker the smell of burning flesh became. Above us loomed the smoking chimneys of the four crematoriums. Gazing up their length, I was reminded of Moloch, the Canaanite god described in the Bible, into whose fiery belly children were thrown as sacrifice.

How could a civilization as advanced as Germany have

descended to such barbarism? This was a nation of poets, composers, authors, and architects. A people advanced in practically every field of human endeavor. How had they become such beasts? How could they justify this slaughter?

Stefan told me he'd come to Auschwitz from Czechoslovakia with his mother and brother. "Both dead, I'm sure. Mother was ill and my brother had a club foot. Walked with a cane. Not much use to the Nazis, either of them."

He was twenty-four, unmarried, and had worked in the family's stationery store. "Father was the one who opened the store. He died five years ago. I had plans of expanding the business, but now..."

He was short and had bright brown eyes and a wide mouth over a round chin. Thin, of course, but not as much as me. His complexion was better too. "The best thing about working here is the food," he said. "All the luggage from the trains goes through here. You won't believe what people packed. If only they knew, eh?" He pressed his lips together, his tone turning solemn. "Mother had made us sandwiches for the trip, but we ate them all on the way."

My wife had done the same, I remembered. The food was all gone by the second day on the train. My daughters were weeping with hunger by the time we arrived.

"Generally, the guards have no problem with us eating what we find," Stefan continued, "but it's forbidden to take food back into camp."

"Do they search you?"

"Not every day, but pretty often. And if they catch you with anything, they beat you or worse."

The gate to Kanada stood open, manned by two SS guards with machine guns slung over their shoulders. Another looked down at us from the watchtower just inside the fence. We entered the compound, and one of the guards swung the gate closed. My breath caught in my throat as I got my first glimpse of Kanada.

There were three rows of large warehouses; I counted ten in the first row. Between them, leaning against the exterior walls in piles as high as the roof, was an incredible amount of property. Sacks, bundles, suitcases, boxes, briefcases, handbags, baskets, and what had to be tens of thousands of clothing items and shoes of varied styles and sizes. All flung together into messy mountains of loot.

"There's not enough room in the warehouses," Stefan said, following my gaze. "Not since the Hungarians started coming."

What I'd seen on the platform yesterday was but a fraction of what was mounded all around me. There had been the spoils of a single train. Here was the plunder of an entire people.

Moving among the warehouses were dozens of women prisoners, some hauling various items of property, others sifting through the mountains of belongings. Each was wearing a headscarf in one of a number of colors. White, red, black.

"Why the different colors?" I asked Stefan.

"They work in groups. Each group has a different headscarf."

We came to a stop before the first warehouse, where the *Kapo* gave us our orders. Stefan and I and a few others were directed to unload a truck packed to the brim with luggage. Probably the same luggage I had loaded onto this truck yesterday.

There were suitcases with names and places painted on them in white block letters. I recognized some of the towns. All in Hungary. Were there any Jews still left in the country I had once viewed as my homeland?

"Come with me," Stefan said, and I followed him up into the bed of the truck. Finding a precarious purchase on the unstable pile of luggage, we began lowering items to other prisoners, who added them to one of the ever-growing heaps leaning against the warehouses.

Stefan had been right. This was easier work than digging trenches. But I still built up a sweat. Partly it was the heat, and partly the fact that the air was so thick with smoke that it was difficult to draw in a proper breath.

Other than that, I was feeling better. The rash on my side still prickled, and my throat was parched, but the pain in my foot had lessened considerably now that my skin was no longer rubbing against the rough interior of my clogs.

The new pair was wider and much longer than I would have liked, but I'd managed to remedy this imperfection by wrapping my feet in rags and stuffing a rolled-up cloth into the tip of the clogs. After weeks of being tightly squeezed on each step, my feet were slowly growing accustomed to their new-found freedom.

As we worked, I saw German guards patrolling among the prisoners, their eyes shifting side to side. Keeping watch. Making sure the Third Reich was not deprived of the spoils of its conquests.

We finished with one truck and moved to another, where the process repeated itself. The *Kapo* came over to inspect our work. Stefan had been right about him, too. He did not beat anyone, nor raise his voice unnecessarily, and if you needed to relieve yourself, he let you, as long as you made it quick. A couple of times, when no guards were around, he even offered a word of encouragement or appreciation. I'd known there were decent *Kapos*, but I'd never worked under one. It made the job easier.

Midmorning, while working on our fourth truck, I heard an unmistakable, terrible sound: a train whistle, shrill and close. For a few seconds, work ceased, and all eyes turned in the direction of the train platform, where soon a new batch of victims would emerge.

"All right, everybody," the *Kapo* said. "Get back to work. Focus on your tasks." His tone did not match his words, though; it was soft and subdued.

We did as we were told. But while earlier there had been idle chatter among Stefan and me and the other prisoners with whom we worked, now there was a grim quiet, each man deep in thought and memories.

Soon, the faint breeze carried over to us the barking of dogs and the tumult of weary passengers disembarking into hell. The same sounds I'd heard yesterday when I'd been working on the platform. The same sounds that had surrounded me when my family and I had arrived in Auschwitz. Confusion, fear, the anguish of separation. Wails, cries, shouts. It took a while for things to settle. For the new victims to be cowed into order.

"Goddamn the Germans," Stefan hissed under his breath. "May they all burn in hell."

Over on the train platform, the first selection was taking place. I could not see it, of course, but I could picture it. Rage and despair swirled and sizzled in my stomach like a lightning storm. My teeth were clenched so tight my jaw ached. Closing my hand around the handle of a suitcase, I imagined it was the butt of a pistol, and that the muzzle was pointed at a Nazi officer who was cowering at my feet. Never in my life had I felt such a desire to spill blood.

"Hey, you sleeping?" came a voice, yanking me back to reality. "Come on, hand it over." It was one of the other prisoners, hands outstretched to receive the suitcase I was holding. I passed it to him and resumed working.

We worked until noon, and then got our soup. It was thicker than my usual fare. And hotter.

"The cooks take care of us, and we take care of them," explained Stefan, which I took to mean that food from the luggage of the dead was being smuggled to the cooks. I thought of Vilmos and wondered how he was doing. What sort of soup was he eating? Or was he already dead? I felt guilty knowing that if he still lived, his meal was poorer than mine.

"You said you could get food from the luggage," I said to Stefan. "What sort of food?"

"Anything and everything," he said, chewing on a potato. "Bread, jam, cans of all sorts, tins of fish in oil, fruit. Chocolate, too. Wine and liquor. But we can't drink those. The Germans take them. Or the functionaries."

I recalled my shock at seeing the food in the *Lagerälteste's* room, the wine bottle on his table. This was where it all came from.

"Doesn't it feel strange, eating the food of the dead?" I asked.

"It's no longer any use to them, is it?" Stefan said, an edge of irritation underlying his voice. Then he took a deep breath and sighed, rubbing his mouth. "At first, I swore I would eat nothing I found, but very soon I was so hungry I couldn't resist. I felt terribly guilty about it for a while. Still do, kind of, but not as much as before. I figure it's better for me to eat it than for it to go to waste or for some guard to enjoy it. That it's what the dead would prefer."

The way he said it, I wasn't sure his conscience was entirely satisfied with this reasoning, though I could find no fault in it.

"What about other things?" I asked.

"You name it. Clothes, of course, and also photographs, documents, perfume, books, diaries, hairpins, hand mirrors, pens, toys. And religious items like yarmulkes and phylacteries. Once I even found a rolled-up Torah all by itself in a suitcase. Most of this is useless to us, of course. Then there's money and jewelry, all of which the Germans take special precautions with. You get caught trying to steal jewelry and you're dead."

"What about medicine?"

"If you're talking about headache powders and the like, then, yeah, you can occasionally find those. If you mean real medicine, that's very hard to get."

"But not impossible."

"No, I suppose not." Stefan looked around to see no one was eavesdropping on our conversation and lowered his voice. "There are people here who know how to organize, how to get stuff. The good stuff."

"Who?"

"A guy named Ludwig is one of the best. He knows how to get stuff into the camp."

There was that name again. Ludwig. Franz's buddy.

"How does he do it?" I asked.

"No idea. I haven't dared to try to smuggle anything in myself."

I was about to ask more about Ludwig when sounds of agitation drifted over from the north—a commotion dotted with barked orders and commands. I rose to my feet, hesitated, and then started walking in that direction, drawn by the noise.

"Adam, don't," Stefan said.

I paid him no heed. Just kept on walking.

He grabbed my arm. "Don't go there, Adam. You don't want to see that."

I gave him a hard glare and yanked my arm free. I hastened my steps, pushed onward by some force I didn't comprehend. With each step, my heartbeat quickened and anxiety constricted my throat further, so that when I got near the fence, my heart was galloping and I was gasping for breath.

A short distance beyond the fence, in a sparse grove of birch trees, were hundreds of Jews. The men were mostly older, but the women were of all ages. All of them were now being herded toward a squat building with two ugly chimneys jutting from its roof. A crematorium. Inside was a gas chamber. And ovens that burned bodies to ashes.

There were a few minor protests, but no real resistance. The people were either unaware of their fate or resigned to it. I saw an elegant elderly couple walk, arms linked, toward their death with an incongruous air of respectability. I saw a blonde toddler sucking on her thumb, her other hand encased in her mother's. I saw a young woman breastfeeding her baby even as she carried him toward the crematorium.

All of a sudden, the docile procedure was disrupted by a dark-haired woman who spun on her heel and slapped a guard across the face. The guard retaliated by smacking the barrel of his rifle into the woman's head, then proceeded to kick her when she dropped to the ground. Finally, he swung his rifle downward and pulled the trigger. The crack of the shot made me jump. Those few Jews who had still not entered the building stopped in their tracks. The baby started bawling. The toddler screamed. A man shouted imprecations at the guards, while another started toward the shot woman, intending to help her.

The guards reacted wildly, beating the startled Jews toward the building with frenzied ferocity, using their boots, their fists, the butts of their weapons.

I stood paralyzed by the fence, watching with unblinking eyes, feeling as small and powerless as an insect. After all the Jews were inside, a few long minutes passed with no activity that I could see. Then two guards approached the side of the building, each carrying a canister. These they upended into two small windows, which they then sealed.

There was a stretch of deathly silence; then the screams began. Muffled by the thick walls of the gas chamber, but still piercing. A tidal wave of death cries.

Upon hearing them, something inside me splintered, then broke, then shattered. As though a small bomb had detonated inside me, leaving a burning wreckage in the middle of my chest.

This was how my wife and daughters had sounded in their death throes. These were the cries I would never forget, never be free of.

I stood bent over, heaving, unable to move. My eyes roved about before latching onto the small body of the courageous woman who had slapped the SS guard. I swore to her that if I lived, I would take vengeance. I would make them pay with their lives.

The screams didn't last very long. An unnatural stillness descended. But it was swiftly ended by the chatter of the guards, their coarse laughter.

How I hated them. How I longed to jump over the fence and rip them to pieces.

A hand on my shoulder made me whirl, fist raised.

It was Stefan, his face pale and his eyes moist. Only then did I register the wet trails down my cheeks, the salty taste in my mouth.

"Now you know why Kanada is one of the worst *kommandos* to be in," he said in a choked voice. "Now you know."

23

"Is this how it is every day?" I asked Stefan, as we walked together back toward the first row of warehouses.

He nodded gravely. "More and more trains keep arriving from Hungary. I can't say how many people"—his voice faltered, and he cleared his throat—"but it has to be hundreds of thousands. Just in the past two months."

It was strange how I could be both unsurprised and shocked by that number.

"How can you stand it?" I asked.

"Sometimes I feel that I can't. That I'll go crazy. But what is there to do? I want to survive, Adam, and it's much easier to do so in the Kanada Kommando than anywhere else in this camp."

Neither of us spoke for about twelve more paces.

"It gets easier," Stefan said, and when I looked sharply at him, he added quickly. "It sounds terrible, I know, but it does. I didn't believe it either when a longtime prisoner told me that, but he was right. You learn to close yourself off to the sounds, the knowledge of what is happening. It helps if you don't watch. Which is why I tried to stop you."

"I'm glad I saw it," I told him, and wasn't sure I was being entirely honest, because I knew that those images and those screams would forever haunt me. "I needed to see it just once. To bear witness."

"Why? You think those bastards will ever face justice? Stand trial for their crimes?"

If I lived, they would. I would be prosecutor, judge, and executioner.

"I don't know about that," I said. "I was talking about the victims. I want to remember them."

Stefan rubbed his forehead. "Maybe it would be better to forget."

We were back near the trucks by now. The *Kapo* took one look at my face, and I could tell that he knew where I'd been and what I'd seen. He gave me a heavy nod, like a taciturn father would give a son who had endured a grueling rite of passage and was now considered mature.

"Head on over to the latrine if you need to," the *Kapo* said. "We start again in a few minutes."

On the train platform, another cargo of Jews was being processed. More cries and yells. More victims. How many Jews had already died here? How many would die?

Stefan and I were pointed toward a huge pile of belongings. Another prisoner gave us directions: suitcases to that warehouse, clothes to another. Stefan and I each grabbed a pair of suitcases and hurried to deliver them.

"Where can I find this Ludwig?" I asked him.

Stefan was sweating profusely, straining with the weight of the suitcases. "This one feels like it's filled with bricks," he said, but he didn't dare set it down to catch his breath, because an SS guard was standing in the doorway of the warehouse, eying us.

Inside was a hive of activity. Wooden worktables were scattered about the large interior. Standing at each of them was a woman prisoner, sifting through an open suitcase and sorting its contents. More women sat on the floor, doing the same. There were not enough tables for all the loot. The air smelled of leather, unwashed fabric, and sweat.

"Take them there," an older woman prisoner told us, pointing toward a nearby wall, where suitcases were stacked four rows deep. "And don't just toss them. Put them up tidily."

As we walked through the warehouse, I was struck by the immense range of belongings being sorted. I saw cigarette cases, shaving kits, fur hats, handkerchiefs, candles, plates, bowls, utensils of every kind, wristwatches, and a remarkable number of books. Over by the door, there was a barrel filled with them, like an overflowing garbage can. They would probably be burned later. The Nazis had a fondness for burning books.

"Where can I find Ludwig, Stefan?" I asked again, once we'd set the suitcases in their place.

Stefan wiped his brow with his sleeve. "He's around here somewhere. If I see him, I'll tell you. If not, we'll go look for him when we get a break, okay?" He glanced around. "Now stand over here, will you? Shield me from view."

He undid the clasps on one large suitcase and flung it open. Inside were clothes, folded neatly, and a small round tin. Stefan ran his hand among the clothes, finding nothing, then unscrewed the lid of the tin and peered inside. He flashed me a toothy grin over his shoulder. "Could be you bring me luck, Adam." He closed the tin and hid it in his sleeve, then shut the suitcase. "Let's go," he said.

Outside, he pulled me between two warehouses and showed

me his find. Inside the tin was a batch of cookies—oatmeal dotted with puffy raisins. Instantly my mouth watered.

"Four for you and four for me," Stefan said, handing me my share. He jammed a cookie in his mouth, chewing rapidly. I stared at my prize as a treasure hunter might stare upon a chest full of gemstones. Four cookies. An unbelievable sight.

"Hurry up," Stefan said, stuffing his mouth with another cookie. "We gotta get back to work before the *Kapo* notices."

I needed no further prompting. I tore off half of one cookie with my teeth and gobbled it, barely chewing before swallowing. The other half I ate more sensibly but still very quickly, the taste flooding me with a pleasure so intense that I felt woozy. A second cookie swiftly followed the first. The third was already between my lips when I stopped with a pang of guilt.

Vilmos. I'd almost forgotten Vilmos.

"What are you waiting for?" Stefan said. He had finished all of his cookies and was rubbing his mouth clean.

"I'll keep these," I said. "For a friend of mine."

"They might search you. They often search the new guys."

I might have asked Stefan to smuggle these cookies for me, but I didn't want to put him in that position. Vilmos was my friend. If anyone was to risk his life to bring him this food, it should be me.

"How thoroughly do they search you?" I asked.

"Pretty thoroughly," Stefan said. "It can get demeaning."

I had until the end of the workday to figure out a solution. In the meantime, I rolled the cuffs of my trousers, stashing the cookies among the folds.

Stefan said, "That must be some friend."

"The best a man could wish for," I said.

We hauled suitcases for a while, then switched to clothes. These we rolled into irregular bundles and took to a second warehouse, where more women prisoners were working. Some were tying strings around batches of trousers or shirts or dresses, while others were examining items for tears. And yet others were removing yellow stars from jackets, erasing their Jewish provenance before shipment to Germany.

"What is she doing?" I asked Stefan, gesturing toward a woman who was running her hand along the seams of a woman's coat.

"Looking for hidden treasure," he said. "You wouldn't believe where people hid money or jewels before boarding those trains. They knew the Germans would take anything that wasn't concealed, and they hoped they'd be able to secure better conditions for their families wherever the Germans ended up resettling them. That's what we all believed, right? That we were being resettled. We thought it was the same centuries-old story of Jews being driven out of one place and into another. Anyway, people sewed rings and pearls and rolls of currency into their clothes, their luggage. She"—he indicated the woman—"needs to make sure there's nothing hidden in that coat. And he"—he gave an almost imperceptible nod toward an SS guard who was eying the woman—"is making sure she does her job and doesn't steal anything."

We stepped out of the warehouse and into the sunlight. The day was another scorcher. Again I thought of Vilmos. How was he handling this heat? Was he still alive?

"What are you looking to buy from Ludwig, Adam?" Stefan asked. "Medicine? You got a sick relative or something?"

"A friend," I said. "The same one I'm keeping the cookies for. I also want to talk to Ludwig about a boy named Franz, who used to work here. You know who I'm talking about?"

"A Dutch boy? Ludwig's friend?"

"That's the one."

"I heard he was working for the *Lagerälteste*."

"He used to. He's dead."

"Really? How? I don't imagine he was working too hard, and he must have been eating properly."

"Someone killed him. Stabbed him in the throat."

Stefan stopped walking. "What do you mean, someone? Not a guard?"

"Have you ever seen a guard stab a prisoner?"

"No," Stefan said slowly. "So a prisoner killed him. Is that what you think?"

"That's right. Someone who had it in for him. Can you think of anyone like that?"

Stefan gave me a look. "Why are you asking this?"

"Because he was a boy, just fifteen, and someone butchered him. I want to know who did it and why."

"What are you, a policeman?"

"No. I used to be a lawyer. A criminal lawyer. But I don't like murderers. Especially murderers of children."

Stefan resumed walking. He didn't speak again until we had both loaded ourselves with more clothes and were on our way back to the warehouse.

"There was someone," he said at length, "but not in Kanada."

I stared at him. His expression was troubled. "Where, then?"

"Back in camp. Two weeks ago, I think. In the evening. I saw Franz and another prisoner talking by one of the blocks. Or maybe it would be more accurate to say the other prisoner was doing all the talking. Franz had his back pressed to the wall and the other prisoner was standing very close to him, their noses almost touching."

"What were they talking about?"

"I couldn't hear. Didn't try to. But Franz looked distraught, and the other prisoner had a finger pointed at his face."

"He was threatening Franz?"

"Could have been. I don't know."

"That's all it was? Talk? No fighting?"

"None that I saw. I didn't stick around for long."

"You didn't think to intervene?"

"Why should I? Franz and I weren't friends. It was none of my business. You're new here, so let me give you some advice: You try to break up fights in this place and you're liable to get hurt."

I thought of Gyuri and Hendrik, and how it was only a matter of time before I would have to deal once more with the latter.

"What did this other prisoner look like?" I asked.

"I only caught a fleeting glimpse of his face. I remember he had reddish stubble, and... something about his nose. Yeah, it was very big. Very thick at the base." He looked at me. "What is it?"

"Nothing," I said. But it wasn't nothing. Because I had seen such a prisoner recently. I was sure of it. I just didn't remember where or when.

24

"There he is," Stefan said at some point in early afternoon. "That's Ludwig."

I turned and saw a man enter one of the warehouses. Tall, young, with black stubble on his face. I continued unloading the truck, keeping an eye on the warehouse's door, and when Ludwig emerged some minutes later, I asked the *Kapo* for a latrine break.

"Make it quick," he said.

I hurried after Ludwig and saw him slip between two warehouses. I glanced behind me to make sure the *Kapo* wasn't watching and followed.

Here was a long passage bordered on both sides by warehouses and more tall piles of loot. There were no prisoners about, though. I didn't see Ludwig either.

Just then, my ears picked up a pair of faint voices from up ahead. A dozen more steps and I could tell one voice was male, the other female. They were speaking German; he with an Austrian accent, she with a Hungarian one.

"Not now," came the female voice. "I have to go."

"Just a little, my love. I can't wait till later."

I removed my clogs and padded forward on bare feet. The voices were very close now, off to the left, their owners hidden from view behind a mountain range of clothes.

I crossed to the other side of the passage and crept closer. Ducking behind a small stack of suitcases, I peeked at the couple whose voices I'd heard.

The man was Ludwig. The woman—no, girl was the better word, because she could not have been older than sixteen—was pressed against the side of a warehouse. Ludwig was standing very close to her, their bodies almost touching. One of his hands was on her waist, the other was cupping her cheek. She had one hand on his arm. Her other arm hung by her side.

"I have to go back, Ludwig," she said.

"Just a minute, Aliz," he said. "Don't I take good care of you?" And before she could answer, he edged even closer and kissed her long and hard on the lips. She didn't resist, didn't push him away, but neither did she appear to reciprocate his passion.

When he finally broke off the kiss, Ludwig said, "I love you, Aliz. Do you love me back?"

"Yes," Aliz said, but her eyes were lowered, her voice tremulous.

"Tell it to me again. And look at me this time."

Aliz raised her eyes, and I saw they were a vibrant green. I also saw that she was very pretty, with a heart-shaped face and small features, and skin that was somehow still rosy despite her living here in Auschwitz.

"I love you, Ludwig," she said, but she didn't smile one bit.

It appeared that Ludwig hadn't noticed the discrepancy. He kissed her again, even harder this time, mashing his lips on hers. One of his hands found her breast, and I thought I heard a tiny gasp emerge from her throat.

"I'll see you later, my love," Ludwig said, caressing her cheek. "I'll bring you something good to eat, okay? Some chocolate, maybe. You'd like that, wouldn't you?"

"Yes," Aliz said, her lips reddened by the kiss. "I would like that very much, Ludwig."

"Go on now," he said, kissing her hand. "And think of me until we're alone together again."

"I will. Goodbye, Ludwig."

Then Aliz was walking away, back in the direction from which Ludwig and I had come. I crouched behind the stack of suitcases, hoping she wouldn't look back at her paramour. She didn't. Not even once.

Ludwig watched her go, love glowing on his face like a street lamp. Then he turned and headed in the opposite direction toward the third row of warehouses. I considered following, but I'd already been away for a few minutes. I needed to get back, or the *Kapo* would get upset.

It was two hours later, more or less, when I saw Ludwig again.

He came over and asked our *Kapo* if he could spare a man for a few minutes. Our *Kapo* agreed so readily that I thought he had likely been on the receiving end of some of Ludwig's smuggling.

"I'll do it," I said, already stepping toward Ludwig.

The *Kapo* frowned in irritation. "Next time, wait until I pick you, understand? Now go, and come right back here when you're done."

I hurried after Ludwig. He had widely spaced brown eyes set in a narrow face composed of sharp features. His cheeks were fuller than most prisoners', his shoulders wider. His uniform was free of tears and major stains and was obviously newer than mine. He was also one of the lucky ones whose shirt resembled a jacket, equipped with two pockets at the waist and another over the left breast. Mine was devoid of pockets entirely.

Clearly, Ludwig's reputation was justified. He knew how to organize stuff. Both clothes and food, judging by his attire and the promise of chocolate he'd made to Aliz.

"I don't think I've seen you before. You're new?" he said.

"Yes."

"What's your name? Where you're from?"

I told him. He gave me his name and said the job he had for me wouldn't take long. "Just a few suitcases, no more than twenty-five in total."

The suitcases in question were heaped near the westernmost warehouse in the middle row. Beyond the nearby fence was the central sauna, the large shower facility I'd gone through on the first day in Auschwitz-Birkenau as part of the induction process. There, I and a multitude of other prisoners had showered together after being stripped of our old clothes and much of our dignity. A little to the west, black tongues of smoke licked the sky, towering from the fire pits.

"We need to take all these into the second warehouse," Ludwig said. "All the way to the rear. Grab two and follow me. We need to be quick."

The suitcases in question were all of the expensive variety, made of fine leather with large buckles, the stolen property of former affluent Jews. Someone had taken the trouble to set these pieces of luggage aside and had them brought here.

I remembered the story Jakob had told me. How Franz had separated the expensive suitcases from the rest of the luggage and had taken them to a specific truck. Now I understood the reason he'd done so. It made it easier to check these suitcases—where one might expect to find worthwhile items—back in the warehouses.

I grabbed two suitcases and followed Ludwig. He hadn't taken a single one. We entered the second warehouse, this one far less busy than the rest, and went all the way to the rear. There, a few tables had been set up in a corner, away from prying eyes.

"Put them down here and go fetch the others," Ludwig told me, before hoisting one of the suitcases onto a table.

When I returned, he was pawing through the second suitcase. Off to the side were a bottle of brandy, a pair of gleaming leather gloves, a few packs of cigarettes, and a small silver goblet, the sort used for *Kiddush* on the eve of the Sabbath and Jewish holidays.

Ludwig saw me eying the items and offered a tight-lipped smile. "If you work quickly, and we're lucky, you'll get something good to eat for your trouble, okay? So get cracking."

I didn't move. "I see that what I was told about you is true—that you're a guy who can get stuff."

A crafty gleam entered his eyes. "Yeah, that's right. You need something in particular?"

"Medicine."

"What sort of medicine?"

"The sort that cures fever and coughing."

"That's very hard to get. But maybe there's some in the hospital."

"My friend can't go to the hospital," I said, remembering what the SS doctor had told Vilmos.

"That's too bad. But that sort of medicine would be very expensive to buy, if you could get it at all."

"Please," I said. "My friend is very sick. He may die."

Ludwig had opened another suitcase and was looking through it. "Sorry, but there's nothing I can do. Even if one of my contacts had such medicine to sell, you don't look like you have anything to trade for it."

He didn't sound sorry, he sounded uncaring. It made me angry, even though I knew that none of us was as empathetic as we'd been before we got here. You couldn't care about everyone. If you did, you'd come apart from the inside out.

"Couldn't you trade these items for medicine?" I said in frustration, gesturing at the table.

His face hardened. "It seems that I should have picked another man to help me. Just so we're clear: This is mine, as are those other suitcases outside. Go back to your regular work unit. I don't want your help anymore."

Again, I didn't move.

"Are you deaf or stupid? Do as I say. Get out of here."

"There's another thing I wanted to talk to you about."

"What?"

"Franz," I said.

Ludwig froze for a second. Then he lowered his eyes to the open suitcase before him. "Franz is dead."

"So you know."

"Yes."

"How? Who told you?"

"Someone I know. What do you care?"

"Do you know how he died?"

"No."

"He was murdered. Someone stabbed him and left him to die in that ditch behind the latrines."

Ludwig's throat moved as he swallowed. "I didn't know that."

I wasn't sure I believed him. His expression seemed too controlled, as did the tone of his voice, as though he were making a conscious effort to hide his thoughts.

"You don't seem stunned by the news," I said.

"Why should I be? I heard Franz was dead two days ago."

"I'm talking about the fact that he was murdered."

"Most people who die here are murdered. You could say all of them are."

"Most aren't killed by another prisoner for personal reasons."

Ludwig shifted his mouth. "What do you mean, personal reasons?"

"I'm saying that Franz was killed by someone who knew him. Someone who targeted him specifically."

Ludwig was frowning at me now, his eyes seemingly darker. "Who are you? Why are you asking me about Franz?"

"I'm the man who's going to find out who murdered him. I understand you and he were partners."

"Where did you hear that?"

"It's not a secret. A lot of prisoners here know about the two of you. You organized things together, didn't you?"

"That's right. He and I got plenty of items into camp, into the hands of prisoners who needed them."

"For a price," I said. "Don't make it sound like a charity."

"All right, I won't. We didn't give things away. We sold them. And why shouldn't we? We were taking a risk every time we smuggled something into camp. I don't know of a single organizer who does it for free." He glowered at me. "I don't know what you're playing at, but I'm done talking to you. Now get out of here, or I'll have a talk with your *Kapo* later and make sure you get punished for not bringing in the luggage like you were supposed to."

I clenched my teeth in fury. There was just one way to get Ludwig to cooperate with me. I had to make him scared. "You asked me before why I was asking questions about Franz. The answer is that I was instructed to do so. Want to know by whom?"

"You're very stupid, aren't you?" he said. "I told you to leave and you're still here. You're going to regret—"

"It was the *Lagerälteste*," I said, and nearly smiled at seeing Ludwig pause in mid-sentence with his mouth hanging open. "That's right. I'm asking these questions because the *Lagerälteste* is pretty upset that someone murdered Franz. He wants to know who did it. And I'm thinking you had a lot to gain from Franz's death."

"Me?" Ludwig said. Gone was the self-assured demeanor and arrogant tone. Now he both looked and sounded horrified. "Why would I want to kill Franz?"

"The oldest, most common motive: greed. You and he were partners. Now that he's dead, the organizing operation you and he ran is solely yours."

Ludwig stared at me for a second, then let out a short laugh. "And what? Do you think I'm taking Franz's share and putting it in the bank? Or maybe I plan to buy some fancy clothes and a new car? Have you forgotten where we are? There's only so much you can use in this place, and, believe me, I manage to get enough of it."

It was true. He did not look like he lacked for anything, or at least, none of the narrow range of things prisoners could use.

"Besides," he said, his confidence firmly back in place, "Franz had been out of it since he started working for the *Lagerälteste*. I wouldn't have needed to kill him. And I didn't. I never would have, I swear. Not for anything."

"You don't seem upset by his death," I said, struggling to ignore the fact that my hypothesis had crumbled. Because what Ludwig said was true. When he died, Franz was no longer in the organizing business. He'd said as much to Zoltan on their last meeting when the latter had attempted to buy medicine for Vilmos.

"Like I said, I heard about it two days ago," Ludwig said. "I did my mourning then."

"And you're over it now, is that it?"

"Of course not. Just like I'm not over my brothers and parents who went up the chimney. But it wouldn't do me any good to fall apart in tears, now, would it?"

No, it wouldn't. In Auschwitz, one did not have the luxury of grieving properly. There was no funeral, no *shiva*, no grave to lay flowers on. Those who wallowed in bereavement could not focus on survival; they shattered into a million tiny pieces shaped like broken hearts. They lost the will to live and died very quickly. I thought of Gyuri and felt a sting of loss and guilt.

I said, "Where were you during the afternoon and evening four days ago?"

"The same as every day. Here until the end of the workday. Then back in camp."

"Was someone with you at camp all during that evening?"

"Every minute of it? No. But that doesn't mean I killed Franz. I assure you I didn't."

He sounded sincere, and his eyes were steady, but down on the table, his hands were fidgeting. It could have been innocent nervousness or a sign of deceit. I was quiet for a moment, hoping he'd feel compelled to fill the silence, but he didn't.

"Can you think of anyone else who had reason to murder Franz?" I said at length.

Ludwig shook his head.

"Maybe someone who wanted to buy something from him and was turned away?"

"He didn't tell me about anyone like that. And our prices are fair. You may not believe it, after what I said about the medicine, but it's true. Medicine is very expensive and hard to come by. If you can get it at all, it takes time—unless you're very lucky."

"Lucky how?" I asked, a pang of worry for Vilmos biting me on the inside.

"Like finding a fully stocked doctor's bag before anyone else gets the chance to poke through it. Something that's never happened to me, I can tell you that." He paused and added, "I'm sorry about your sick friend."

Again, I didn't believe him, though unlike the first time he'd said he was sorry, this time he'd made an effort to sound sincere. Back then, he hadn't cared what I thought of him. Now that he knew I was working for the *Lagerälteste*, he cared quite a bit.

"What was Franz like?" I asked.

"What was he like?" Ludwig seemed bewildered by the question.

"Yeah. You were his friend. Tell me about him."

Ludwig took a second before answering. "He was hardworking. Very smart. Far beyond his years. And very creative at finding ways to fool the guards when he smuggled things into camp. He was also brave. And there was something free about him, even here." He ran a hand over his face, and when he spoke next, he sounded grief-stricken for the first time. "It's terrible that he's dead."

"Was there anyone else he was friends with?"

"He got along with pretty much everyone. But friends? I think I was the only one."

"What about the female prisoners? Did he have a sweetheart?"

Ludwig shook his head. "No one."

Which left me with very little to go on. And time kept slipping by, taking my life with it.

"Maybe Franz was robbed?" Ludwig suggested, and I might have been wrong, but he sounded almost hopeful. "That could have been it, couldn't it?"

No, it couldn't. Because in that case, there wouldn't have been any bread for Vilmos to find.

Then I remembered what Stefan had told me earlier.

"The man who accosted Franz in the camp about two weeks ago, do you know who he is?"

Ludwig's forehead creased. "What man?"

"Franz didn't tell you?"

"No."

"How can that be? I thought you were his only true friend."

"Last time I spoke with Franz was two and a half weeks ago, a few days after he started working for the *Lagerälteste*."

"How come?"

"He said I should stay away from his block, to not come near him."

"What reason did he give?"

"None. He just told me to steer clear of him. To forget about him."

I gave him a look of incredulity, and he responded with a small shrug. "I know it's odd, but that's how it was. He was adamant. Made me swear on it."

"Was he angry with you?"

"No. Not at all."

"How did he seem, then?"

"Scared," Ludwig said. "Very, very scared."

25

Shortly before the end of the workday, our *Kapo* gave us a few minutes to use the latrine.

"I told you he was a good fellow," Stefan said. "He does this every day so we don't have to squabble with the rest of the prisoners back at camp."

I relieved myself quickly, then ducked behind a corner and hid the two cookies I'd kept for Vilmos. Then I joined the rest of the men in our group and started back for camp.

Ahead of us, other prisoners, men and women, were plodding toward the Kanada gate or passing through it. About fifteen SS guards were standing at the gate, and every few seconds, one of them would motion at a prisoner to step aside. Then that prisoner would undergo a search.

Fear wrapped its cold, slimy fingers around my neck and squeezed. I prayed that I would be allowed through without being searched. A shrill, panicked voice in my head shrieked that I had been a fool to keep the cookies, to take such a risk. *Get rid of them,* the voice urged me, *before it's too late.*

Clenching my jaw, I squashed the fearful voice, tamping it down until it was but a bothersome murmur at the back of my mind. Vilmos was my friend, and he needed whatever extra nourishment he could get. I was going to give these cookies to him.

As long as he was not dead already.

There were about fifty prisoners between me and the gate now. Another two prisoners were pulled off the path to be searched. I struggled to compose my features into what I hoped was a blank, innocent cast, when I heard a cry from my left.

A male prisoner was cowering before an SS guard, who was whipping him with a riding crop. At the guard's feet was evidence of the prisoner's crime: a can of food—I could not make out of what—the size of a man's fist and lying on its side. For this tiny measure of food, the hapless prisoner's raised arms were now being ripped to shreds. For this, he would be removed from the Kanada Kommando and assigned to one in which the life expectancy could be measured in weeks if not days.

Fear tightened its grip further, compressing my Adam's apple. My stomach contracted, and my hands turned clammy with icy sweat.

Keep calm, I told myself, don't let them see you're scared.

Only ten meters separated me from the gate. Just a few more steps and I would be in the clear. I swallowed hard and strove to keep my breathing even. Head up, eyes straight ahead, mustn't look shifty or like I had something to hide.

Seven meters to go now. Six, five, four, three...

I saw it in my peripheral vision. A rigid finger pointed my way, accompanied by a sharp command to step aside. I stifled the urge to run. There was no place to run to. With my heart lodged firmly in my throat, I obeyed.

The guard was a mean-faced man of about thirty-five, with a spray of small pimples marring his cheeks and dull brown eyes behind round spectacles. He had cut himself shaving that morning, I saw. Tiny blood clots on his neck.

He had a small mouth and a long nose that wrinkled in disgust at the sight of me.

"Are you carrying something that isn't yours, Jew? Something you stole? Reich property?"

I said that I'd stolen nothing.

"If you hand it over now, things will go easier for you than if I have to find it myself."

"I've taken nothing, sir," I said, my tone respectful and obsequious. To my cop ears, I sounded like a horrible liar, but perhaps that was merely due to the terror roiling inside me. *He's going to find the cookies*, that voice in my head said. Speaking softly now, with a satisfied, I-told-you-so edge. *You're a dead man.*

I had removed my cap and was standing at attention with it clutched in my right hand. How I longed to be able to squeeze and twist it in both hands, to relieve some of the tension. But instead, I didn't move, staring straight ahead, while the guard moved in so close I could smell sausage and onions on his breath.

"I think you're lying, Jew. I can see it on your face." He tapped his temple with two fingers. "You think you can trick me, but you're wrong. Last chance or I won't be merciful."

I repeated my claim that I'd stolen nothing. The guard nodded as though he'd expected no better from me.

"Drop your cap to the ground," he said, and when I did, he prodded it with his boot. There was nothing there.

"Take off your uniform," he said.

I hesitated. I had long since abandoned all vestiges of modesty at being naked around other men, but on the path just two meters from where I stood, scores of women were trudging by as well.

The guard backhanded me across the face. My head spun with the force of the blow. Needles of pain stung my cheek and mouth.

"Do as I say, Jew!" the guard snarled.

Tasting blood, I undid the buttons of my shirt, pulled it off, and let it fall to the dirt. Then I stepped out of my clogs, pushed down my trousers, and kicked them off. I made sure to not look at the prisoners who could now view my nakedness. Shame spread its warm, uncomfortable glow over my face.

The guard proceeded to step on my uniform, rubbing the soles of his boots back and forth as though cleaning them of mud.

There was nothing in my clothes.

I hoped that would be the end of it. But the guard was not done with me yet. His eyes roved slowly up and down my body. His lips curled in disdain, though everything he saw—the filth, the bruises, the bones jutting under the skin—was his and his comrades' doing. But he did not see it that way. He was not seeing a man at all, but a creature of a lesser order. That's how he had been taught to view a Jew: as a dangerous vermin that polluted the Aryan blood and corrupted the society in which it lived. A vermin that needed to be exterminated.

"Raise your hands. Spread your fingers."

I did. My hands were empty.

"Turn around," he said.

I obeyed, my fear sharpening now that I couldn't see him.

"Bend down and spread your buttocks."

For a second I wasn't sure I'd heard him correctly, so shocking was the command. Then came the harsh blow to my back as a reminder that nothing in Auschwitz was shocking or beyond the pale. Because everything was.

Shutting my eyes tight, I did as commanded. The moment, the most vulnerable and humiliating moment I'd ever known, seemed to stretch forever, crushing and suffocating my spirit bit by bit.

Finally, came the guard's voice again.

"Turn around."

I did, my face scorched with embarrassment. The guard's face was a mask of revulsion and bewilderment. He eyed me suspiciously. He had found nothing, but some wicked instinct was telling him that he had simply not looked hard enough.

Then his eyes alighted on my clogs, and his forehead smoothed. He picked up first one clog and then the other and gave each of them a good, hard shake. Two thin strips of filthy rag floated out. These I'd used to cushion the sides of my feet, including where my wound was. Neither would be wanted by the officials in Berlin.

The guard ran a finger under his nose, over a toothbrush mustache similar to the one Hitler wore. He scratched at his temple, the same one he'd tapped to indicate his superior intelligence. He gave me a final sneer, swiveled, and walked off without another word.

I let out a shaky breath, gathered my clothes, and with trembling fingers, put them on again. Then I joined the other prisoners leaving Kanada toward the men's camp.

26

Upon returning to camp, I rushed to the appointed meeting place with Vilmos. He wasn't there. Turning around in a circle, I scoured the crowd of returning prisoners for my friend, my dread that Vilmos had not survived the day growing with each passing second.

I didn't see him. He wasn't there. He was dead.

I should have been there with him, to help him get through the day. I knew this was an illogical thought, but guilt is an insidious creature. It makes its own rules.

The weight of despair grew heavier across my shoulders and back, and a painful void expanded in my stomach. Burying my face in my hands, I felt tears wetting my palms.

Then came a voice from behind. "Been waiting long, Adam?"

Jerking my hands off my face, I whirled—and saw Vilmos standing there with a weary smile on his face.

"Remember, Adam," he said, his tone part amusement, part admonishment, "there is always hope."

I threw my arms around him and hugged him as tightly as I

could. The pressure of his arms was weaker than mine, and when I released him, I could see why. Vilmos looked exhausted, drained. There were deep circles under his eyes, and lines of fatigue gouging his face. His shoulders slumped, arms drooping at his sides. I noticed blood on his dirty fingers.

"What happened?" I asked.

"I had to dig out a big rock," Vilmos said. "Bruised my hands a bit. It's not serious."

But his illness was. I could hear it in his voice; see it in his eyes.

"Come on," I said. "I've got a surprise for you."

He followed me to a shadowy spot between two blocks and there, after checking no one was spying on us, I retrieved the two cookies from their hiding place.

I removed my clogs, reached deep inside each, and pulled out the rolled pieces of cloth I had stuck into their tips. I held each clog upright, and out slid the cookies, slightly battered and misshapen from being squeezed tightly behind the cloth, and most likely not smelling all too great after being at such close proximity to my toes, but still marvelous.

Vilmos's eyes widened as I handed over the cookies. "How? Where?" He was finding it hard to form full sentences.

"Go on," I said. "Eat them. We've only got one or two minutes before roll call."

Vilmos brought a cookie to his mouth, then paused. "What about you? You should have one."

"I already ate my two," I told him, astounded that even as tired and hungry as he was, Vilmos would still think of my well-being. "Hurry up now."

Vilmos bit into the first cookie, and a small moan of pleasure sounded deep in his throat. He consumed both cookies quickly and gave me a smile full of crumbs, like a child's.

"Those were heavenly, Adam. Thank you so much. How did you get them?"

"From a suitcase in Kanada."

"And you hid them in your clogs?"

I told him about being searched by the SS guard, how he had shaken the clogs. "I'd stuck the cloth in so tightly that it was like a stopper, and the clogs are so damn long that there was room for the cookies. The son of a bitch didn't think to check inside."

I started laughing, and Vilmos did too, the sort of liberating laughter that surges from the pit of your stomach and bends you over and rattles your bones good and hard. We held onto each other as we laughed, and for a tiny stitch of time, our troubles were forgotten.

Then it was time for roll call, and reality reasserted itself.

We stood for the count, immobile, while before us a sentence was carried out. The guilty party was said to have stolen a potato. The punishment was *fünf-und-zwanzig*, twenty-five lashes with a cane. The prisoner was stripped of his trousers, bent over a table, and a burly SS guard delivered the blows to his buttocks with maniacal ferocity.

We couldn't cover our ears nor shut our eyes. We were ordered to watch the punishment and hear the victim's cries. So that the lesson would sink in.

When it was done, the prisoner was pulled off the table and thrown to the ground. He lay there in a crumpled heap until the count was complete.

After roll call, we received our bread rations. In the normal world, a display of horror as the one I'd just witnessed would have robbed me of my appetite. In Auschwitz, there was no room for such squeamishness. You got a chance to eat, you took it.

I offered Vilmos a portion of my bread, saying I would likely be able to get more food in Kanada tomorrow, but he steadfastly refused.

"You need it just as much as I do, Adam. I'm feeling better, honestly."

He didn't look it. Vilmos's cough was as nasty as it had been that morning, and when I snuck a hand onto his forehead, before he could knock it away, I felt the heat of his fever. He was still sick. Just putting up a brave front for my sake.

"I hope to see Mathias, the man who got me the clogs, a little later," I said. "I'll ask him to move you to an easier *kommando*."

"I don't think that would be wise, Adam."

"Why not?"

"The SS doctor from the selection was at the gate when I returned to camp. I think he was there to see if I made it back. Like it was a game or a wager he needed to settle."

"The filthy pig," I muttered.

"And there's every chance he'll be there tomorrow as well. If I'm not there..." Vilmos left the end of that sobering thought unsaid. We both knew what it meant. The SS doctor was having a bit of fun, waiting to see how long it would take Vilmos to die digging trenches. If Vilmos did not show up for work in his regular *kommando*, that would be the end of the game, and Vilmos would be sent to the gas chambers.

It was cruel and inhuman, just the sort of entertainment an SS doctor would appreciate. I glanced despairingly at Vilmos, and he said, "Let's just eat, Adam, okay?"

Just as we were finishing our bread, before I had the chance to tell Vilmos what I'd learned during the day, a familiar figure approached. It was one of the *Lagerälteste's* henchmen, the one with the conjoined eyebrow, one of the pair who had taken me to the *Lagerälteste* the night I was put on Franz's murder case.

"He wants you," he said. "You need to come with me."

There was no need to specify who *he* was. I stood up, alarm spreading its icy tendrils over my limbs. "What's happened?"

"He'll tell you," the man said, and gestured for me to follow.

He led me not to the *Lagerälteste's* block but toward the latrines, and then behind them. I realized where we were going—the ditch where Franz had been killed.

Had the *Lagerälteste* changed his mind? Had he decided to abort my investigation? Was I to be killed where Franz had been, in some sort of demented symbolism?

When we got to the ditch, there were three men in it. The *Lagerälteste,* Mathias, and a regular prisoner whose face I couldn't see. That was because he was on hands and knees, shaking and weeping.

"Ah, here's my clever Jew." The *Lagerälteste* clapped his large hands together. He was all smiles, all teeth. "Didn't I tell you he was a clever Jew, Mathias?"

Mathias's expression was placid as he confirmed that the *Lagerälteste* had indeed told him precisely that.

"What's going on?" I said, breathing a bit easier now that it appeared I was not about to die. Not right then, in any case.

"We found Franz's murderer," the *Lagerälteste* said. "That's what. Just in the nick of time for you, eh?"

"Him?" I said, pointing at the weeping prisoner.

"Yes, that's the *schweinehund*," the *Lagerälteste* said, calling the prisoner a pig-dog before planting his boot in the prisoner's backside, causing him to drop flat in the dirt.

I glanced a question at Mathias, who explained, "We followed your suggestion and ran a search in the camp for a bloody shirt, and—"

"And this *schweinehund* had it," the *Lagerälteste* completed. His teeth were bared, and there was foam on his lips. If anyone looked like a dog around here, it was him. A rabid one.

A jolt of pure relief streaked through me. The case was over. I'd succeeded. I was going to live. I could hardly believe it, and couldn't wait to tell Vilmos the good news.

"Where is it?" I asked. "Where's the shirt?"

"He's wearing it," the *Lagerälteste* said. "That's how we know it was him. I called you here because I figured you'd want to be here when I killed him."

I could not imagine why he thought I'd wish to witness that.

"And also because I want to know why he did it. Why he killed Franz. But the idiot speaks hardly any German. Mathias says he's Hungarian, so you ask him. Ask him why he killed Franz."

I crouched beside the prisoner, grabbed his arm, and pulled him to his knees. He was a sorry sight. One eye was bruised and on its way to swelling shut, and tears and snot were smeared all over his face. A wet circle on his lap told me he had wet himself.

The prisoner was hugging himself with both arms. I told him to move them away from his torso.

His eyes were wild and unfocused, and he was trembling like a drenched child. I had to repeat myself and tug on his arms to get a clear view of his shirtfront. When I did, I saw a large rust-colored stain stretching all the way from his collar to the middle button. It was undoubtedly blood. A few days old, I thought. The amount was consistent with a spurting neck wound.

The *Lagerälteste* loomed over my shoulder. He was practically vibrating with blood lust. "Go on, ask him already. I want to know why he did it."

I asked the prisoner his name. Through quivering lips, he stammered that he was called Pista.

"Well, Pista, why did you kill a boy here four days ago?"

Pista stared at me with huge wet eyes. "I... I... I know nothing about no boy. Nothing. Please tell them I know nothing."

"His name was Franz," I said. "You stabbed him in the throat right here."

Pista shook his head. "No. No. I know nothing about no boy, I tell you. Nothing."

"What's he saying?" the *Lagerälteste* asked.

"That he didn't do it."

The *Lagerälteste* huffed. "Of course he did. Filthy, lying Jew. Tell him that if he doesn't come clean, I'll make his death especially painful."

I said to Pista, "There's blood on your shirt. A good deal of it. How did it get there?"

Shrinking under the *Lagerälteste's* boiling fury, Pista gulped. "It happened four days ago. A member of my *kommando*, he didn't jump to attention fast enough when an officer was walking by. The officer shot him with his pistol. I was standing right next to him and got blood all over me." He licked his lips. "I've killed no one. You got to make him believe that. Please. I swear. I don't know anything about no boy."

I studied his terror-stricken, pleading face. And like sand through an hourglass, grain by grain, my relief drained away. Because, despite not wanting to believe it, my instincts were telling me Pista was being truthful.

"Well, what's his story?" the *Lagerälteste* asked.

"He says the blood got on his shirt when he was standing close to another prisoner who was shot by an officer. Says it happened the same day Franz was murdered."

"He must think we're all fools if he believes we'll fall for that. I'll show him."

"Wait a minute. Ask him where it happened; at what time of day." It was the man with the conjoined eyebrow.

"What the hell for, Rolf?" the *Lagerälteste* said.

I didn't wait for an answer. I relayed the question to Pista.

"It was in late afternoon. On the other side of those blocks," Pista said, pointing a shuddering finger at the row of residential blocks to the side of the latrines.

I translated the answer, and Rolf said, "I saw it happen. An *Untersturmführer*. He was passing by a group of prisoners when he pulled out his pistol and shot one of them. No idea what provoked him."

"Did the blood splatter any other prisoners?" I asked.

"Yeah. There was a lot of it."

The *Lagerälteste* looked ready to burst. A bloated vein pulsed in his forehead. His face was changing color, the broken capillaries on his nose and cheeks standing out like tributaries of blood. "Did you see this man? Did you?"

"Well, no. I was behind the prisoners, so I didn't see any of their faces. All I saw was one of them get shot and the blood spraying."

"So you don't know it was this guy who got splattered, do you?" the *Lagerälteste* shouted.

"No. I guess I don't," Rolf said, taking a step back. He looked scared for his life, and I didn't blame him. He was ruining the *Lagerälteste's* moment—an action likely to result in severe bodily injury or worse. "I'm just telling what I saw. For all I know, the blood on his shirt is Franz's, just like you think."

"What do you think, Adam?" Mathias said. He was the only one who seemed calm about the whole business. "You think he's the killer?"

I looked at Pista. He was still kneeling, eyes darting from one person to the next. The rest of us were speaking German, which meant Pista didn't understand the bulk of our conversation, so he didn't know what was going on. But he must have sensed that the atmosphere had shifted.

He was very thin, I noticed, his neck scrawny, and his color was terrible, a lackluster gray. He was also older than most prisoners—in his late forties, I thought. If he somehow survived the day, chances were he would perish from exhaustion or starvation in the next few weeks.

If I said that he did it, I'd be in the clear. I would have fulfilled my mission. Pista would die today, as he likely would anyway in the near future. Perhaps a bit more painfully, but dying of starvation was terrible as well. Who could say with certainty which fate was worse?

And I would live.

If I said that he was innocent, however...

"It's not him," I said, pushing a long breath through my nose, feeling both incredibly foolish and incongruously happy with the decision I'd made.

"What?" The *Lagerälteste* couldn't believe his ears.

"He didn't do it. He didn't kill Franz."

"How can you be sure? Maybe he heard about that business with the shot prisoner. Maybe he saw it happen and used it to explain the blood on his shirt. Franz's blood. You said we should look for a shirt with blood on it. Well, there it is."

"I didn't expect the killer to still be wearing it. Whoever killed Franz had planned it. He knew who he was. He knew you might get upset about it. He would have gotten rid of any bloody clothes."

"You don't know that for sure."

I did. Because I knew the killer hadn't searched Franz's body, which was why Vilmos had found bread on it. The motive was personal.

"Look at him," I said, gesturing at Pista. "You really think he's your killer?"

The *Lagerälteste's* fists bunched and released, bunched and released. He so wanted Pista to be guilty; had already imagined what it would feel like to exact vengeance on him. He could still kill him, of course. He didn't need a reason. But it wouldn't be the same.

"You understand what you're saying, Jew? What it means? It means you still have to find this killer. And you have until tomorrow night to do it, or I kill you."

The *Lagerälteste* locked eyes with me. His rage was turning his face into a roiling sea, his facial muscles twitching and jumping, the broken capillaries wriggling like snakes.

"I understand," I said, not breaking eye contact.

The *Lagerälteste* nodded. "All right, then. But I'm not entirely convinced you're right." He took a step toward Pista, fists balled.

"Let him go," I said. "He's innocent."

"Maybe he is, and maybe he isn't. It makes no difference to me."

Pista scooted away on his ass, raising his arms in a pitiful attempt to shield his head. I couldn't let this happen. Couldn't let the *Lagerälteste* kill him. Because if he did, I had just sacrificed myself for nothing.

"Wait," I said, with enough force that the *Lagerälteste* paused to look over his shoulder at me. "Listen, all right? Just listen. I'll find the killer, okay? I'll do it by tomorrow. If I fail, make my death twice, no ten times, as painful and long as you planned on making it. Just let this man go. He's not a part of this."

It was an empty offer because the *Lagerälteste* could do to me whatever he wished, could kill me in whatever fashion he devised. But I was desperate for Pista to live. It was vitally important. I had failed to save Gyuri; I could not fail to save Pista as well.

"What do you care what happens to him?" the *Lagerälteste* said, eyes narrowing in suspicion. "You know him?"

"Never seen him before in my life."

"Why, then?"

"Because he's a human being," I said, my voice ringing with conviction. "An innocent human being. He doesn't deserve to die."

The *Lagerälteste* stared at me with his intense eyes for a long moment. He was breathing hard, his large chest rising and falling like crashing waves. At his sides, his arms hung like battering rams, ready to break and smash and shatter. My argument might have moved an ordinary man, one with a conscience, but the *Lagerälteste* was a different sort of creature. He had no morality to speak of. To him, other human beings were worthless—unless, like Franz, they belonged to him.

Which was why I knew with gut-wrenching despair that I could not sway him.

But then he surprised me. His face broke into a grin, and he unclenched one of his fists to rub his jaw.

"I'll tell you what, my clever Jew," he said. "I'm going to grant you your wish. I'm going to let this *schweinehund* live. But you owe me a death now, so here's how it's going to be. You find Franz's killer by tomorrow, or I won't just kill you—I'll kill your friend, too." The dawning horror in my eyes made his grin widen. "Yes, I've seen you two together. Good buddies, aren't you? You and the short one with the face of a bookkeeper."

Vilmos. He was talking about Vilmos. I felt the earth being pulled from under my feet. Then I was falling headfirst into a bottomless abyss. What had I done? How could I have been so stupid?

"I'll kill you both, and like you suggested, I'll take my time doing it. And just so we're clear, if you're thinking of tricking me, of hurling yourself at the fence if you fail to find this killer, you better think again. Because I won't be satisfied with such an easy death for you. Nor for your friend. If you kill yourself, either one of you, I'll kill ten prisoners in your place, including the one you just saved. Do you understand me?"

I fought the urge to leap at him, to punch him until his face was nothing but raw, bloody meat. But it wouldn't do any good. He had all the power here. Rolf and Mathias would pull me off him, and then they would kill me. And afterward, they would kill Vilmos, too. Choked by guilt, fear, and impotent rage, I was unable to utter a sound, so I just nodded.

"Very good. Now tell this *schweinehund* to get out of my sight before I change my mind."

I swallowed, cleared my throat, and told Pista, "You can go. Hurry!"

It took a second for Pista to register that he'd been spared. Then he scrambled out of the ditch like an animal, stumbled and fell flat on his chest, rose again, and sprinted as though Satan himself were at his heels.

The *Lagerälteste* was still grinning at me. "By tomorrow, Jew. Or you and your friend both die."

27

The three of them turned to leave.

"Wait," I said. "I need to ask you some questions. You and the other *Stubendienst* who slept in the same room with Franz."

I was talking to Rolf, he of the conjoined eyebrow. He looked at the *Lagerälteste*, who grumbled, "Answer his damn questions and then come to the block." To me, he said, "Don't take too long, Jew. Rolf's got work to do." Then he and Mathias walked away, leaving Rolf and me alone.

"I understand you were a defense lawyer before you got here," Rolf said.

"That's right."

"Were you any good?"

"Not bad."

"My lawyer was a scumbag. Took my mother for everything she had, then showed up at court stinking drunk. No wonder I got sent up."

"Were you guilty?"

Rolf threw his head back and laughed. "Of more than they got me for."

He was a man of crude features: a lantern jaw, bulging cheekbones, and a crooked mouth brimming with crooked teeth. The finishing touch was that eyebrow, of course. That face must have come in handy in his criminal career. A single look was all it took to make you terrified.

"Did you meet the *Lagerälteste* in prison?"

"No. That happened here. The only one of us who knows him from before is Mathias. But the *Lagerälteste* had a reputation, so I knew who he was."

"What did you do time for?"

"Murder and robbery."

"Who did you kill?"

"I was robbing a store and the dumb owner put up a fight. Just eight marks in the till and he comes at me with a hammer. I stabbed him in the heart."

"So you have experience with knives."

His eyes flared. "Hey now, don't go jumping to wrong conclusions. I had nothing to do with what happened to Franz."

"Relax, Rolf. You've been around. You know how these things go. Until I know otherwise, everyone who knew Franz is a suspect. If you didn't do it, you've got nothing to worry about."

Rolf squinted at me, his single eyebrow curling like a caterpillar. "Way you talk reminds me of the bastard detective who made the case against me."

I gave a half smile. "I picked up a few things sitting in on police interrogations. You got an alibi for the time Franz was killed?"

"All afternoon I was with Mathias. Ask him; he'll tell you."

"Where were you?"

"All around. We do a tour of the camp every couple of days, to check on things."

"You were together the whole time?"

"Every minute. From say, three hours after lunch until shortly before the first *kommandos* started returning to camp. And Franz was alive when we set out. He was in our room at the block. Mathias can confirm this too."

"What about later? Because Franz might have been killed at any time before curfew."

Rolf rubbed his chin. "I had dinner, then roamed about for a while, then returned to the block."

"Were you with someone?"

"Not all the time. But that doesn't matter because I didn't kill Franz. Why would I? I had nothing against him."

His harsh features made it difficult to read his expression. He was worried about my questions, but that might have been solely because he knew what the *Lagerälteste* was capable of. Rolf had killed before, and with a knife, no less. Therefore, he was certainly a suspect. On the other hand, Franz's killing seemed to have been planned and executed meticulously. I wasn't sure Rolf had the intelligence for such an undertaking.

"When you got back to the block that evening, was Franz there?"

"No."

"What about the others—Mathias and the other *Stubendienst*?"

"Mathias was with the *Lagerälteste* in his room, drinking. Otto was in our room with me or we were together in the block or thereabouts."

"This was after dinner, you said?"

"Yeah, but the *Lagerälteste* and Mathias had been drinking from beforehand."

"Was that usual?"

Rolf grinned. "Oh yeah. The *Lagerälteste* likes to drink, and a lot of bottles come in on the trains. When he gets some good ones, they can drink all evening long."

He made no mention of the people to whom those bottles used to belong. Apparently, they did not enter his thoughts at all.

"You didn't see Franz all that evening, is that right?"

"Yeah. Like I said, the last time I saw him was before Mathias and me went to tour the camp."

"At what time did you go to sleep? After curfew?"

"That's right. First we made sure the prisoners were all settled, and then we turned in."

"And Franz wasn't there?"

"Yeah. Like I told you."

"Didn't you wonder where he was? Worry about him? It was after curfew, after all."

"I thought he was with the *Lagerälteste*," Rolf said.

"In his room?"

"Yeah."

"So Mathias was already back in your room by then?"

"Yeah. He must have thought Franz was with the *Lagerälteste*, too."

"What was Franz doing in the *Lagerälteste's* room that late?" I asked.

Rolf's eyes twitched. Then he ran a slow hand over his mouth and looked off to the side. "Whatever the *Lagerälteste* told him to."

I said nothing, just kept my gaze on Rolf's face. He shifted his feet, then scratched his forearm. His eyes met mine and darted away. Here was a man who had laughed at the recollection of the murder he'd committed, along with other crimes, and yet he was now uncomfortable.

"Anything else?" he asked. "I need to head back."

I considered asking him if he knew the redheaded man with the thick nose whom Stefan had seen pointing a finger at Franz's face, but I feared that Rolf would pass on my question to the *Lagerälteste*, which would likely lead to the redheaded man's death. I was not about to jeopardize his life before I knew whether he was guilty or innocent.

"Just one more thing," I said to Rolf. "The previous boy, the one before Franz, what was his name?"

"Bruno."

"What happened to him?"

"He died."

"Yes, I know that. But how did he die?"

Rolf thought for a second or two, then turned his palms up and shrugged. "He just died. Any other questions? Because the *Lagerälteste* might get upset if I don't get back soon."

"No, that's everything, Rolf. You go ahead. I'll come over in a few minutes to speak to Otto."

Rolf climbed out of the ditch and walked away. I stayed where I was, just me and my thoughts, staring at the spot where Franz had died. I had learned a few things, despite Rolf's attempt to keep them from me. They made me very angry and very sad, and I wished I could do something about them, but I knew full well that I couldn't.

28

Coming to the block where Franz had lived, I was met by the *Lageralteste.*

"So, my clever Jew, learn anything interesting from Rolf?"

"Not really," I said. "But maybe Otto will prove more useful."

I moved to go inside, but the *Lageralteste* blocked my path. His eyes were bloodshot, and he reeked of alcohol. He must have guzzled an entire bottle in the short time that had elapsed since he'd left me and Rolf at the ditch. His lips were pulled back into what I imagined a hungry tiger's smile would look like.

"You better hope you'll find this killer, or I will take great pleasure in killing you. And your friend too."

"I hope the same," I said. "For Franz's sake. May I go talk to Otto now?"

The *Lageralteste's* grin widened. "By all means. Go right ahead."

Otto was the square-jawed functionary who, along with Rolf, had taken me to the *Lageralteste* that first night.

A squat, wide-shouldered man with tar-colored stubble that

started halfway up his scalp. A wide mouth with thick lips. Ears that jutted out like oars. Dark eyes that gleamed with the light of a pair of candles burning on a narrow board that served as a shelf.

He was sitting on a low wooden chair, legs crossed at the ankles and stretched under a small table on which sat a fat loaf of bread. The loaf was missing a quarter of its former length. The culprit was a sharp knife currently resting next to its victim, a spray of crumbs around it, evidence of its crime.

A pang of hunger clawed at my stomach. Almost an entire loaf! It was the stuff of dreams.

Otto saw me looking and flashed me a warped grin. "Hungry, eh? Well, you're better off than I thought you'd be when I brought you here the other night. I was sure you'd be dead within the hour."

"I was too," I said.

"You handled it pretty well. Most people would have started blubbering, begging for mercy, making all sorts of promises."

"Has it ever worked for any of them?"

He shook his head slowly. "Not a single one."

"I didn't think it would."

"Would you have begged if you'd thought it would save you?"

"Maybe."

"You're not sure? You want to die? Maybe that explains what I heard you just did. You must be the dumbest Jew in all of Auschwitz."

"Who told you?"

"Rolf. He said you persuaded the *Lagerälteste* to let a prisoner go. A prisoner you didn't know. Even though it would have gotten you off the hook if you'd let him die."

"What else did Rolf tell you?"

"That you ask pretty good questions. Like a police interrogator."

I fed him the lie about my being a defense lawyer, and he nodded his head and said he knew that already.

"I need to ask you a few questions about Franz," I said.

"Go ahead. I got nothing to hide." He spread his arms wide as though to illustrate the point.

"I understand he slept with you here."

"That's right. That's his bunk over there."

It was a double bunk, with far greater vertical space between the beds than the regular triple-level bunk afforded.

"Which level was his?"

"The top one. Rolf sleeps on the bottom."

I peered at where Franz had slept. A pretty luxurious set up, by camp standards. There was a mattress, a real one, though not very thick; a light blanket; and a small pillow, which once might have belonged to a child. No clues to the identity of the murderer. But then, I hadn't really expected any.

"Who sleeps there?" I asked, pointing at the double bunk on the opposite side of the room.

"Mathias and me. The top bunk is mine."

Which fitted with what Mathias had told me.

"I was told you got up that night to take a leak."

"That's right."

"You didn't notice Franz wasn't here?"

"Why would I? It was dark, and I wasn't looking for him."

"It's a small room. You might have noticed the absence of his breathing."

Otto smiled. "The way Rolf snores, a Panzer tank could be rolling outside and I wouldn't hear it."

"Where were you on the afternoon and evening Franz was murdered?"

"Part of the time, I was here in the block with Rolf, either playing cards or making sure everything was tidy and neat. Otherwise, I was around."

"By yourself?"

"I visited the kitchen at some point in the afternoon. The cooks can vouch for that. But otherwise, yes, I was by myself."

"No alibi, then?"

"Not for the whole time, no."

"What did you do time for back in Germany?"

"All sorts of things. I've been to prison a number of times."

"What was the big one, the one that eventually got you sent here?"

"I raped a girl. Beat her pretty badly, too. From what I heard, she can no longer walk properly."

Otto sank a little lower in his chair, lacing his fingers behind his head. The candles flickered, making shadows scuttle across his face.

"She wasn't my first," he went on, "just the only one they could pin on me. In prison I got into a few fights, killed a few prisoners. The guards didn't mind. It saved the state money not having to feed them. It showed those in charge I had what it takes to be useful here." He smiled. "Want to know why I like it here? Because every once in a while they let me go to the main camp, to the brothel. Full of young Polish women. It's fun, even though you're not allowed to beat them. They have to stay pretty, you see."

He said all this with a satisfied air. He wanted to shock me with his depravity. I had met criminals like him back in Hungary—those who embraced their roles as outcasts, as those who lived outside the boundaries of society. They were invariably cruel, violent, and utterly indifferent to the suffering of others.

"That's nice to hear," I said, feeling sick to my stomach and wishing like hell I could kill this despicable creature then and there. "But let's get back to Franz, shall we? That's why I'm here."

"All right. What about him?"

"How did you and he get along?"

"I didn't hate him, if that's what you're getting at. Though he did annoy me the first few days with his weeping."

"What was he crying about?"

"What do you think? Being here."

"He didn't like being the *Lagerälteste's* servant?"

"No, he sure didn't."

"Why not? I suppose he got good food and proper clothes."

"He didn't enjoy what he had to do in order to get them."

Otto was smiling again. A taunting smile, daring me to voice the conclusion I had already reached.

"What he had to do with the *Lagerälteste,* you mean?"

He nodded slowly, the smile still plastered on his ugly face. I wanted to push him to the floor and wipe that smile off with my foot.

"Which was what you and Rolf and Mathias thought he was doing that night, the reason he wasn't in this room?"

"Yes."

The sick feeling in my stomach grew. I glanced across the room at the closed door. Beyond it was the *Lagerälteste's* room, where Franz had gone through hell the last few weeks of his life.

No one dared say it plainly. Not Mathias, not Rolf, not even Otto, though he came closest of the three due to his provocative nature. They all knew what the *Lagerälteste* was, what he'd done to Franz, but all adhered to a code of silence. If they didn't, they might incur the *Lagerälteste's* wrath, though he must have known full well that they were not ignorant of his proclivities.

It was strange, and a testament to the nature of these evil men, that the *Lagerälteste* didn't feel the need to hide the murders he'd committed and eagerly flaunted his cruelty. But he didn't flaunt this particular perversion, and acted as though it was a secret.

Other prisoners must have known, including regular ones. I hadn't been aware of it before I'd taken this case, but eventually, I supposed, word would have reached me. Now I understood the comment made by the *Blockälteste* after he'd hurled my new clogs at my chest, the one about my being too old to bend down with my trousers by my ankles.

The *Lagerälteste* wasn't interested in men, just boys like Franz.

"It doesn't sound like you pitied him at all," I said.

"Why should I? He had it better than most prisoners. He ate well and didn't have to work too hard. So he had to do that one unpleasant thing—that's not too bad."

"Some would say it's the worst thing a boy could be made to do against his will."

"I wouldn't know," Otto said. "I only have experience with girls."

My heart was beating slowly but very hard, thumping like a giant's footfall. I felt very cold and very sad and gripped by the worst sort of anger, the sort that has no outlet or hope of resolution. I could do nothing to the *Lagerälteste*. Just as I could do nothing to the SS personnel who had killed my family. I was merely a slave, after all. And I did not wish to die.

At that moment, I was grateful to have never laid eyes on Franz. Otherwise, I might have been tormented with images of him being molested by the *Lagerälteste*.

"You said you didn't hate Franz. Did anyone else?" I asked.

"Nah. He was all right. Even stopped crying after a few days, which I guess means he was stronger than he initially looked. Rolf was indifferent to him, I think, and Mathias liked him. Tried to cheer him up."

This did not surprise me. Among this sordid bunch, Mathias appeared to be the least cruel.

"Mathias always had a weak spot for the boys," Otto said.

"Oh? Did he also try to cheer Bruno up?"

"You know about Bruno, huh?"

"Yes. Including how he died."

It was like throwing bait in the sea and hoping a fish would nab it. I held my breath as I prayed Otto would bite.

"You have been busy," he said. "Well, it could have been worse. Usually is. He's never as gentle as he is with his boys. They're the only ones he strangles instead of beats to death."

He was slouching now, totally relaxed. Now that he believed I already knew what the *Lagerälteste* did to his boys, all restraint on his speech had disappeared. He could talk freely now, without fear, relishing the effect he could see it was having on me.

"How long do they last, usually?"

"Until he gets tired of them. Then he starts hunting around for someone new. About six months, usually. But Bruno lasted just four."

"Why so little?"

"I don't know. It's none of my business. Anyway, they should be grateful. Six months, even four, is longer than most prisoners live. And most of them live much more poorly than they do."

"Did Franz know he was living on borrowed time?"

"I didn't tell him."

"How many boys has it been till now?"

Otto looked at the ceiling, his lips moving silently. "Nine, including Franz."

Nine boys, I thought, feeling as though I could drown in sorrow. Though why I should feel this way, I didn't know. Nine was a minuscule number compared to the wholesale slaughter that went on in Auschwitz, which included the murder of babies and small children, like my two daughters. Yet the sadness that now pressed upon me was so keen, it was as though my skin was about to tear under its honed blade.

"He killed all nine boys?" I asked in a disbelieving voice, though why I should have found this difficult to accept was a mystery.

"Well, not all of them," Otto said.

Of course. What a foolish question. After all, the *Lagerälteste* hadn't killed Franz. Which, I suspected, explained a portion of his rage. For this murderer hadn't simply taken the living Franz from him, he'd also robbed him of his right to eventually murder Franz himself.

The *Lagerälteste's* words rang in my head, their terrible meaning now laid bare. *I am king here. If I want something, I take it. If I want someone dead, I kill him.*

I kill him. No one else.

This case wasn't about Franz, not as far as the *Lagerälteste* was concerned. He didn't care about him one bit. Franz had simply been another boy to exploit for his perverse pleasure. This murder wasn't a crime against Franz, but against the *Lagerälteste* and his absolute authority.

"I'm glad that at least one of you showed him some kindness," I said.

Otto sneered. "Don't let Mathias fool you. He's no different than the rest of us. At least I didn't kill my mother."

"Mother?"

"You heard me. He killed his own mother. Stepfather, too. He's no better than any of us."

Yes, he was. Because he'd tried to keep Franz's spirit up. Bruno's, too. And perhaps he'd done the same for the boys who came before them. He'd also brought me my new clogs. All these were acts of kindness.

I wondered why Mathias hadn't told me about his mother. Perhaps he'd been ashamed. Or perhaps if he'd told me about her, he couldn't have pretended all the people he'd killed were deserving of their fate. Though why he should have cared what I thought about him at all, I couldn't say.

As I was leaving the block, I saw Mathias approaching.

"You're walking better," he said.

"Because of you. Thank you for the clogs."

He nodded. His expression was as flat as ever.

"Why did you give them to me?"

"Their previous owner had no more use for them."

"Yes, but why go to the trouble of bringing them to me?"

"I figured you already had enough problems without every step causing you pain."

"Why do you care about my problems?"

"I don't. But why should a man who has so little time to live not walk comfortably?"

I had no answer. I wanted to ask him about his mother, why he had killed her, but that might have upset him, and I wanted him on my side as much as it was possible.

"I have a request, Mathias," I said, hoping I wasn't overstepping the mark but feeling I had no choice in the matter.

"Oh?"

"My friend is sick. He has a fever. He needs medicine."

"The friend who is to join you in death this Sunday?"

I nodded.

"What good would medicine do him?"

"If I solve the case, it might save his life."

"I don't have any medicine. Occasionally, the hospital has some."

"He can't go to the hospital."

Mathias didn't ask me why. He simply accepted it as a fact.

"I'm sorry, Adam, but I can't get you any medicine. Not quickly, anyway, and probably not at all."

I inhaled slowly and nodded, despair cloaking itself around my shoulders and chest.

He began to move past me but halted when I asked, "Mathias, did Franz looked scared in the final days of his life?"

"Why do you ask?"

"I was just wondering if he felt threatened by anyone."

"Not that I know. Franz didn't look any different than usual."

I wanted to ask him why he had tried to cheer Franz up, and Bruno too. But what did it matter? Perhaps it stemmed from the same notion that had led him to gift me my new clogs. Whatever the reason, I was grateful to him. For my sake, and for the sake of the dead boys too.

29

I found Vilmos in our block. He had taken off his shirt and was inspecting it for lice. I joined him, squashing the little creatures between thumb and forefinger, unable to stop thinking about the nine boys who had been molested and killed.

"What is it, Adam?" Vilmos asked.

"It's the case. I don't have much time left."

"You'll figure it out. I'm sure of it. Anything you want to share?"

"Let's find somewhere private to talk," I said.

We headed toward the northern fence, close to where we had talked with the Mumbler. Again I scanned the drooping, staggering figures of the women prisoners in Mexico, hoping I'd see one of my sisters. And again, I did not.

I told Vilmos about my day. Working in Kanada, seeing the people being marched into the crematorium. Talking to Ludwig and Stefan. The redheaded man Stefan had seen threatening Franz. The man with the bloody shirt, and how I'd told the *Lagerälteste* that he was innocent.

"You did a brave thing, Adam. The right thing."

I wondered if I should tell him that I had inadvertently put his life at risk too—that if I failed to solve the case, he and I would both die a horrible death.

But what would be the point? Why pile more worry on his narrow shoulders? Either I solved this case and we lived, or I didn't and we died. Like me, Vilmos would not choose the only escape if it meant that ten innocent prisoners would die. Yet I found it difficult to look at him without being gnawed by guilt.

Then I told him what I'd learned from Rolf and Otto, and what the *Lagerälteste* did to his boys.

Vilmos shut his eyes. "Dear God, such cruelty. Such evil."

I said nothing, thinking that because of me, Vilmos might soon fall prey to that same cruelty, that same evil.

"Those poor boys," Vilmos murmured.

"Maybe Franz is better off dead," I said, gazing at the fence.

Vilmos rested a hand on my arm. "Here in Auschwitz, Adam, each of us makes a decision every day. A decision whether it is better to struggle on living or to end the suffering by dying. And who can say with certainty which decision is the better one? But it's a decision that belongs to each man and no one else. It's one of the only things we still own. Whoever killed Franz robbed him of that decision."

I nodded, massaging my forehead. "I'm just worried that I don't have enough time to catch this killer. I have no leads apart from the redheaded man Stefan saw threatening Franz, and I have no idea how to find him among all the thousands of prisoners. But I'm sure I saw such a man recently."

"It's odd, but I have the same feeling. Like you, I just don't remember where or when it was."

"We could go block by block and ask. But if word reaches the *Lagerälteste,* every redheaded man in the camp would be at risk. I don't want that on my conscience."

"I understand," Vilmos said. "Perhaps it'll come to you soon. Or to me."

We walked a few more steps before I spoke next. "There are a few things that are bothering me."

"What things?"

"The knife or whatever was used to stab Franz. The killer took a big risk by taking it with him. If he was caught with it, he would have died terribly. So why didn't he leave it at the murder scene?"

"A knife is a valuable thing," Vilmos said. "Perhaps the killer didn't wish to part with it. Yes, he took a risk, but once the blade was wiped clean of blood, it would no longer be incriminating."

"That's only true if the killer is a regular prisoner, one who would find it difficult to obtain a replacement. Prisoner functionaries could get another knife pretty easily. And so could Ludwig, I imagine."

"You're probably right."

"So here's the problem, Vilmos. You told me that the bread you took from Franz's body was easy to find."

"It was."

"Then why was it still there? If the killer was a regular prisoner, would he have kept the knife, knowing the risk, but not taken two seconds to search the body? I don't think so."

"You're right," Vilmos said. "It's strange. What else is bothering you?"

"The fact that Franz was carrying bread in the first place."

"We all save a portion of our bread every now and then, Adam."

"But we don't work directly for the *Lagerälteste*. Whatever horrors Franz endured, he didn't lack for food. He had no reason to keep bread for later, unless he was planning on giving it to someone else."

"Who?"

"I don't know. Ludwig said Franz had no friends but himself. And if any of the prisoner functionaries had seen him with another prisoner, the *Lagerälteste* would have killed him by now, just to be on the safe side. And we know from Zoltan that Franz was not in the selling business anymore."

I paused to squint at a woman dragging her feet near the fence of Mexico. Something in her build and the set of her shoulders reminded me of my sister Sarlota, but then I saw, with a twinge, that the woman was not her.

"Which means," I said, "that somewhere in this camp, there's a prisoner who had some sort of a connection with Franz. But I don't know who he is. Nor do I have any idea how to find him."

"You think this mystery man is the killer?"

"It's possible. Or he might know something that would lead me to him."

Vilmos coughed long and hard, half bent with his hands on his knees. When he straightened, I noted how drawn his face was, how the skin under his eyes was black with fatigue. "You're very ill, aren't you, my friend?"

Vilmos wiped spittle from his lips. "Don't you worry, Adam. One day we'll play chess as free men. In Jerusalem. Or Tel Aviv."

I wished I could believe that. I wished I could believe that this coming Sunday, Vilmos and I would still be alive.

30

Last day to solve the case. Last day to catch a murderer, or Vilmos and I would both die. That was the thought that greeted me as I opened my eyes onto another day in Auschwitz. Though when I thought of it, I had less than even that.

It was Saturday morning. I had until curfew tonight to catch this murderer. Less than a day.

Vilmos had been quiet during the night, so quiet that a few times I had been certain that he'd died in his sleep and had to bring my ear close to his lips to catch his breathing. But there he was, feverish and looking on his last legs, but still alive. He read my mind and smiled. "You're not going to dump more water on my head, are you?"

I smiled back. "You bet I am. And don't complain so much this time."

On the way to the latrine, with Vilmos hanging onto my arm for support, Hendrik caught sight of us. His hateful eyes traveled from me to Vilmos, and his lips curved into a nasty smile. He had seen how sick Vilmos was, and the son of a bitch was happy about it. I gave him a hard look, and he quickly turned away.

He was scared of me. Good. I had enough problems without worrying about him.

After the latrine, we went to the washroom. There, after dousing Vilmos, I washed myself and examined the wound on my foot. It was still painful, and far from healed, but the swelling was down, and the skin around the wound appeared less inflamed.

The rash on my side had subsided as well, though the skin still itched. Overall, if my best friend hadn't been so ill and I had more than a day to live, I might have felt a glimmer of optimism.

But as we joined the lines for breakfast, I was swamped by despondency. Vilmos might not survive the day, and even if he did, it would take a miracle to obtain the medicine he needed. As for me, I had no idea where to go next in my investigation, and each passing second brought me closer to the deadline set by the *Lagerälteste*. Closer to my violent death, and Vilmos's too.

While we waited for our coffee, I searched the faces of the prisoners around me for the redheaded man, but I did not see him. For all I knew, he might have been dead. If he was, and if he had indeed killed Franz, then all hope was truly lost. Because the *Lagerälteste* wanted his pound of flesh. He would not be satisfied with my presenting him with a murderer whom he could not punish.

I turned to Vilmos. "You just make it through the day, you hear me? I'll bring back something good to eat—and medicine, I hope."

"I'll be here when you get back," he said. "I haven't beaten you at chess nearly enough to give up on life yet."

At the *Appellplatz*, a few SS guards and officers stood surveying the gathering prisoners like herdsmen deciding which cows would go next to the slaughterhouse. Among them was the SS doctor from the selection. When his eyes alighted on Vilmos, the corner of his pink mouth drew upward.

"I want to kill the bastard," I hissed under my breath.

"Focus on staying alive, on solving your case," Vilmos said. "That's more productive."

We bade each other good day and went to join our *kommandos*. Stefan and I shook hands.

"Here's to finding something tasty to eat today," he said.

Or a doctor's bag full of medicine, I thought. And Franz's murderer.

As we entered Kanada, the whistle of an incoming train bombarded our ears. My back stiffened, but I did not turn to look. Neither did any of the others.

We started the day shifting luggage into warehouses. I kept my eyes peeled for a doctor's bag, but there was none. As the minutes dragged by, my anxiety heightened, and with it my despair. Time was running out, and I had nothing to go by.

Franz had been surrounded by men who'd committed murder and wouldn't think twice of doing so again. None of them had an alibi, apart from Mathias, but none had a reason to kill him either. No reason that I knew.

That left Ludwig, but he had no motive either. And there was, of course, the redheaded man. If he was still alive, he was somewhere back at camp, one of the thousands of prisoners who were hard to tell apart in their striped uniforms and caps. I needed to find him today, and I could not ask for help from Mathias or any of the *Lagerälteste's* men. I had to do it by myself and had no idea how.

What irked me the most was that I had seen that man recently. I was sure of it. But the time and location continued to elude me.

Apart from him, Ludwig, and those few prisoner functionaries who lived in the same block as Franz, there was an untold number of prisoners who might have committed this murder. This included the dozens of other prisoner functionaries who might have come into contact with Franz and the many prisoners to whom he had sold contraband. Hundreds of possible suspects, and not enough time to eliminate from suspicion hardly any of them.

To these I might add all of the male prisoners who worked in Kanada. Any one of them might have held a grudge against Franz. Any one of them might have killed him.

As we carried, hoisted, and hauled, I questioned a few of my fellow prisoners about Franz, hoping I'd get lucky and stumble upon the killer. This did not happen, and as we broke for lunch, I could not escape the dispiriting thought that I had learned nothing useful that day and that my deadline was mere hours away.

As we received our soup, yells and shouts and cries buffeted us from both the north and south. On either side of Kanada, the gas chambers were busy devouring our people. Flames and smoke shot up from the chimneys, casting a gaudy glow to the cloudless sky. The sun stood high above us, a silent witness to all that transpired in Auschwitz.

I recalled tales of sun-worshipers in ancient times. Perhaps it would prove more fruitful to pray for deliverance to the sun than to God. At least the sun was present here. God did not appear to be.

I ate my soup mechanically, burdened by thoughts of the dying and the smell of their burning. Some of the other men were as silent as myself, but others chatted amiably and occasionally even laughed. They had grown callous. If I worked in Kanada for long enough, I'd likely come to resemble them.

After I'd finished eating, I went to the latrine. On the way back, my stomach tight with anxiety and my head filled with grim images of imminent death, I heard a female voice calling my name.

I stopped in surprise and turned my head in the direction of the voice. A woman prisoner was walking briskly toward me, a broad smile on her face.

It took me a second to recognize her. She looked quite different in her prisoner's dress and black headscarf. And, of course, she had lost some weight.

"Gisella?"

"Hard to believe, isn't it?"

It was, but that wasn't the reason my heart was drumming in my chest. Every day in camp, I would stare south at the women's camp across the rail spur, or north into Mexico, or east into the women's transit camp, where fresh women prisoners often stayed but for a few days before being shipped to work camps throughout the Third Reich. I kept searching for my four sisters, but I never saw any of them.

Gisella was a good friend of my sister Sofia. She had come on the same train as the rest of us, so she might know what happened to my sisters.

"I'm so glad to see you alive," Gisella said. I could tell she wanted to hug me, but she dared not. It was not allowed.

"Let's go here," I said, gesturing to a space between two warehouses, but even there we didn't touch. "What became of your family?"

Her eyes welled up. "Mother and father were sent to the gas chambers. My sister and I were spared. A week after our arrival, she was sent away on a train. I don't know where. You look so thin, Adam. Are you feeling well?"

"I'm fine. What about my sisters? Do you know what happened to them?"

Tears meandered down her cheeks, and a choked sob croaked

from the base of her throat. She gave a shaky nod, but it took a few seconds for her to be able to speak.

"Blanka was carrying her son when she went through selection. The SS doctor told her to give him to your mother, but Blanka refused, so he sent them all to the gas chambers. She would have lived if she'd agreed."

I would have expected nothing else from Blanka. She had suffered three miscarriages before finally giving birth to Gabor, her only son. He was three years old, a beautiful, intelligent child with soulful eyes and a mischievous smile. Blanka was a devoted mother, the sort of mother who would die before parting with her son.

"Sofia was already showing," Gisella went on. "Her pregnancy doomed her." She wiped her eyes, but the tears kept coming.

"What about Sarlota and Julia?" I asked.

"Julia lied about her age. Said she was sixteen. But you know what she looked like."

I did. Julia was slight and short. She was often mistaken for twelve instead of her real age, which was fourteen.

"She was also sent to the gas chambers," Gisella said.

"And..." I had to clear my throat. "And Sarlota?"

"Sarlota made it through selection. She and I were in the same block. She got sick our second week here. I don't know with what. She went to the hospital and never came back."

Gisella did not need to tell me what this meant.

"I'm so sorry, Adam," she said.

I didn't answer straightaway. Nor did I weep, though my eyes were lakes of salt. I just stood there as a gaping hollowness in my center threatened to suck me into its nothingness.

They were all gone. My wife, my daughters. My mother, my sisters. My father too, though he had died naturally years before.

I was the only one left. A single remnant of a loving family. A family of laughter and joy, of kisses and warmth, of friendship and support and loyalty. All gone. All dead. I wanted to scream and rave, to bust something to pieces with my fists. Instead, I kept quiet. I dug my nails into my palms and focused on the stinging pain they brought me, so I would not be drowned by the larger, suffocating pain of my loss.

There was only me now. And I would soon be dead too. And then there would be no trace of my family left. It would be as though none of us had ever existed.

I could not let this happen. I owed it to my parents and sisters, to my wife and daughters. I had to survive, so at least a memory of them would remain.

I let out a low breath and dried my eyes. "How long have you worked in Kanada, Gisella?"

"About six weeks," she said.

"Ever met a Dutch boy named Franz?"

Gisella nodded solemnly. "He's no longer here. He's dead."

"How do you know?"

"From a friend of Franz. A man named Ludwig."

"Why would he tell you about Franz?"

"He didn't," she said. "He told a friend of mine."

31

I stared at Gisella. "What friend?"

"A girl I work with. Her name is Aliz."

I sucked in a breath. "Why would Aliz care what happened to Franz?"

"Because they were sweethearts. Before Franz was taken to work for the *Lagerälteste* of the men's camp."

So Ludwig had lied to me. He'd told me Franz did not have a romantic relationship with any female prisoner. But he'd had such a relationship with Aliz, the pretty girl whom I'd seen Ludwig kiss just yesterday. The girl Ludwig was clearly in love with. Which gave Ludwig a powerful motive to murder Franz, a motive he'd lied to hide from me.

"What is it, Adam?" Gisella asked. "Why are you interested in Franz?"

"Because Franz was murdered by another prisoner," I said. "I'm trying to find out who did it."

Gisella covered her mouth. "No."

"You know what I did before the war, don't you?"

"Yes, you were a—"

"Don't say it. Not to anyone. It will cause me great trouble if anyone knew, understand?"

She nodded. "Yes, I understand."

"Now what I need you to do is bring Aliz to me. Tell her what I'm doing and that I need to talk to her, but do it so no one else hears. Can you do that for me, Gisella?"

She said that she could and told me to wait there. I did, my brain humming with fragmentary thoughts that now locked together like puzzle pieces, forming a picture.

Ludwig. That wily, treasonous, lying bastard. He had killed Franz. And his motive was as old as the world: a woman.

Or in this case, a girl. A girl who was now walking hesitantly toward me, checking behind her that no one was following. A girl who now stood before me, obviously agitated, her breathing quick, fingers laced before her.

Gisella was at her side. "This is Adam, Aliz. I've known him for years. You can trust him."

Aliz's green eyes glittered wetly, like a pond canopied by foliage. This close, she looked even prettier than yesterday. I could well understand Ludwig's infatuation.

"Gisella told me Franz was murdered," she said in Hungarian. Her voice was soft and quivering. "Is this true?"

"Yes. I'm sorry. I understand you and he were close."

She smiled a sad smile. "We loved each other. I still do. I—" she paused to collect herself. "He gave me hope for the future. Even though we were both young, we knew we wanted to be together forever."

I could tell that she meant it, and that she believed Franz had meant it too. I doubted neither of them.

"I'm trying to find out who killed Franz. I promise you he'll pay dearly for what he did."

"Why? Why do you care about Franz? Did you know him?"

"No," I said, and hesitated before telling her the truth. "The *Lagerälteste* ordered me to discover who murdered Franz."

Her eyes flashed, and her full mouth tightened. "You're working for that man?"

"I don't have much choice in the matter. If I fail, I'll be the one to pay dearly."

Aliz nodded understanding, but her fury did not abate, merely redirected its focus. "That man took Franz away from me. He's an animal. A cruel beast. Do you know what he did to Franz?"

"Yes," I said softly. "I do."

"It's worse than death, that's what I think. It's better that Franz is dead. At least he no longer has to endure that."

She broke into quiet sobs, and Gisella rubbed her back. I could feel Aliz's pain, but I also knew that we didn't have much time. Lunch break would soon be over, and who knew if I'd get the chance to speak to Aliz again.

"I know this is difficult, Aliz, but I need to ask you some questions. Can you answer some for me?"

She nodded, wiped her cheeks, and looked steadily at me. She was a strong girl. Tough to begin with, probably, and made tougher by her time in Auschwitz. Franz had likely been the same. I imagined the love they'd shared was beautiful.

"How did the *Lagerälteste* know about Franz to begin with?" I asked.

"It happened three weeks ago. He just showed up here in Kanada. A horrifying, beastly man. He stomped around like he owned everything he saw. Franz was in one of the warehouses, and the *Lagerälteste* walked straight there. It was the only warehouse he went into. He was there a few minutes and then he came out again. The smile on his face... it made my skin crawl."

Aliz shut her eyes and took a deep breath before continuing.

"Once the *Lagerälteste* had gone, Franz came to see me. I'd never seen him so pale, so grim, so scared. He told me about the *Lagerälteste*, what he did to his boys. He said that in the men's camp, he always made sure to hide whenever the *Lagerälteste* or one of his underlings was around, and that Ludwig was the one who dealt with them and gave them food and alcohol from the luggage. Franz was terrified because of how the *Lagerälteste* had looked at him. How he'd leered at him. The next day Franz was gone. He never came back to Kanada. The *Lagerälteste* had taken him."

To a fate worse than death, I thought. Aliz was right about that. I said, "What did the *Lagerälteste* do after he exited the warehouse where Franz was?"

"He left. Walked straight out. And he was laughing. He had the most horrible laugh."

"How often does he come to Kanada?"

"I'd never seen him before, and not since. I was told he hadn't been here for months before that day."

Which led me to one conclusion: The *Lagerälteste* had come to Kanada to see Franz. He knew where he would be, at which warehouse. Someone had told him. Someone who could get Franz into that warehouse and keep him there until the *Lagerälteste* arrived.

The *Lagerälteste* could have seen Franz in the men's camp, of course. Could have been led to him there. But someone wanted it to be done in Kanada. I had a pretty good idea who it was, and why he had done so.

"Aliz, was Ludwig in the warehouse with Franz when the *Lagerälteste* arrived?"

"Yes," she said. "Why?"

"I saw you two together yesterday. You and Ludwig. You seemed pretty intimate."

Her face reddened. "That means nothing to me. Nothing. I love Franz. Only Franz."

"I don't doubt it. Seeing you and Ludwig, it was clear to me he feels more for you than you do for him."

"It's not easy living here," she said. "Surviving. I have two sisters who work in other *kommandos*. Ludwig gives me food, which I take to them. I do what I must. For them. Do you understand?"

I nodded. "You have nothing to be ashamed of, Aliz. Nothing at all. I just need to know how soon after Franz was gone your relationship with Ludwig began."

Her beautiful eyes were large circles now. Perhaps she was beginning to suspect what I was almost certain of. "Very soon," she said in a quiet voice. "Two days at most. Ludwig made his feelings known to me and said he would take care of me, that he'd bring me food I could take to my sisters. All I needed to do was give him what he wanted."

Gisella looked horrified. She too had understood. "Adam, you don't think that Ludwig—"

"I'm not sure of anything right now," I said, though of course I was. Right then, I wanted to hear what Aliz had to say.

"Franz wanted no contact with me," Aliz said in a voice that was dreamy and disbelieving. One hand was pressed to her throat. Confusion and horror stormed in her eyes. "Ludwig saw Franz in the men's camp and told me that was what Franz had said. That I should forget about him. That he and I were finished." Her mouth tightened. "That bastard."

"Listen to me, Aliz," I said. "You mustn't say anything to Ludwig. Nothing about me, and nothing about what we've just talked about. You need to act as though nothing has changed. It's important. Can you do that, Aliz?"

She nodded. "Oh yes. I've been acting with him for a while now. I can do it for a little longer. But only for a little."

"That's all you need to do," I said. "Just until the end of the day. Then it will be over. I'll see to that."

32

The afternoon dragged on. Another train arrived, and more innocent people entered the crematoriums and left as smoke and
ashes. There was no wind, and the smoke lingered in the sky
above Kanada like a bad omen. The air smelled charred and
malignant.

At one point, I saw Ludwig slip into a warehouse only to
emerge from it shortly after, followed by Aliz. Another tryst
among the loot. Another grope and unwanted kiss, and hopefully
nothing more. I prayed Aliz would have the strength to act her
part.

I did not find any medicine, but a quick sifting through a suitcase yielded a box of hard sweets, each wrapped in flimsy paper
and smelling like a tiny piece of paradise. The taste of sugar was so
sharp, my breath caught in my throat. My tongue had forgotten
the taste and was shocked by it.

Stefan grinned. "Like something you've never tasted before,
huh?"

"Yeah," I said. "It's been a long time."

Again, I kept half of the sweets for Vilmos, stashing them in the tip of my clogs. But this time, my precaution proved unnecessary, for I was let out of Kanada without being searched.

I kept my eyes on Ludwig as we walked the short distance back to the men's camp. There was a spring in his step, and why wouldn't there be? He was a man in possession of the woman he loved. Had he fooled himself completely? Come to believe that she truly loved him back? Or did he hope she would grow to love him, now that Franz was out of the picture? Either way, it was clear Aliz had kept up the pretense. Ludwig had no idea that she knew what he'd done. Or that I knew it, too.

When the *Kapo* wasn't looking, I sidled up to Ludwig and murmured in his ear, "I know, Ludwig."

His eyebrows knotted. "Know what?"

"Everything. I know about Aliz. And about Franz."

His face lost its color, and he nearly tripped over his own feet. I grabbed his forearm and steadied him.

"Meet me after dinner at the ditch behind the latrines," I said. "You know the place. It's where Franz died. And don't keep me waiting, understand?"

He gulped and nodded. I let go of his arm and nudged him ahead of me. He turned once to look at me, fear etched all over his face.

This should have been a moment of triumph, of surpassing relief, but instead I was gnawed on the inside by worry. Was Vilmos still alive?

My heart was pounding as we entered the camp. I hurried to the meeting place, and only realized how certain I'd been that Vilmos was dead when my pent-up breath escaped my lungs upon seeing him.

He was sitting on the ground, head buried in his hands. A picture of exhaustion. Yet before I could call out his name, he raised his eyes and stood. His face was dripping with perspiration, but he was smiling. At my frown, he grabbed my hand and pressed it to his forehead. It was damp and cool. The fever had broken.

"How?" was all I could say.

"I told you there is always hope, Adam. Never forget that."

As we did yesterday, we found a secluded spot, and there I gave him the sweets I had smuggled for him. He put one in his mouth and, leaning his head against the side of a block, closed his eyes and let the candy melt on his tongue. He looked utterly serene, as though the sweet had transported him to another place.

"Kanada is truly a place of wonders," he said after he opened his eyes.

"And of horrors," I replied, remembering the people I'd seen being herded into the crematorium.

Vilmos understood what I was referring to. "Yes. Of horrors too. But tell me, what about the case? Have you made any progress?"

"I've solved it, Vilmos."

His face lit up. "Good job. Who did it?"

I was about to answer when the gong for roll call sounded.

"Will you be okay on your own after roll call?" I asked, as we hurried to the *Appellplatz*. "I have some business to attend to."

"I won't be on my own," Vilmos said. "I'm to meet Zoltan."·

"Good. But don't come to the ditch behind the latrines."

He frowned at me, but didn't ask for a reason.

After roll call, we stood in line for dinner. Vilmos wanted to know the identity of the killer, but we were surrounded by prisoners and couldn't speak.

When I got my bread, I pushed the entire portion into Vilmos's hand. I couldn't eat. My stomach was seething with excitement and anger.

"Adam, what—" Vilmos began.

"I'll explain everything later," I said, and hastened away before he could ask any more questions.

After a single stop, I walked over to the ditch where a fifteen-year-old boy had been stabbed in the throat. There, standing on the lip of the ditch and kneading his hands, was Ludwig.

He stopped fiddling when he saw me, drew his hands apart, and rubbed them dry on his trousers. He pulled back his shoulders and tilted his chin up, but he couldn't hide his nervousness. He crackled with it. When I stopped before him, I could see his forehead and upper lip were damp. The odor of sour, anxious sweat wafted off him, easy to pick out even over the stench of the nearby latrines.

"Listen," he said. "Don't tell Aliz, okay? I'll make it worth your while. Here." His hand dipped into one of his pockets and came out holding a half pack of chocolate, which he held out to me. I wanted it, so I took it. It was as simple as that. "And I'll get you your medicine. I promise."

That was a lie. I could tell by the way his eyes went on a trip before returning to mine. He would string me along until he found a way to get rid of me, just as he'd gotten rid of Franz. There was no moral boundary he wouldn't cross to have Aliz.

"There's something else I want," I said.

"Anything. You name it, I'll get it for you."

"I want you to tell me exactly what happened."

"I thought you already knew."

"I want to hear you say it. I want to understand."

He sucked his lower lip into his mouth and rolled it between his teeth. His hand went to his cheek, and he rubbed it like he was trying to remove a stain that wouldn't come off.

"I saw her first," he began at last. "Aliz. The day she came to work in Kanada, I saw her and knew immediately that she and I belonged together. I'd never felt anything like that. Never. She was mine."

"But she fell in love with Franz instead of you."

His mouth twisted. The thought of Aliz with Franz, with anyone but himself, cut deep.

"The bastard knew how much I wanted her, and he didn't care. He still went for her, and she fell for his charms." He gritted his teeth. "I saw her first."

"Couldn't you let it go? Be happy for them?"

"No. But I made Franz believe that I was. I pretended to be okay with it."

"And at the same time, you decided to get rid of him."

He nodded.

"Why not just kill him and be done with it?"

"Because I'd never killed anyone in my life. And because what he'd done to me was the ultimate betrayal. Death was too good for him. So I decided to make his biggest fear come true."

"The *Lagerälteste*," I said.

"Yes, the *Lagerälteste*. We'd heard warnings about his affinity for pretty teenage boys. Franz was terrified. He became quite adept at hiding his face whenever the *Lagerälteste* or one of his underlings was around. And he never bribed them with any of the stuff we found in Kanada. I took care of all that."

"Why did you have the *Lagerälteste* come to Kanada to see Franz? Why not arrange for it here in camp?"

"I wanted her to see him."

"Aliz?"

"Yes. I wanted her to see the *Lagerälteste*, how big and frightening he was. I wanted her to know that Franz was gone forever. I wanted her to harbor absolutely no hope that he would ever return. I wanted her to need comforting, consoling, and I planned on giving it to her."

Sour bile rose in my throat. It hurt when I swallowed it down. What Ludwig had done was completely unnecessary. He had hurt Aliz for no reason. Which made me think that he had wanted to hurt her; to punish her for loving someone else. This wasn't love that he felt for her, but a perverted possessiveness, akin to that felt by the *Lagerälteste* toward Franz.

"You should have seen Franz," Ludwig said, a small sinister smile playing on his lips, "how he turned white the second the *Lagerälteste* entered that warehouse. I thought he might faint. I don't blame him. The *Lagerälteste* looked at him like he wanted to devour him whole. I admit that I felt a twinge of remorse at that moment. But it passed when I remembered that Franz had stolen Aliz from me."

"He didn't steal her. They fell in love."

"He bewitched her with his good looks. So I made sure he paid for those good looks." Ludwig's eyes blazed. "I saw her first. He should have respected that."

I drew in a breath, conscious of time running out and still needing to know everything.

"Was it true what you told me, about Franz not wanting to see you?"

"Yes. I don't know why he said it. I was disappointed. I enjoyed visiting him every day and seeing him suffer."

"Did he ask you to pass on any messages to Aliz?"

"I thought he might, and of course I wouldn't have done it, but the only thing he wanted me to tell her was that she should forget him. I was astonished, and delighted. It meant I didn't have to lie to her."

You lied to her every day, I thought, when you pretended to still be Franz's friend. But of course, Franz and Aliz weren't the only victims here.

"Did you know what would happen to Bruno, Franz's predecessor? That he would be killed to make room for Franz?"

At first Ludwig didn't answer. Then he gave a quick, almost furtive nod. He had persuaded himself that Franz had been deserving of his fate, but he couldn't do the same in Bruno's case. Bruno had simply been in the way, so he'd had to die.

"So that's it," Ludwig said. "Now you know everything. So just keep your mouth shut, and I'll make it worth your while."

"That's not everything," I said. "You still haven't told me why you killed him."

Ludwig frowned. "What on earth are you talking about?"

"How did you get Franz to meet you here? Why did you take the murder weapon with you?"

"You think I killed Franz? Whatever gave you that stupid idea?"

"Did you kill him because you realized Aliz still loved him? And would always love him as long as he lived?"

"She loves me."

"No, she doesn't. She just tells you she does so you'll bring her food. She loves Franz."

"You're lying."

"Not only does she not love you, Ludwig, she hates you. Want to know why? Because she knows what you did to Franz. I told her."

For two seconds, Ludwig stood utterly frozen. Then his face contorted and he let out a bellow. His hand went into his other pocket, and I caught a glint of steel in his grip. Then he charged me. Still roaring, he whipped the short blade at my face, but he clearly didn't know what he was doing, and I easily sidestepped his attack and buried my fist in his kidney.

My muscles had dwindled in the camp, but my fury lent me strength. Ludwig cried out as the punch connected, and the knife dropped from his grasp. He fell to his knees, one hand clasped to his side. He looked at me with unalloyed hatred. But then his expression turned to dread.

"I thought I made it clear that he was mine," came the menacing voice from behind.

"I had no choice," I said, turning to the *Lagerälteste*. "He came at me with a knife."

The *Lagerälteste* wasn't alone. Mathias and Otto were also present. They stood a little behind their boss.

"A knife, eh? That thing? Is that what he used to kill Franz?"

It was a switchblade with a brown handle and a blade about as long as my forefinger.

"I didn't kill Franz," Ludwig said. "I swear it."

The *Lagerälteste* sneered. "You hear that, fellas? He swears it."

He took a step toward Ludwig, who scrambled back on his ass.

"I didn't," Ludwig whined. "I had no reason to." He was crying now, fat tears pumping out of his eyes.

But the *Lagerälteste* wasn't listening. I had stopped by his block before coming to meet Ludwig and told him that Ludwig was the killer. The *Lagerälteste* didn't doubt it for one second. After all, he knew how much Ludwig had hated Franz. Enough to bring him to the *Lagerälteste's* attention. More than enough to kill him.

And there was another reason he believed me. Because I'd shown him that I would not let an innocent man die to save my own skin.

Ludwig was still protesting when the *Lagerälteste* kicked him in the face. The crunch of bone gave me shivers. Ludwig fell back with a groan, rolling over the lip of the ditch and down its slope to the spot where Franz had died. The *Lagerälteste* followed him down. Otto moved closer for a better view. I stayed where I was, and so did Mathias. The heavy thuds of punches and kicks, coupled with the *Lagerälteste's* grunts and curses, floated up to us from the ditch. At first, there were also Ludwig's screams, but these died down very quickly.

A number of prisoners started to come over to see what the raucous was about, but quickly scattered when they saw Mathias.

I wished I could shut my ears, block out all sound, but I didn't. When you bring about the death of a man, you shouldn't shy away.

Finally, the *Lagerälteste* climbed back out of the ditch. He was breathing hard, and his face was drenched with sweat and spattered with blood. Red streaks covered his boots, matching the blood smeared on his hands.

He looked like a wild animal directly after a feed, vicious and untamed and gruesomely sated.

Flashing me a grin, he said, "You did well. I knew you could do it."

"Are we good?" I said.

He wiped at a red spot on his chin, but that only served to transfer more blood onto it from his hand. "You mean, will I let you live?" He paused, drawing the moment for effect. "Yeah, sure. You did your part. You earned it. I might even consider letting you stay in the Kanada Kommando, if you beg me to."

I shook my head. "Thank you, but I'd rather return to my old one."

He looked both surprised and disappointed, and I realized that he had been playing with me, that he'd wanted me to ask him only to refuse me. "Why the hell would you want that?"

What was the point of explaining it to him? How could a man like that understand what being in Kanada was like? Surrounded by the possessions of the dead, hearing the cries of the victims as they were led to the gas chambers, and breathing air so foul with the stench of burning flesh that your mind felt as though it would tear itself asunder if you remained there a minute longer? There was food in Kanada, but in many ways working there was worse than digging trenches under the blazing sun.

"It's simply what I prefer," I said.

He huffed and shrugged and grunted. "Have it your way, Jew." To Otto and Mathias, he said, "Let's go."

The *Lagerälteste* and Otto started off, but Mathias said, "I'll come over in a couple of minutes. I'll get some prisoners to clear the body."

"Fine, fine," the *Lagerälteste* said without turning around. Then he clapped Otto on the back. "Make sure they have strong stomachs. Ludwig's not a pretty sight." He and Otto laughed. Mathias and I waited quietly until they had disappeared from view.

"Congratulations, Adam," Mathias said.

"Thanks."

"You don't look happy."

I wasn't. The only thing I felt, apart from relieved that I had kept Vilmos and myself alive, was an insistent sense of wrongness, of something that did not quite fit.

I bent down and picked up the knife Ludwig had wielded. I turned it over in my hands, while turning other things over in my mind, and that sense of misalignment only grew. I looked toward the ditch where Ludwig lay dead, then at the smoke rising from the crematoriums, then at the knife again.

And I knew, though I wished I could pretend that I didn't, that I had made a mistake.

33

Vilmos was waiting for me outside the block. We started walking, and I told him what I'd learned about Ludwig and how the *Lagerälteste* had killed him. The sky was darkening now. Soon it would be curfew and we would be confined to our block for the night. Within me, rivaling emotions battled. On the one hand, I was overjoyed that Vilmos and I would live. On the other, I could not shake off my certainty that I had been wrong.

"I don't think Ludwig killed Franz," I said.

"Why not? He certainly had motive."

"Did he?"

In a nearby watchtower, an SS guard was peering down at us. We turned and walked away. One could never know when one of them would get itchy fingers and start shooting.

"The girl," Vilmos said. "He wanted the girl, and he decided it would be best if Franz was gone."

"Franz was already gone. He couldn't go to Kanada anymore, couldn't see Aliz, and there was no hope that would change. Ludwig had her all to himself."

"You said so yourself—Ludwig came to the conclusion that the only way Aliz would let go of Franz completely was if he was dead."

I shook my head. "Ludwig had managed to persuade himself that Aliz loved him. And there are other things that make me believe he wasn't the killer."

"Such as?"

"When I asked Ludwig why he didn't simply kill Franz in the first place, he said he'd never killed anyone in his life. I think he was telling the truth."

"But he was talking about the time before he sacrificed Franz to the *Lagerälteste*."

"That's a possible interpretation, but I think he was speaking generally."

"That's not very persuasive, Adam," Vilmos said gently.

"True. But that's not the main reason I think he wasn't the killer."

"So what is?"

I paused, kneading the back of my neck. "Franz was killed by a single stab wound to the throat. That's not an easy way to kill a man. A killer might get lucky, of course, but usually such a killing requires proficiency with knives."

"And?"

"And Ludwig wasn't proficient. Not even close. He held the knife wrong, and he'd telegraphed his move so early, I could have smoked a cigarette and still evaded him. I'd wager that he'd never used a knife on a human being before attacking me."

We resumed walking, while Vilmos contemplated this.

Eventually, he said, "If not Ludwig, then who?"

"I don't know. The redheaded man, perhaps."

Again I wondered how I might find him among the thousands

of prisoners in the men's camp, and whether he had been transported to another camp—if he was even still alive, that is.

"I hope you don't feel guilty about Ludwig," Vilmos said.

"I don't. Ludwig got what was coming to him. What he did to Franz was unpardonable. But that leaves the question of who murdered Franz."

"You still want to find the man who did it?"

"I do. Even though one death shouldn't mean much in this horrible place. I'm already invested, you see. I want to see this through. I feel like I owe it to Franz."

We walked a few dozen paces in silence before Vilmos said, "There's a good chance, Adam, that you'll never discover who killed him."

I gave a wry smile. "There's always hope, Vilmos. You taught me that."

34

The next day was Sunday, and officially it was a day of rest. But actually, it was just another day of torment.

Right after breakfast, a bunch of us were ordered to the *Appellplatz*, where we were subjected to a vicious session of *hinlegen*, a particularly cruel type of exercise devised by the warped minds of the SS. *Hinlegen* required us to fall to the ground, stand up, jump high in the air, and fall to the ground again. This was done over and over until the SS guards tired of it. Those prisoners who broke down in the course of this torture were dragged aside and lashed with whips or beaten with truncheons. A couple were shot.

A number of times I thought I was going to faint, that my muscles would tear, my lungs would burst, or my heart would explode in my chest. Small cuts opened on my palms and fingers as I dropped down again and again on the dry earth. It would have been so easy to give up, to just lie there, but I forced myself to continue. Against all odds, I had survived the passing week. I would not die today.

It was a wonder that Vilmos, weak as he was, did not collapse. My friend had incredible strength.

Once that was over, we were marched to the shower rooms, where cold water pelted our bodies for a minute before we had to put on our stinking uniforms and go out to dry in the sun. In summer, this was but a minor discomfort in the grand scheme of things. In winter, one could easily catch pneumonia and die. Winter was like a catastrophe rolling inexorably toward us. Whenever I thought of it, my heart would lurch and my intestines convulse.

As we were coming out of the shower block, Vilmos and I heard a commotion. A knot of prisoners had gathered not too far from the fence. We made our way over there and encountered a familiar, grisly sight.

A prisoner had leaped at the fence and been electrocuted to death. He lay with the fingers of one hand still clutching the deadly metal links.

"Dammit," I said, fury humming through my veins.

"It's right where Gyuri did it," Vilmos mumbled.

I realized he was right. And also that we were standing just about where I'd nearly run into a passing prisoner as I was chasing Gyuri to stop him from killing himself. And as I recalled this, an image of that prisoner bubbled up from some hidden corner of my memory and flashed before my eyes.

He had reddish stubble on his face, a tall forehead, and a prominent pear-shaped nose. No wonder he'd sounded familiar when Stefan had described him to me.

My heart rate jumped. I gazed around me, eyes darting from face to face, sure I would see the redheaded man right there. But he was nowhere to be seen.

"What is it, Adam?" Vilmos asked.

I told him, and his mouth dropped open. Then he asked me to

give him a minute and closed his eyes and stood stock still for what seemed like an hour. Just when I was about to ask him what the hell he was doing, he opened his eyes and pointed toward the nearest block.

"That's where he came from."

"The redheaded man?"

Vilmos nodded. "I was running behind you, remember? I saw you and him nearly collide. I wasn't focused on him at all at the time, but now that I'm running that moment through my head, I remember seeing him exiting that block and walking in that direction."

"Are you sure about this, Vilmos?"

"Just as I'm sure where all the pawns, rooks, knights, and bishops stand on a chess board."

Which was all the convincing I needed. If Vilmos remembered it, that's how it was.

"Let's go," I said.

The block was identical to our own. It even smelled the same —unwashed skin, blood, urine, sickness, and filth. Dust motes floated thickly in the heavy air. Vilmos and I treaded slowly down the center of the block, searching for the redheaded man with the large nose.

Some of the prisoners were busy doing various chores— checking their bedding for lice, tidying the block, mending their clothes. Others were talking in hushed voices. And then there were those, the weaker ones, who did nothing but lie listlessly in their bunks, their huge eyes blinking the seconds away.

We were more than halfway down the block when we saw him. He was sitting on the heating duct, clipping his nails with the only tool he had in his possession—his teeth. He was just as Stefan had described him: a man of average height, with red stubble on the back of his head and face. And in the middle of that face, like a mountain rising up from a plain, was a nose that was narrow at the bridge and very wide at the nostrils. And flanking it, a pair of slate gray eyes that were assessing us warily.

"What are you guys looking at?" he asked.

"We want to talk to you for a few minutes," I said. "Outside."

"Talk to me about what?"

"Franz."

The gray eyes flared for a second. "I don't know anybody by that name."

"Yes, you do. You can either talk to us about him or the *Lagerälteste*."

His jaw tightened, more in hate than in fear, which surprised me. "You work for him?" The way he said *him* was like he was spitting the word out.

"No, but I know for a fact that he would be interested in you. It would be better if you talked to us instead."

The way he looked at us, I could tell he wanted nothing more than to knock our teeth in. But the threat of the *Lagerälteste* was a powerful incentive for cooperation. The redheaded man stood up and said, "Fine. Let's go."

We followed him out and found a secluded spot.

"What's your name?" I asked him after Vilmos and I introduced ourselves.

"Konrad," he said. He had a clear German accent and a voice made scratchy by cigarettes. "What do you want?"

"Like I said, we want to talk about Franz."

"What about him?"

"Do you know he's dead?"

"I heard about it."

"Do you know he was murdered?"

"I took it as a given that he was."

"Why would you think that?" Vilmos asked, sounding as surprised by the answer as I was.

"That's what he does, isn't it? That's how all his boys end up."

Vilmos and I exchanged a look. The conversation had taken an unexpected turn.

"You're talking about the *Lagerälteste*?" I said.

Konrad's face turned even more hostile. "Who else?"

"The *Lagerälteste* didn't kill Franz. Someone else did. Someone stuck a knife in Franz's throat."

Konrad's eyebrows notched upward. "You're serious? Someone stabbed him?"

"That's right. And we want to know who it was."

He looked from me to Vilmos and back again. "You're doing this for the *Lagerälteste*?"

"We're doing it for Franz," I said, which was the truth. Because as far as the *Lagerälteste* was concerned, the killer had already been punished. "The *Lagerälteste* doesn't know about you."

"You think I stabbed Franz? You couldn't be more wrong."

"We have a witness who saw you threaten Franz about two weeks ago. What was that about?"

Konrad took a long breath and let out an equally long sigh. "I wanted to hurt him. That's the truth."

"Why?" Vilmos asked.

"Because I blamed him for my nephew's death. Which was stupid of me, but I was crazy with grief and rage. And I didn't know Franz then."

"Your nephew?" I said.

"His name was Bruno. My sister's son. He was—"

"The *Lagerälteste's* servant before Franz," I completed in a murmur.

Konrad looked at me. "You knew Bruno?"

"No, but I heard about him. I know what the *Lagerälteste* did to him."

"He murdered him. He was just a boy."

"And you blamed Franz for this?"

"The *Lagerälteste* killed Bruno to make room for Franz. That's the way he does it with his boys. He kills one before moving on to the next. I was devastated when Bruno died. He was the only family I had left. The rest... well, you can imagine what happened to them. I wanted to kill the *Lagerälteste*, but I didn't dare. Because I knew I'd likely fail, and I would be dead even if I succeeded. Do you understand?"

He sounded ashamed of himself, as though it were cowardice to wish to survive.

"Yes, we do," Vilmos said. "We all feel this way."

"So what happened two weeks ago when you talked to Franz?" I asked.

"I saw him walk by, and I snapped. I wanted to hurt him, maybe even kill him, but all I ended up doing was cursing him a little. Once I had vented some of my anger, I could see he was a victim too, just like Bruno. An innocent boy being put through hell. So I just walked away, thinking I was a dead man."

"Why would you think that?"

"I was sure Franz would tell the *Lagerälteste* about me and the way I'd talked to him. I figured I'd soon get a visit from his goons, maybe the son of a bitch himself. I thought of killing myself beforehand, figuring it would be an easier death, but I couldn't bring myself to do it. Which was lucky, because Franz never breathed a word about me to the *Lagerälteste*. Not only that, but he came to see me two days later to tell me I had nothing to worry about. To say how sorry he was about Bruno. We talked for a while. He told me about himself, and I told him about Bruno. And the day after that, he brought me some bread."

A surge of excitement sizzled over my skin. "Why did he do that?"

"I told him how Bruno used to bring me bread, so Franz said he would do the same. In Bruno's memory. Franz was a terrific boy. Every couple of days he would bring me a piece. You can imagine how much it helped. It was terrible what the *Lagerälteste* did to him, what he did to Bruno and all the boys who came before."

"Yes, it was," I said. "I'm sorry about your nephew."

"Bruno was a great kid. A beautiful kid. It would have been better for him if he'd been ugly. The way the *Lagerälteste* treated him, the things he made him do, it would have been better for Bruno if he'd died. But he couldn't die, which was my fault."

"How so?" Vilmos asked.

Konrad's jaw tightened. He was angry. Angry at himself. "Because as long as I lived, Bruno couldn't kill himself, which I could tell he wanted to do. The *Lagerälteste* had made it clear that if Bruno took his own life, I would be killed in the most horrible fashion. Apparently, one of the previous boys had done just that— escaped the *Lagerälteste* the only way possible, by committing suicide. So after that, the *Lagerälteste* made sure his boys knew that if they dared kill themselves, their families and friends would pay dearly."

Which reminded me of what the *Lagerälteste* had told me after I had persuaded him to spare Pista, the innocent prisoner with the bloody shirt. The *Lagerälteste* had said that if I failed to find the real killer, he would brutally kill both Vilmos and me, and if either of us committed suicide beforehand, he would kill ten other prisoners in our place.

He must have made a similar threat to Franz. But who had he threatened to kill? I realized with horror that one of the people had to be Ludwig, the same man who had betrayed Franz. Only Franz hadn't known that. He'd believed Ludwig was his closest friend. The *Lagerälteste* must have gotten a real kick out of playing this cruel trick on Franz.

This was why Franz had told Ludwig to never talk to him again. And also why he'd sent a message to Aliz that she should forget about him. He had been trying to distance himself from them, to protect them.

I realized two other things, too. The first was that when Otto had told me that the *Lagerälteste* had not killed all his boys, he had been thinking about the boy who had killed himself, not about Franz. The second was the answer to one of the questions that had been bothering me.

"You and Franz were supposed to meet the day he died, weren't you?" I asked.

Konrad nodded. "He was supposed to bring me some bread, but I was ordered to go fix a broken wall in the quarantine camp. I'm a carpenter, you see. I missed our meeting, and only got back here at dinnertime. I looked for Franz, but I couldn't find him. I figured he'd come see me the next day, but then I heard he was dead."

"You said he would bring you a single piece of bread. Was that always the case?"

"Yeah. He apologized a few times about it—said he was scared to bring more because someone might notice it gone. Like I said, he was a terrific boy. A brave boy."

My mind was racing, assumptions crumbling one by one like buildings in an aerial bombardment. It was disorienting, like being flipped over and having to look at the world upside down. My heart was skittering. I had to slow it down just to be able to begin examining the facts from a new angle.

"Are you all right, Adam?" Vilmos asked.

I nodded slowly. "I think so. I think it all finally makes sense."

35

We bade Konrad goodbye. He shook our hands and wished us all the best, and then Vilmos and I were alone again.

Vilmos said, "You know what happened, don't you? You know who killed Franz?"

"Yes. I think I do."

"You're not sure?"

"I'm almost sure. It's just nothing like what I'd expected."

"So who is it? Who's the murderer?"

I told him. I explained my reasoning. At first Vilmos was skeptical, but gradually he became as convinced as I was.

"But why would he do that?" Vilmos asked.

I thought I knew the answer, but I could not be entirely certain.

"What's important, Vilmos, is that you stay out of it. I'm going to do this alone."

"Do what?"

"Talk to him."

"What good would that do? It would only put you in danger. He might kill you, Adam."

"Perhaps. Which is why I want you as far away as possible. But I need to know for sure. It's foolish, I realize that, but I can't help it. I have to see this through."

"I still say you're making a mistake. A possibly fatal mistake."

I smiled. "I can only hope that's not the case. And we always have hope, don't we?"

Vilmos shook his head. "You're a stubborn mule, you know that? You be careful, understand?"

"I will. I'll see you later at the block." Then I walked away, alone in my mad, perilous quest.

I found him outside his block, smoking a cigarette. Upon seeing me, he blew out a ring of smoke and said, "Want one, Adam?"

I hadn't had a cigarette in a long while, and the old craving lit up like a torch. He ignited my cigarette with his, and I suggested we stroll off together. Which we did, walking side by side and smoking like old friends.

After a minute, I asked him, "Was your family rich?"

He frowned at the question. "Dead poor. Why?"

"I was just wondering if you killed your mother and stepfather for the inheritance, or if there'd been another reason."

He stopped and stared at me in shock, his cigarette suspended between two fingers en route to his mouth.

"Who told you about my mother?" Mathias asked.

"Otto. I don't think he likes you all that much."

Mathias swore. "He has a big mouth, that one."

"He's also crazy. And violent."

"Yes, he is. But why do you care about my mother?"

"I was just curious why you didn't tell me about her."

He shrugged and took another drag. "I don't like talking about her, that's all."

"Was that really the only reason? Or were you worried I might figure out something about your past? Something you wish to keep secret?"

His eyes narrowed to slits, and for the first time, I saw the killer in him. Not the crude, brutal animal the *Lagerälteste* was, but a sleek, crafty, elegant predator. Vilmos was right. I must have been mad to confront Mathias. But now it was too late to back out.

"What are you getting at, Adam?" he said, his voice like the whisper of a blade as it slides out of its sheath.

"I know what happened, Mathias. I know who killed Franz."

Mathias took a final pull on his cigarette, dropped the remnant on the ground, and crushed it with his shoe. "Ludwig killed Franz. That's what you said, wasn't it?"

I had been too nervous to smoke since I'd asked Mathias about his mother, and my cigarette had burned nearly all the way to my fingers. I flicked it away. "That's what I thought yesterday, but I was wrong. I know the truth now."

"Are you sure about this, Adam? Because in that case, the *Lagerälteste* might decide to kill you after all."

"Only if you tell him, Mathias, and I don't think you will. Because then he might decide to kill you."

Mathias looked ready to tear my throat out. There was fire in his eyes, and his scar had turned purple. "Are you threatening me, Adam?"

"Not at all. I just want to know the truth. All of it."

"You better not be thinking of telling lies about me. I have an ironclad alibi, remember? I couldn't kill Franz."

"I don't think you did. But you were involved."

"Involved? You think this was some kind of conspiracy?"

"That's exactly what it was."

"Let me guess—you think I hatched some plot with Rolf? That he lied about my alibi, is that it?"

"No. It wasn't with Rolf."

"With whom, then?"

I told him.

Mathias laughed. "Have you lost your goddamn mind?"

"I don't believe I have." And I told him who had killed Franz.

Mathias laughed again, but this time his laughter was brittle and unconvincing. For the first time, I saw the glint of fear in his eyes. "You have gone crazy."

I shook my head. "It's the only thing that makes sense."

"Why can't it be Ludwig, like you thought yesterday?"

"Because Ludwig had no real reason to kill Franz. I see that now. Franz was already out of his way. And Ludwig didn't know the first thing about using a knife. But the biggest clue that Ludwig hadn't done it was that he would never have taken the murder weapon with him. He would have left it by the body."

I paused to draw in a breath and try to slow my galloping heart.

"You see," I went on, "that's the thing that bothered me the most from the start. I couldn't see a reason for the killer to take the murder weapon. You might say that a knife is a valuable thing to have here in Auschwitz, and you'd be right, but there's a problem with that explanation. You don't know this, Mathias, but Franz was carrying two pieces of bread on his person when he died. A prisoner I know who came by the body that night took them. Which was what the killer would have done if he'd been a regular prisoner, the sort who couldn't get a replacement knife easily. But the bread was still there."

Mathias said nothing. His lips were parted and his brow furrowed. I could tell he was making an effort to keep his expression as flat as usual, but he failed to banish a small quiver of anxiety from his face.

"You didn't know about the bread, did you, Mathias? Franz had planned on giving it to a prisoner he knew. Every few days he would bring that prisoner a single piece of bread. Only that day, he was going to give him two. There's only one reason that explains why Franz would do so. He knew that would be the last time he would deliver the bread. Because he knew he was going to die that day."

Mathias's shoulders sagged, and I knew I had called it right.

"But something happened," I said. "The prisoner who was supposed to get the bread couldn't meet Franz, so Franz died with the bread still on him. You didn't know that, so when you took the knife, you left the bread where it was."

Mathias shook his head, but it was a cursory gesture, with no real conviction behind it. "You've got it all wrong. I didn't take any knife. The first time I was at the murder scene was when I found the body the morning after Franz died. I have an alibi, remember? I was with the *Lagerälteste* the entire evening, and before that I was with Rolf."

"You arranged that beautifully," I said. "You spent the afternoon with Rolf inspecting the camp, and later you got the *Lagerälteste* so drunk that he passed out and didn't call Franz to his room. So Rolf and Otto thought Franz was with the *Lagerälteste*, and you had the perfect alibi."

"Which means I couldn't have taken any knife from the murder scene," he said.

"Yes, you could. Because you weren't with Rolf throughout that afternoon. There was a short time you were apart, and I know when it was."

"What are you talking about?"

"Do you remember Pista, the man with the bloody shirt? Rolf

saw him get splattered with blood that afternoon when you and he were supposed to be together. But you didn't see it happen, did you? Otherwise, you would have said something when Rolf told the *Lagerälteste* about it."

Mathias was quiet. He was barely even breathing.

I said, "The shooting that got Pista splattered happened not far from the latrines, just a short distance from the ditch where Franz had died. What happened is that you made some excuse and slipped behind the latrines to get the knife. It would have taken you no more than two or three minutes, and you figured that short interval wouldn't be enough for Rolf to say that you two were ever apart. After all, he had an interest in giving you an alibi, because it meant he had one himself. And you weren't gone long enough to kill Franz. Not without changing your clothes, which were free of blood."

Mathias said nothing. Fresh sweat beaded his forehead.

"It would have worked," I continued, "if not for what happened to Pista. I'm guessing that by the time you came back from the ditch, the prisoner who got shot had already been dragged away, so you didn't know it had happened until Rolf told us about it. Maybe you didn't hear the shot because an incoming train was blowing its whistle. Or maybe a selection was taking place on the train platform and all the shouting and screaming masked the report. Or maybe you did hear it but were too involved in what you were doing to pay it any mind. It's not as though gunfire is all that rare around here. This is all pure conjecture, of course, but if I were to ask Rolf, I'm positive it would evolve into a certainty."

"Even if I had gone to take a leak or something, it doesn't mean I took the murder weapon," Mathias said.

"Someone saw you do it. A *muselmann* called the Mumbler. Do you know who I'm talking about?"

Mathias didn't answer, but I could tell that he did.

"I guess you didn't see him, but he was there, and he saw you. The Mumbler's mind was very muddled, so the story he told me was pretty confused. He said he saw a knight in shining armor with a sword in his hand. A sword he quickly sheathed. That was you, putting the knife away as you were climbing out of the ditch."

"A knight? Why on earth would I be a knight?"

"Partly it was the knife, which the Mumbler remembered as a sword. And partly it's your clothes. You're dressed very well, very elegantly, compared to the rest of us. I think that's why the Mumbler imagined you as a knight in shining armor. He also said the knight had been to war. That's because of your scar, I think. In his befuddled mind, that translated to a war injury."

Mathias shook his head and gave a small chuckle. Some of his confidence had returned. "You're basing your case on what a half-witted *muselmann* said? Are you serious?"

"Completely. Let's cut with the pretense, Mathias. I know you took that knife, and I know why you took it. Because it was the only way to make sure the *Lagerälteste* did not entertain the notion that Franz killed himself."

Mathias swallowed hard. The fearful glint in his eyes was now a full-blown blaze.

I said, "I know that the *Lagerälteste* threatened his boys that if they committed suicide, their loved ones would be killed. Franz wanted to die, but he needed to do it in a way that wouldn't look like a suicide. So you and he devised a plan in which it would look as though Franz had been murdered. It would have worked, too, if a certain prisoner hadn't told you that I'd been a police detective in Hungary. You wouldn't have told the *Lagerälteste* about it if you'd thought he might put me on the case. You assumed he would just kill me."

"Why would I risk my neck for Franz?" Mathias asked, his tone so soft that I knew this was his final gasp of denial.

"Because you were molested as a boy yourself."

He looked as though he'd seen a ghost; perhaps the ghost of the boy he'd once been. "How do you know that?"

"That's why I asked you if you came from a rich family. In my experience, a person only kills his parents for one of two reasons. The first is money. The second is because they abused him during his childhood. I'm guessing that your stepfather forced himself on you, and that your mother did nothing to stop him. You stressed to me that you only killed people who deserved it. A mother who turns a blind eye when her son is raped certainly deserves to be punished."

Tears appeared in Mathias's eyes, as clear and as fragile-looking as crystals. The tears of the boy in the man's eyes.

"Otto told me you had a weak spot for the *Lagerälteste's* boys," I said. "You see yourself in them, don't you?"

Mathias stuck his hand between his teeth and let out a stifled cry. Then he was sobbing and nodding. It took a couple of minutes for him to regain control of himself.

"What do you want, Adam? Medicine? I wish I could get you some, but I can't."

"I don't want anything from you, Mathias. And I'm not going to tell anyone what you did. I just wanted to know the truth."

"Well, you know it. It happened exactly like you said. Franz asked for my help. It was the only way he could escape the *Lagerälteste* without others getting hurt."

"Did you know it was Ludwig who had told the *Lagerälteste* about Franz?"

"Not at the time, no. I only learned about it when you came to tell the *Lagerälteste* that Ludwig was the killer."

"Why do you let him do it to boy after boy after boy? Why don't you kill him?"

"For the same reason you don't," Mathias said, his eyes wild and pleading for understanding. "I want to live, Adam. And without the *Lagerälteste*, I'm a dead man. Other prisoner functionaries don't like me, and they're not scared of me either. But they know I'm protected by the *Lagerälteste*, and they are scared of him. The second he's gone, they'll come for me. I wouldn't last a day."

"So what's going to happen to the next boy?" I asked. "And the one after that? Or are you planning on staging more murders?"

"The war is going very badly for Germany. With luck, the next boy would survive to see this place liberated."

"And until then, he'll suffer as no boy should ever suffer."

"Most prisoners in Auschwitz suffer as no one should ever suffer," Mathias said. "Only the dead don't."

36

Before Mathias parted, I considered asking him another question —whether on the first day of the investigation, he'd deliberately sent me to the train platform instead of the Kanada warehouses, where Franz had worked. It had cost me a precious day.

In the end, I didn't suppose that it mattered one way or the other. The only way Mathias could have saved my life would have been to commit suicide by confessing to the *Lagerälteste*, and I could not expect him to do that. Besides, he'd helped Franz stage his murder and he'd given me my clogs, so he wasn't all bad.

Mathias might have proved to be a valuable source of food and other items, but after the past few days, I decided it was safer to steer clear of the *Lagerälteste* and his men as much as possible.

Alone once again, my thoughts drifted to Franz, the dead boy I had never seen but had grown to know. I now knew why he had seemed scared when Ludwig had last spoken with him. He had been frightened for Ludwig's and Aliz's safety. Perhaps he had already begun contemplating suicide and knew that unless he had a foolproof plan to make it look like murder, their lives would be in jeopardy.

I had solved the case, but I felt very little satisfaction. For I had not provided Franz with the justice he deserved. Ludwig had been punished, yes, but the real culprit was the *Lagerälteste*, and he was invulnerable. Because Mathias had been right: I wanted to live.

It was a few minutes before lunchtime, and I started heading back. Partway to my block, I heard a man calling my name. It was Hendrik, and he had a smug smile on his face.

I stopped, not smiling back. "What do you want, Hendrik?"

"To show you something." He tilted his head to indicate the space behind him, a long and narrow passageway between two blocks, like an alley.

"I'm in no mood for your games," I said. "I'm in no mood for you, period. I thought I'd made that clear."

Hendrik touched his throat, the skin bruised red and blue by my fingers. "You shouldn't have done that. Especially not in front of everyone. Now you're gonna pay."

"I don't want to fight you, Hendrik. If you force me to, you'll regret it."

Hendrik dropped his smile, and a malevolent light entered his eyes. "You're the one who's going to regret things. Come on, take a look and see what I have for you."

He moved backward into the passageway. He was a few meters away from me; too far to be a threat. I didn't come closer, just edged sideways to get a better view. When I did, and saw what Hendrik had arranged for me, my heart dropped.

Vilmos was on his knees halfway down the passageway. Behind him stood Jan, Hendrik's pal, and he was holding something metallic to Vilmos's throat. Marco, Hendrik's other buddy, stood to the side, shifting his weight from one foot to the other and looking kind of pale. He didn't appear to be armed.

"Three against two," Hendrik said. "Like that night, remember? Only I don't think your friend is in any position to help you now."

I turned my gaze to Hendrik, fury radiating off me like heat from a fire. I began moving toward him. "You son of—"

Hendrik raised a hand. "One more step, and Jan will rip your friend's throat wide open."

I stopped, trembling with rage.

"Follow me," Hendrik said. "Slowly and quietly."

He walked backward a few dozen paces, not taking his eyes off me. I followed, matching him step for step. Since most of the prisoners had already gone to queue up for lunch, there weren't a lot of people to witness this. Still, behind me I could sense the movement of a few stragglers. Some must have glanced over and seen that something bad was happening, but no one came to my help. No one would risk his life for me. No one but Vilmos, and he was in no position to offer any assistance.

"That's far enough," Hendrik said, and he drew a shiv from under his shirt. A pointed piece of metal, black and wickedly sharp, similar to what Jan was now pressing to Vilmos's throat. Not as good as a knife, but more than enough to pierce skin and muscle, to tear an artery to shreds. I could only imagine how much bread it had cost Hendrik to procure these weapons. That was why it had taken him this long to initiate his revenge.

"Are you all right, Vilmos?" I asked.

"Yes," he said. "I'm okay."

His mouth was bloody, his cheek was swollen and red, and there were scratch marks on his neck. I was not yet sure how, but I was going to kill Hendrik for this. But first I had to make sure Vilmos was safe.

"Let him go," I told Hendrik. "He has nothing to do with this. This is between you and me."

"I'll let him go," Hendrik answered pleasantly, "if you do exactly as I say."

"Don't do it, Adam," Vilmos called.

"Shut him up, Jan!" Hendrik said, and Jan pressed the tip of his shiv into Vilmos's throat, drawing a thin trickle of blood.

"What do you want?" I asked Hendrik.

"A little payback. No more than you deserve. You humiliated me, and I can't have that, so I'm gonna mark you. With this." He brandished the shiv. "You're going to come over here and drop to your knees when I tell you to. Then I'm going to mark your face, so everyone will know what happens to someone who wrongs me. If you try anything, Jan will kill your friend, and I will kill you. If you behave, you'll walk away with nothing but a few scars for a souvenir."

He was lying. He wasn't going to let me live. The reason he'd set things up this way instead of ambushing me or attacking me at night was that he was scared of me. Twice he and I had come to blows, and twice I had bested him: the first time the night I had defended Gyuri; the second when I grabbed Hendrik by the throat and humiliated him in the block.

When he saw how weak Vilmos was, he realized he didn't need to attack me directly. He could go after Vilmos and use him to force my surrender.

If he let me live, I would seek vengeance. He couldn't risk that. He wouldn't dare let me live. He was going to kill me, and Vilmos, too, probably.

I swore inwardly. I should have seen this coming. I should never have left Vilmos alone. Now, I was going to have to save both our lives. Somehow.

"All right," I said. "But you have to promise to let Vilmos go."

Hendrik grinned. "Oh, I promise. You behave and we won't lay another finger on him."

"Don't, Adam—" Vilmos began, but I raised a hand to shush him.

"It's the only way, Vilmos. It'll be all right. Stay hopeful." I put a little emphasis on the word *hopeful* and gave Vilmos a meaningful look. He couldn't move his head to indicate that he'd understood me, but he blinked a long blink, which I took to mean that he had.

I took a step toward Hendrik. My pulse was beating frantically, and I could feel the blood rushing through my veins.

Another step.

Sweat was dripping down my back. Every sense was heightened. My fingers tingled with anticipation of what would soon happen.

A third step.

Against my belly, I felt the reassuring presence of Ludwig's knife. My secret weapon. I could whip up my shirt and have it ready to slash in less than a second. I hoped I would be fast enough. Hope was all I had right now.

Another step.

Just two meters away from Hendrik. A couple of seconds to go. I rehearsed the movements in my head. Left hand grabbing the hem of my shirt and yanking it up. The right already moving toward the knife. My thumb pressing the button to release the blade. And then the slashing motion at Hendrik's throat.

"Stop right there!" Hendrik's voice cut through my mental preparation.

His head was notched to the left, and he was squinting at me. Dammit. He sensed something was amiss.

"Lift up your shirt," he said, and what little hope I'd been feeling shattered to bits.

There was no point in playing dumb. I obeyed.

"My, my," Hendrik chuckled. "Were you meaning to surprise me?"

I said nothing. An icy feeling of despair swamped my chest, making it difficult to breathe. It wasn't fair. I had escaped death by solving Franz's murder, and now, just a day later, I was about to die. I had been foolish to hope.

I glanced apologetically at Vilmos. The blood from the cut on his throat had dripped to his shirt, painting a stitch of red down his collar.

"Very slowly, take out the knife and toss it to me," Hendrik said.

I did. He bent down and picked it up. He pressed the button that sprang the blade loose and grinned. "This will do even better. Now come on. Just a little closer."

I let my shirt drop and rubbed both hands along the sides of my trousers. A couple of steps, and Hendrik commanded me to drop to my knees. I did, raising my hands, semi-closed, on either side of my head in a gesture of surrender.

Hendrik raised the knife. "This is gonna hurt quite badly." He sounded eager, ravenous, barbaric. He was aching to cut me open, to spill my blood and end my life. He moved around me, standing at my back. My entire body was rigid. My lungs strained to pull in air. My heart beat like cannon fire in my ears. Hendrik grabbed the back of my neck hard, immobilizing my head. Ahead of me, I saw Jan had loosened his hold on Vilmos, the tip of his shiv no longer pressed to Vilmos's neck. There was a gap between Jan's lips, and he looked entranced by what Hendrik was about to do.

As Hendrik's hand rounded my neck, bringing the knife toward my throat, I gave Vilmos a wink. And simultaneously I grabbed Hendrik's wrist with my left hand, and with my right jabbed the sewing needle I had liberated from the seam of my trousers into the soft part between his thumb and forefinger.

JONATHAN DUNSKY

Hendrik yelled and tried to tear his arm away, but I held on tight, pushing the needle deeper into his flesh. At the same time, Vilmos drove the back of his head straight into Jan's groin. Then he turned, pushing Jan away.

Hendrik screamed, smacking me on the back of my head again and again. Stars exploded all over my vision, but I maintained my hold on his arm, pushing the needle in all the way, so its tip broke the skin on his palm.

The knife dropped from his hand. I let go of him, seized the knife, and jumped to my feet, whirling around.

Blood was pouring down Hendrik's hand. He gazed at it in shock. Then he saw me, and with his uninjured hand reached for the shiv he had stuck in his waistband. Before he could get it out, I pounced. The first swing gouged a deep line across his brow. The second sliced one cheek apart. His hands flailed blindly to stop me. He couldn't see for the blood spilling into his eyes. His nails scratched my cheek, my nose, my chin. Half my face erupted in pain. I jabbed the knife once, twice, a third time—each thrust cutting his swirling arms, spattering my face with blood. Then, with a cry, I plunged the knife between his hands, finding his throat. The force of the thrust pushed him backward, ripping the knife from my grip. The blade jutted from his flesh. Hendrik dropped to the ground. For a second, his limbs twitched and jerked, not unlike the way Gyuri's limbs had done the night he cried in our block. Then, with a gurgling inhalation, Hendrik let out a groan and was still.

I retrieved the knife and turned in time to see Jan and Vilmos fighting. Jan was on top of Vilmos, who was struggling to keep Jan from stabbing him with his shiv. I watched Jan punch Vilmos in the face, then ram the shiv into Vilmos's side.

"No!" The yell came from the deepest place within me, searing my vocal cords. I sprinted forward, the knife dripping a trail of Hendrik's blood.

Jan raised his shiv over his head for a second stab. I was too far away to stop him.

Then came a blur of motion from the side, and Jan was thrown off balance. It was Marco, the one who had declined to come to Hendrik's aid the night I had humiliated him. He had pushed Jan off of Vilmos.

With a snarl, Jan leaped at Marco, driving him to the ground, spitting and cursing. He raised the shiv, but I was already there. I stuck the knife between Jan's shoulder blades all the way to the hilt, then pulled downward as hard as I could, ripping a deep gash. Jan howled, twisting. I heard a snap as the blade broke free from the handle. Then Jan was on the ground, twitching. He did not twitch for long.

I looked at Marco, who held both hands up.

"I didn't want to do it," he said, "but Hendrik would have killed me if I refused."

Maybe it was the truth. Or maybe Marco had decided to switch sides only when I had killed Hendrik. I didn't care either way right now. I was satisfied that Marco posed no threat. I rushed to Vilmos, falling to my knees by his motionless form.

With eyes that had gone blurry with tears, I searched for blood on his torso, but there was none. Frowning, I was about to raise Vilmos's shirt, when I heard a loud groan. "Ahhh. Ooh, my head."

It was Vilmos. He was shaking his head, hand pressed to his face. He let out another groan, blinking rapidly as though emerging from a deep sleep.

"Vilmos?" I asked stupidly. "Vilmos, you're okay?"

"Yeah. Yeah, I think so. But my head hurts like mad."

I helped him to a sitting position and his eyes focused on me. "Are you hurt? There's blood on your face."

"It's not mine. It's theirs." I pointed at Jan and Hendrik.

"How?" Vilmos asked.

I touched his collar. "The blood from your neck dripped right over where I sewed your collar a few days ago. It reminded me of my needle. Hendrik hadn't expected it. But I don't understand—I saw you get stabbed. How come you're not wounded?"

Then I caught sight of Vilmos's bowl. Like mine, it was tied to the loops of his waistband. Only now it sported a large dent near its center, as though it had been punched by something hard. Like a shiv.

I looked from the bowl to Vilmos. "A knight in shining armor," I said, and we both started laughing. A laughter of pure relief and amazement.

It didn't last long; less than a minute. When we were through, Vilmos glanced at Marco and looked questioningly at me.

"He saved your life," I said. "He pushed Jan away from you."

"I didn't want to do any of this," Marco said, trembling. "But I had no choice. I swear."

Vilmos and I exchanged a look, followed by a nod.

"You can go, Marco," I said. "There's been enough death here today."

EPILOGUE

Hope is a deceitful, fickle creature. Like a disloyal lover, she makes you believe she will forever be at your side, only to desert you when you least expect it.

Two days after I'd killed Hendrik, Vilmos's fever returned. Like a firestorm, it erupted in the morning and burned through him in a matter of hours. That afternoon, after sinking the blade of his shovel into the earth, he paused, leaned on the handle, turned his weary head my way, and gave me a small smile that I would remember till my dying day.

Then he collapsed, his depleted body giving a small thud as it hit the ground.

I rushed over, falling to my knees beside him and clasping his hands. I watched the life go out of his eyes and take a piece of my heart with it.

At the end of the workday, I carried his body back to camp, refusing to relinquish him when others sought to relieve me of my load.

In camp, I laid his body with care alongside the other dead of the day. I smoothed his clothes, caressed his cheek, and wet his forehead with my tears. And then, even though it wasn't the time or place for such a prayer, I murmured the *Kaddish*. And I swore to him that I would survive this place.

The day after Vilmos had gone, what little hope remained in me suffered another blow. A few dozen men and teenage boys arrived at the men's camp. They had come from the Czech family camp. The Nazis had liquidated it, sending a few hundred prisoners to other work camps to the west. Most of the thousands who had resided there, including all the small children, were gassed and burned.

Trains from Hungary ceased coming, but Jews continued to arrive in Auschwitz, and kept on dying in their multitudes.

The weeks dragged on. In August, the gypsy camp was also liquidated. Thousands of gypsies—young and old, male and female—were devoured by the gas chambers.

Summer drifted into autumn. News of Russian advances abounded, yet the death machine rattled on. Whether by hunger, disease, punishment, or selection, our numbers continued to dwindle. Every day, I awoke to find a familiar face missing, another life extinguished.

In October, we heard a terrifying blast and saw a different sort of fire paint the western sky red. It took a couple of days for the story to filter back to us.

Members of the *Sonderkommando*, those miserable men working in the crematoriums, who witnessed up close the gassing of the victims and were later tasked with burning their bodies, had revolted. They blew up one of the crematoriums, had managed to kill a number of soldiers and *Kapos*, and attempted a mass escape.

It was said that all the prisoners involved, over four hundred of them, were captured and killed. They were the only ones to strike a real blow against the Germans in the entire history of Auschwitz.

Winter arrived, and it was every bit as bad as the old timers had said. At night, we shivered in our bunks, the cold enveloping us like a blanket of ice. In the evening, we stood at roll call as snowflakes the size of fists pummeled our shaking bodies. The guards had us clear snow with our hands, which quickly turned blue and numb. Men died as though the Angel of Death himself were swinging his scythe through our ranks.

I came very close to dying myself one day when a vicious guard whipped me into unconsciousness. If I had not made that oath to Vilmos, I would not have found the strength to carry on living.

Eight months after I arrived at the camp, in January 1945, in the face of approaching Russian divisions, the Nazis vacated Auschwitz. In thick snow and bone-shuddering cold, they ordered us—the weak, hungry, bereft, and exhausted—to begin marching. We left Auschwitz for the last time, leaving behind the sick in the hospital.

We walked for days through the frigid countryside with almost no food or rest. Those who faltered were shot without mercy. The sides of the roads were littered with frozen bodies. One of those bodies belonged to Vilmos's lover, Zoltan; and another to Andris Farkas, the man who had ratted me out as a policeman to the *Lagerälteste*.

After many tribulations, I and the rest of the survivors staggered into Buchenwald, a concentration camp near Weimar, Germany. Among our number was the *Lagerälteste*.

There, stripped of his position and authority, reduced to a common prisoner, he was finally vulnerable to our vengeance. On the second night, we set upon him, giving him the sort of treatment every tyrant deserves. It took four men to hold him down, and four more—armed with makeshift daggers—to stab him to death. I was one of the four assassins. Another was Mendel, the fifteen-year-old boy who had replaced Franz as the *Lagerälteste's* servant.

Rolf suffered a similar fate to that of his erstwhile master, though I took no part in his death. As for Mathias and Otto, they did not arrive in Buchenwald, and no one in the camp seemed to know what became of them.

There was very little food, and the guards were sadistic beasts, driven to even greater cruelty by the disintegration of their beloved Third Reich.

Each day, waves of airplanes flew overhead from the west—allied bombers and fighters, en route to destroy another piece of Hitler's Germany.

One needed to control one's reaction at the sight of these airplanes. The guards would beat or shoot any man who allowed his excitement and happiness to show.

Optimistic rumors pervaded Buchenwald. Germany was on the brink of defeat. The Allies were closing in. Some said British troops would liberate us, while others believed it would be the Americans. These rumors seemed more plausible than the ones that had circulated in Auschwitz the previous summer. But would we still be alive when Allied soldiers finally got here? Or would the SS guards kill us all beforehand?

Around me, men kept on dying. I, too, felt my life grow more tenuous with each passing day. Food became scarcer. Living conditions deteriorated. Hope grew fainter.

Each morning as I lay in my bunk, so weak that a part of me wished to just stay there and let my life slip out of my body, it was Vilmos's voice that nudged me to my feet.

L'Shana Haba'ah B'Yerushalayim, Adam.

Yes, Vilmos, I thought. Next year in Jerusalem.

Or, perhaps, Tel Aviv.

Thank you for reading The Auschwitz Detective

Please review this book!

Reviews help both readers and authors. If you enjoyed *The Auschwitz Detective*, please leave a review on Amazon. I would greatly appreciate it.

Want a free short story by Jonathan Dunsky?

Join Jonathan Dunsky's readers' newsletter and get a free copy of The Favor.

Go to JonathanDunsky.com/free to claim your copy.

Looking for more Adam Lapid?

Grab your copy of *The Unlucky Woman*, the first Adam Lapid short story, available in paperback on Amazon.

Or, if this was the first Adam Lapid novel you've read, I recommend reading *Ten Years Gone*, book 1 in the Adam Lapid series, available in paperback on Amazon.

AFTERWORD

Dear reader,

Some books are born out of compulsion. When I first got the idea of writing an Adam Lapid mystery set in Auschwitz-Birkenau, I knew that I was setting myself up for a difficult task. It would have been much easier to write another novel set in 1950s Israel. Yet once the idea took root in my mind, it could not be dislodged or ignored. It demanded to be written.

Every Adam Lapid novel involves meticulous historical research. But never have I devoted more time, effort, and care than I did with The Auschwitz Detective. I watched many videos of survivors, read multiple books, consulted the websites of leading museums, and pored over historical accounts, all in order to paint an accurate picture of life in Auschwitz-Birkenau in the summer of 1944. Visit www.JonathanDunsky.com/AuschwitzResources for a list of resources that I used, if you wish to learn more on this topic.

I'm not a historian but a storyteller, so I'm sure that some small errors have infiltrated this book. For that I apologize, dear reader. It was not for lack of trying.

There are various challenges in conducting research on Auschwitz-Birkenau. First, no story of survival is identical to another. Much depends on when a person was imprisoned in Auschwitz, which *kommando* they worked in, who their *Blockälteste* and *Kapo* were, and myriad other circumstances, small and large.

For example, the experience of a prisoner who worked in the Kanada Kommando in 1943 was vastly different to that of a prisoner working in the same *kommando* in the spring and summer of 1944, when the extermination of Hungarian Jewry was taking place.

Second, some small details were difficult to uncover. For instance, it took me several weeks to learn what prisoners did with their bowls during the workday.

And third, despite the abundance of academic research that has been done on Auschwitz, much remains unknown.

Still, despite these difficulties, I feel that I have succeeded in rooting this story in an accurate, realistic setting. I wanted to give you a glimpse into what life was like for a prisoner of Auschwitz—the tastes, smells, sounds, and various hardships that made up the fabric of one's time in that horrific place. And, of course, I wanted to tell a gripping story as well.

I realize that certain parts of The Auschwitz Detective might have been difficult to read. All I can say is that I did not exaggerate anything negative. For instance, the *Lagerälteste* may seem like an over-the-top villain, but I read accounts of prisoner functionaries who were every bit as bad if not worse.

There are a few clarifications I wish to make regarding spelling and historical detail:

1. In certain books and texts, you may find the word *Lagerälteste*

appear as *Lagerältester*. Both mean the same position in the camp. The same goes for *Blockälteste* and *Blockältester*.

2. In the second half of 1944, new Jewish prisoners in Auschwitz were marked with a yellow stripe above an inverted red triangle. Since The Auschwitz Detective takes place in early July 1944, Adam Lapid might have seen some prisoners marked that way. I chose to leave out this alternative marking so as not to impede the flow of the novel.

3. It is not uncommon to read references that state that prisoners' uniforms included a jacket. I opted for the word *shirt*, because I believe the word *jacket* is misleading. For one thing, many uniform *jackets* were shaped like a regular work shirt, with no pockets. For another, the word *jacket* implies that prisoners wore a shirt underneath, which they did not.

4. Many survivors describe the horror of morning roll call, and you may be wondering why Adam and Vilmos did not have to stand in one. The reason is that morning roll call was abolished in early 1944, in an effort by the Germans to prolong the prisoners' workday.

5. If you were wondering how it was possible for characters such as Jakob, Hendrik, Stefan, Aliz, Vilmos, and Adam to speak German, despite not having lived in Germany or Austria, you should know that the German language was quite common in many countries outside the boundaries of the Third Reich. Many Jews in Poland, Hungary, Czechoslovakia, and the Netherlands, as well as other countries, were fluent in it. This gave them a great advantage in Auschwitz. Prisoners who did not speak German, such as most Greek Jews, suffered for it.

6. You may have encountered testimonies by survivors who describe SS personnel dumping pellets of Zyklon B through openings in the roofs of the gas chambers. This was done in the two gas

chambers to the south of Kanada. In the two to the north, Zyklon B pellets were poured through small windows.

In no other death camp did more people die than in Auschwitz. Current estimates state that at least 1.1 million people died there, ninety percent of them Jews. Much of the killing was done in just under two months, between May and July 1944.

In that period, over 400,000 Hungarian Jews arrived in Auschwitz-Birkenau. The vast majority were gassed on arrival. Survivors say that the crematoriums worked around the clock to dispose of the bodies, and that fire pits were employed to deal with the overflow. The amount of loot in Kanada was far greater than the capacity of the warehouses.

Auschwitz-Birkenau was a factory of death, and during those two months in 1944, the machinery of murder worked at its most efficient level. It says a lot about the priorities of Nazi Germany that even as it was losing the war on two fronts, it dedicated considerable resources to murdering as many Jews as possible.

It was a terrible time. One which we must learn from. One which we must make sure is never repeated.

Dear reader, if you enjoyed reading The Auschwitz Detective, I ask that you take a moment and leave a review on its Amazon page. It doesn't need to be long. A couple of sentences should suffice. Your review is very important. Not only will it help the book reach more readers, it will also motivate me to continue writing, since I'll know my words have reached a wonderful person like you.

If The Auschwitz Detective is the first Adam Lapid novel you've read, I invite you the read the other installments. In each, Adam Lapid tries to rebuild his life in Israel, while solving mysteries. Here are the other books in order:

1. Ten Years Gone
2. The Dead Sister

3. The Auschwitz Violinist

4. A Debt of Death

5. A Deadly Act

6. The Unlucky Woman (a short story)

I have already begun working on the next Adam Lapid mystery, which will also be set in Israel. Please join my readers' club at www.JonathanDunsky.com/free to be informed when it is published. You'll also receive a free short story and the occasional email regarding news, sales, and other information.

I also invite you to join my readers' Facebook group at Facebook.com/JonathanDunskyBooks and connect with other readers of my books.

If you wish to contact me, please write to Jonathan@JonathanDunsky.com, and I'll get back to you as soon as I can.

For those of you who are members in a book club, I've compiled a list of questions that you can use for a discussion. You can find them on the next page.

Finally, I'd like to say a big thank you to Jeannie Blau, Otilia Rossetti, and David Lee for their kind and wonderful assistance in the editing process of this novel.

That's it for me, dear reader. I hope to see you again in another book.

Yours,

Jonathan Dunsky

BOOK CLUB DISCUSSION QUESTIONS

1. What feelings did The Auschwitz Detective evoke in you?
2. Did reading this novel give you a better sense of what life was like for Auschwitz prisoners? What new things did you learn about their daily lives?
3. What did you think about Adam and Vilmos's friendship?
4. In the scene with Pista, the prisoner with the bloodied shirt, Adam can save his own life by condemning Pista, who he believes would soon die anyway, but he doesn't. What is the significance of this scene?
5. How well did the author combine the mystery elements of the book with the historical setting?
6. One of the main themes of the novel is hope. Discuss the manner in which Vilmos and Adam view hope and the ways in which each of them struggles to cling to it.
7. Did reading this novel change how you view Auschwitz

survivors and the things they had to do to remain alive? If so, in what way did your views change?

8. When he works on the train platform, Adam saves two boys from selection, even while he does nothing to try to save the rest. Discuss his actions, his options, and his thought process and subsequent guilt.

9. What is the true meaning of the phrase "Next Year in Jerusalem" to Adam and Vilmos? How does it connect to the meaning of this phrase for Jewish diaspora across two thousand years of exile?

10. How would you describe Adam Lapid's character? What are his main attributes?

11. What is the significance of Gyuri's suicide and Adam's reaction to it? How does it connect to the rest of the novel?

12. What did you think of the relationship between Adam and Mathias?

13. Did the solution to the mystery surprise you? What did you think of the clues the author included in the plot?

14. Which scene resonated the most with you, and why?

15. If you could pick a character from the book and have a story written from their point of view, who would it be?

16. Were there any quotes or passages that stood out to you?

17. Have you read any other books in the Adam Lapid series? If so, how did The Auschwitz Detective compare?

18. What were the main themes of the book?

19. If this book were adapted into a movie, who would you cast as the lead characters?

20. If you could talk to the author, what questions would you ask him?

21. Would you recommend this book to a friend? How would you describe it when you recommended it?

ABOUT THE AUTHOR

Jonathan Dunsky lives in Israel with his wife and two sons. He enjoys reading, writing, and goofing around with his kids. He began writing in his teens, then took a break for close to twenty years, during which he worked an assortment of jobs. He is the author of the Adam Lapid mystery series and the standalone thriller The Payback Girl.

Made in the USA
Columbia, SC
22 January 2021

31409695R00167